26/5/22
8/6/22
27/6/23
9/8/23
3d/9/23

D0130034

Please return/renew this item by the
last date shown to avoid a charge.
Books may also be renewed by phone
and Internet. May not be renewed if
required by another reader.

www.libraries.barnet.gov.uk

BARNET
LONDON BOROUGH

'Evaristo remains an undeniably bold and energetic writer, whose world
view is anything but one-dimensional' *Sunday Times*

ABOUT THE AUTHOR

Bernardine Evaristo is the Anglo-Nigerian award-winning
author of several books of fiction and verse fiction that
explore aspects of the African diaspora: past, present, real,
imagined. Her novel *Girl, Woman, Other* won the Booker
Prize in 2019. Her writing also spans short fiction, reviews,
essays, drama and writing for BBC radio. She is Professor of
Creative Writing at Brunel University, London, and Vice Chair
of the Royal Society of Literature. She was made an MBE in
2009. As a literary activist for inclusion Bernardine has founded
a number of successful initiatives, including Spread the Word
writer development agency (1995–ongoing), the Complete
Works mentoring scheme for poets of colour (2007–2017) and
the Brunel International African Poetry Prize (2012–ongoing).

www.bevaristo.com

Mr Loverman

BERNARDINE EVARISTO

PENGUIN BOOKS

PENGUIN BOOKS

UK | USA | Canada | Ireland | Australia
India | New Zealand | South Africa

Penguin Books is part of the Penguin Random House group of companies
whose addresses can be found at global.penguinrandomhouse.com.

Penguin
Random House
UK

First published by Hamish Hamilton 2013
Reissued in Penguin Books 2020
012

Printed and bound in Great Britain by Clays Ltd, Elcograf S.p.A.

A CIP catalogue record for this book is available from the British Library

ISBN: 978-0-241-14578-4

www.greenpenguin.co.uk

MIX
Paper from
responsible sources
FSC® C018179

Penguin Random House is committed to a
sustainable future for our business, our readers
and our planet. This book is made from Forest
Stewardship Council® certified paper.

For David, for everything

Not everything that is faced can be changed, but nothing can be changed until it is faced.

– James Baldwin, 1924–1987

Contents

The Art of Marriage

Saturday, 1 May 2010

Morris is suffering from that affliction known as teetotalism. Oh, yes, not another drop of drink is goin' pass his lips before he leaves this earth in a wooden box, he said just now when we was in the dancehall, Mighty Sparrow blasting 'Barack the Magnificent' out of the sound system.

Last time it happen was when he decided to become vegetarian, which was rather amusing, as that fella has spent the whole of his life stuffing his face with every part of an animal except its hair and teeth. Anyways, all of a sudden Morris started throwing exotic words into the conversation like 'soya', 'tofu' and 'Quorn' and asking me how *I* would feel if someone chop off mi leg and cook it for supper? I didn't even deign to reply. Apparently he'd watched one of those documentaries about battery chickens being injected with growth hormones and thereby deduced he was goin' turn into a woman, grow moobies and the like.

'Yes, Morris,' I said. 'But after seventy-something years eating chicken, I notice you still don't need no bra. So, tell me, how you work that one out?'

Get this now: within the month I found myself walking past Smokey Joe's fried-chicken joint on Kingsland High Street, when who did I see inside, tearing into a piece of chicken, eyes disappearing into the back of his head in the throes of ecstasy like he was at an Ancient Greek bacchanalia being fed from a platter of juicy golden chicken thighs by a nubile Adonis? The look on his face when I burst in and catch him with all of that grease running down his chin. Laugh? Yes, Morris, mi bust mi-self laughing.

So there we was in the dancehall amid all of those sweaty, horny youngsters (relatively speaking) swivelling their hips effortlessly. And there was I trying to move my hips in a similar hula-hoop fashion, except these days it feels more like opening a rusty tin of soup with an old-fashioned tin opener. I'm trying to bend my knees without showing any pain on my face and without accidentally goin' too far down, because I know I won't be able to get up again, while also tryin' to concentrate on what Morris is shouting in my ear.

'I mean it this time, Barry. I can't deal with all of this intoxication no more. My memory getting so bad I think Tuesday is Thursday, the bedroom is the bathroom, and I call my eldest son by my younger son's name. Then, when I make a cup of tea, I leave it standing 'til it cold. You know what, Barry? I goin' start reading some of that Shakespeare you love so much and doing crossword. What is more, I goin' join gym on pensioner discount so I can have sauna every day to keep my circulation pumping good, because between you, me and these four walls . . .'

He stopped and looked over his shoulder to make sure no one was eavesdropping. Right, Morris. Two old geezers talking about the trials and tribulations of being geriatric and the whole room of gyrating youth wants to know about it?

'I suddenly noticed last week, mi have varicose vein,' he whispered into my ear so close he spat into it and I had to wipe it out with my finger.

'Morris,' I say. 'Varicose vein is what happen when you is ole man. Get used to it. As for forgetfulness? Likely you got early dementia and nothing you can do about that except eat more oily fish. As for staying sober . . .'

I shut up because Morris, with his eyebrows scrunched up pitifully, suddenly looked like a puppy dog. Usually he will banter right back, whack me on the head with the proverbial cricket bat. Morris is a sensitive fella but not hypersensitive, because that really would make him more woman than man – especially at a certain time of the month when they get that crazed look in they eyes and you better not say the wrong thing, or the right thing in the wrong way. Actually, even if you say the right thing in the right way they might come after you with a carving knife.

'Don't worry yourself. I is joking, man.' I punched him in the chest. 'If you was goin' off your head, I would be the first to tell you. Nothing to worry about, my friend. You as sane as you ever was.' Then I mumbled out of the side of my mouth, 'Which ain't saying much.'

Morris just stared at me in that wounded way that he really should-a grown out of about sixty-nine years ago.

I worked out he must be in the throes of alcohol-withdrawal symptoms. Not that I got direct experience of this withdrawal phenomenon, because I ain't never gone a day without the sweet sauce blessing my lips. Difference between me and Morris is that most days that is all I do, wet my lips with a taster, a chaser, a little something to warm me up. A sip of Appleton Rum, a swig of Red Stripe or Dragon Stout, mainly to support the intemperance industry over there on the islands. Call it an act of benevolence. Only on a Saturday night do I give in to my *bacchanalianese* tendencies. In Morris's case, he don't consume the drink;

the drink consumes him. Pickled. That man is *pickled*. The ratio of alcohol to blood in him must be 90 to 10, a-true. Not that he should worry, he's one of those pissheads who look good on it.

Finally, he decided to lighten up and crack a smile. Nobody can be depressed around me for long. Yesss. I am the Great Mood Levitator. I am the Human Valium.

'We veterans now,' I tell him. 'We have to adjust. What is more, we must believe that our best years are ahead of us, not behind us. Only way to deal with this non-stop train hurtling towards oblivion is to be positive. Is this not the Age of Positive Thinking? You know what they say, glass either half full or half empty. Let we make it half full. Do we have a deal, my man?'

I hold out my hand for a shake but instead he gets the wrong end of the stick and starts acting like a teenager, attempting one of those hip-hop, fist-pump, finger-flick handshakes that we both get all wrong and anybody looking will think we are a couple of pathetic old *dudes* trying to be cool.

Morris, oh, my dear Morris, what I goin' do with you? You have always been a worrier. Who is it who always tell you 'Morris, take it off your chest and put it on mine'?

Now look at you, that welterweight body of yours – selfsame one that used to do the 'Morris Shuffle' around your opponents in the boxing ring to become Junior Boxing Champ of Antigua in 1951 – is still mighty strong in spite of a piddling varicose vein or two. You still the chap I used to know. Still got impressive *musculature* on your arms. Still got a stomach more concave than convex. Still got no lines except those around your neck, which nobody will notice anyways except me.

But, Morris, there is one thing I does know for sure about you – your heart and mind has always liked to travel on that sea-goin' vessel them-a-call Lady Booze. No way are you goin' jump ship for dry land at this late stage in life and end up marooned on a desert island called Sobriety.

This I know without a doubt because I, Barrington Jedidiah Walker, Esq., have known you, Monsieur Morris Courtney de la Roux, since we was both high-pitched, smooth-cheeked mischief-makers waiting for we balls to drop.

I ain't complaining, because, while Morris is planning on bettering himself, he chauffeurs me home in his Ford Fiesta, as I am too plastered to get behind the wheel of a car and negotiate the high roads and low roads of East London without getting arrested by the boys in blue. That's one thing I does miss – drinking, driving and getting away with it, as we all did in the sixties and seventies. No CCTV cameras silently ogling you with their Cyclopean eyes three hundred times a day as you go about your business in London Town. Soon as I leave my door I *watched*. Big Brother come into we lives and none of us objecting. I can't even pick a booga out of mi own nose without it being filmed for posterity.

Morris drives me up to my yard, No. 100 Cazenove Road, Stoke Newington, waits to make sure I go in the right gate and don't collapse in the gutter, then drives off quietly in first gear with a cheery backhand wave.

He should be coming in for some spiced cocoa and some ole man's gentle comfort.

Instead, my heart sinks because I goin' into the lion's den.

This is the story of we lives.

Hellos and goodbyes.

*

I tiptoe up the noisy gravel path and, as Carmel has the hearing of a bat, I am in the Danger Zone. I turn the key in the lock, push open the door and wait, cock-eared. In the old days Carmel sometimes used to bolt it, forcing me to haul my arse over the side-gate and sit on the lawn mower in the shed, waiting for the dawn to rise and for her wrath to descend. Until I kicked the garden side-door down one time to show her that she can't keep the king out of his castle no more.

Once safely inside, I take off my jacket and throw it so it hoops over the coat rack to the left of the door. It falls on the floor. Rack must-a moved. I try again. It lands on the stairs. Third time – back of the net! Gotcha! Yesss. You go-wan, Barry. I high-five myself to the cheers of the multitudes meanwhile catching sight in the hall mirror of the 'dashing gentleman', as the English ladies used to coo back in the day. The ones with polite manners that is, as distinct from those trollops who hurled less flattering epithets at a man innocently strolling down the road minding his own business. Never no mind. Those days long gone. I've not been called no names by nobody except the wife for at least twenty years.

I am still a Saga Boy. Still here, thanks be to God. Still spruced up and sharp-suited with a rather manly swagger. Still six foot something with no sign of shrinkage yet. Still working a certain *je ne sais* whatsit. I might have lost the hair on my head, but I still got a finely clipped moustache in the style of old Hollywood romancers. Folk used to tell me I looked like a young Sidney Poitier. Now they say I resemble a (slighty) older Denzel Washington. Who am I to argue? The facts is the facts. Some of us have it, some of us do not. Bring it on, Barry. Bring it on . . .

Seeing as I been acting like a cat burglar in my own home for fifty years, climbing the stairs towards her lair is fraught with anxiety.

The bedroom door is ajar.

I squeeze myself through and creep inside.

First thing I do in the darkness is slide out the gold clip that holds the two tongues of my blue striped tie together. Only decent thing I got when I retired from Ford Motors in Dagenham. After forty years at the coal face mi get a tie, mi get a rubbish-engraved plate, mi get a watch that is more Timex than Rolex, and mi get a clammy handshake and patronizing speech from the Managing Director Mr Lardy Comb-Over in the staff canteen.

'It is with tremendous sadness, Mr Walker, that we say goodbye to an employee who has given us such dedicated service over such an extended period of time. Your presence on the factory floor has greatly endeared you to your colleagues. You are quite the joker, I hear, quite the anecdotalist, quite the raconteur.'

He paused to study me, like he wasn't so sure I understood words of five syllables or ones that was a bit Frenchified, then added, 'Oh, you know, one who regales others with stories.'

Oh, boy, I catch so much fire when people talk down to me like I'm some back-a-bush dumb arse who don't understand the ins and outs of the Queen's English. Like I wasn't educated at Antigua Grammar School, best one in the country. Like all my teachers didn't come from the colonial mother ship. Like this here Little Englander can't speak the Queen's as well as any Big Englander over there, I mean *here*. And so what if me and my people choose to mash up the *h-english linguish* whenever we feel like it, drop our prepositions with our panties, piss in the pot of correct syntax and spelling, and mangle our grammar *at random*? Is this not our *post-modern, post-colonial* prerogative?

Anyways, when I arrived here on the good ship *Immigrant*, I brought with me a *portmanteau* of school certificates, and the only reason I didn't go to no university was because I didn't score highly enough to get the single government scholarship to a university in England. I been taking evening classes since 1971 to make up for it.

Sociology, Psychology, Archaeology, Oloyology – you name it. English Literature, French Language, *naturellement*. Don't even get me started on Mr Shakespeare, Esq., with *whom* I been having the most satisfying *cerebral* relationship, *sirrah*. I know my Artology too: Miró, Monet, Manet, Man Ray, Matisse, Michelangelo, Murillo, Modigliani, Morandi, Munch, Moore and Mondrian, not to mention the rest of the alphabet. I even dragged Morris to that controversial *Sensation* exhibition at the Royal Academy in 1997 to see Emin's slutty bed, Ofili's elephant dung, Hirst's pickled shark and Quinn's bloody head. Morris scoffed, 'I can do better than that.' To which I replied, 'It might be more concept than craft, Morris, but art would be boring if artists still only painted buff male bodies with rock-hard buttocks, juicy lips and dangling protuberances in the style of the Renaissance.'

Although . . . come to think of it, perhaps not . . .

Morris's final word on the matter? 'In that case I'm goin' piss in a bucket and exhibit it as Art with a capital A.'

Morris's problem is he don't like to go too deep. It's not that he's not capable, because that man is smarter than most. He's the one who got the scholarship to study maths at Hull University, but when he got there he didn't like the cold, didn't like the food, didn't like the course, didn't do the work and, when he was sent down at the end of his second year, didn't want to go home. Lucky fella found work as a book-keeper for a textile wholesaler in Stratford, which was pretty good, seeing it was hard for we people to land such jobs. His boss was a Mr Szapiro, a Polish Jew who'd escaped the Warsaw Ghetto. Morris liked his boss but was bored brainless by the job. Nonetheless, he stayed forty-three years.

All the while, I was getting intellectualized. This here humble engine-fitter can pontificate about all of those chin-stroking armchair philosophizers with the best of them. How Socrates believed we should know ourselves and question everything, break through the limits of we own beliefs. Plato said being a moral person meant not just knowing what is right but choosing it as well. But I eventually realized that if you spend too much time with these Ancient Greek egg-heads, your mind will spin off into the stratosphere. They are so mentalist, you goin' end up demented. So I dropped my philosophy class at Birkbeck and reverted to the most ancient and most reliable kind-a wisdom: homespun.

If only I'd told Comb-Over I'd not even needed to work at Ford's for years, because I'd been building up my property business since the sixties, buying cheap, doing up, getting Solomon & Rogers Estate Agency to rent out. The only reason I continued clocking on at the factory was because I actually liked the work and liked working with my hands. Man must work with his hands, not so? And I would-a missed my work mates too bad: Rakesh, Tommy, Alonso, Tolu, Chong, Arthur, Omar – the United Nations of Ford's, as we dubbed ourselves.

I place the tie clip inside the small bowl on the bedside table, the one with blue storks painted on it à la Chinese porcelain of the Ming Dynasty period, I do believe. Its stem-cup design with peony scrolls is certainly recognizable from my numerous expeditions to the Victoria and Albert Museum, to which I frogmarch Morris. Only difference between this bowl and the original is that Carmel bought this one in Woolworth's for 99p in 1987. That's never no mind, because God will *not* be able to help me should I ever break the damn thing. Selfsame bowl used to hold all of those lemon sherbet sweets I loved exploding in my mouth before I decided to stop taking my pearlies for granted. Just as well, because I can still bedazzle with my indestructible ivories. Must be the only 74-year-old in the land with his own full set, not a single one extracted, capped, veneered or crowned.

Next, I unloop my tie and drape it over the doorknob of the wardrobe just behind me, twisting my torso away from my hip a bit too sharpish. I freeze, turn back and allow my muscles to realign, everything facing in the same direction: head, shoulders, hips. Gotta be careful, because at my age something that should stretch might snap instead.

I ease the gold cufflinks out of my starched white shirt and pop them into the perfect O-shaped mouth of the bowl. I unbutton said shirt and pull its tail out of my baggy grey-green trousers with a permanent pleat down the front and turn-ups at the bottom that always end up full of cigar ash after an all-night bender. It'll soon be time to get Levinsky to make a new suit. Worth the trek across London to Golders Green, because he's the only one I know who can still make suit in authentic fifties style without charging Savile Row price.

Then I wriggle out of the sleeves of my shirt, bunch it up in my hands and throw it into the corner by the window for Carmel to wash.

It lands like . . . an exhalation of breath.

I like *that*. Derek Walcott? You listening over there in St Lucia? Mi no care if you did get the Nobel Prize for poetry, you better watch out, because Barrington Walker's goin' steal the linguistic march on you, fella.

In spite of my efforts, Carmel's deep-sea breathing stops and she comes up for air with a kind of watery spluttering, as if she's just stopped herself from drowning.

Un-for-tu-nate-ly.

Wifey rolls over and turns on the flowery bedside lamp with a click that sounds like the cocking of a trigger. The skin on her underarm sways off the bone.

I goin' get a right reprimandation.

'Is morning time already, Barrington.'

She is using the three-syllable version of my name . . .

'You know how time does pass, dear?'

Statement, not a question.

'Does it?'

Threat, not a question.

'Why don't you go back to sleep, dear?'

Instruction, not a question.

'Oh, I'll have plenty of time to sleep when the Good Lord comes for me and that won't be long now, I am sure.'

Emotional blackmail – pure and simple.

'In which case, I hope he comes for me before he comes for you, dear.'

A lie – pure and simple.

'Unless that one with horns and a pitchfork catch you first.'

I try and concentrate on the job in hand, but when I sneak a glance at Carmel I see she getting ready to invade Poland.

I take off my three rings and pop them into the bowl. My

ruby beauty is like a thimbleful of blood that's been poured into an oval mould of gold. Bought it for myself when my first rental property went into profit. The golden truck tyre was given to me by that German construction worker in 1977. Bit of a knuckle-duster, he was, 'rough trade'. My favourite is a coiled serpent with diamond scales and glinting sapphire eyes, its head poised, ready to take a bite of the apple.

As for my wedding ring? Only a pair of metal cutters could get it off of my fingers.

Many times I have resisted a trip to the hardware store.

'Bringing the stink of cigars into *my* bedroom again.'

'I sorry.'

'And that *renk* rum *narsiness*.'

'I sorry.'

'When you goin' mend your ways?'

'I sorry.'

'You could-a called, at least.'

'I know, I . . . am . . . sorry.'

'I told you to get a mobile phone years ago.'

Am I truly bonkers? A mobile phone so the ole girl can track me down any time of day or night?

Carmel been playing this game a long, long time. Sometimes she let it drop for a few months or even years, like in the 1980s, when she seemed quite content, enjoyed her work, made more of an effort with her appearance, started socializing with her work friends. Me and she settled into a *détente*. Then, out of the flaming blue, she decides to get the hump, when all I want to do is crawl into bed and sleep.

Far as she's concerned, her husband is a womanizer. Out sowing his seed with all those imaginary Hyacinths,

Merediths and Daffodils. On what evidence? Alien perfume? Lipstick on my collar? Ladies panties in mi jacket pocket?

I can honestly say to my wife, 'Dear, I ain't never slept with another woman.'

She chooses not to believe me.

Her big eyes are almost popping out of her head. If she don't watch out, I goin' make a grab and play ping-pong with them one of these days.

What Carmel should be grateful for, what Carmel should realize, is that her man here is one of the good ones, because he been coming home to her bed for fifty years. All right, all right, sometimes it's the next morning, maybe the afternoon, occasionally a day or two might pass . . .

'Yes, my dear. I go get a mobile phone if it make you happy.'

My face said, *Don't you go breaking our Non-Aggression Pact, dear.*

I release my big brass belt. The one with the buffalo-head buckle that splits into two.

We have come to the point in the proceedings where I drop my trousers. For the first time this night. (*Un-for-tu-nate-ly.*)

I got to get my socks off somehow, but I don't feel like bending over, because I might just throw up all over the moulting shag-pile carpet Carmel bought thirty years ago for her knees when she's praying morning, noon and night and even out loud in her sleep. Nonetheless, if I dare sully it, she'll get a rifle from wherever she keeps her arsenal of *metaphorical* weapons and blast me out of the window.

I cross one leg over the other and, wobbling like an out of practice yogi (and feeling Carmel willing me to fall over), I manage to whip them off.

We have reached an impasse.

She is the Sphinx guarding the city of Thebes. Head of a woman, body of a lioness, wings of an eagle, memory of an elephant, bite of a saltwater crocodile with 2,000 pounds per square inch of pressure, ready to snap my head off.

In order for me to get into bed, I got to give the right answer to the riddle she not even asking, because she think she know the answer.

On the wall opposite is the damned wallpaper she loves so much. It has a certain *theme*: garish flowers, jungle vegetation, tropical animals. It begins to sway, and I steel myself for the herd of elephants that's about to stampede all over me.

I'm so tired I could sleep standing up in my white Y-fronts and string vest.

That's when I realize I still have my hat on. I take it off and bow with grandiose hat-waving flourishes, like an eighteenth-century gentleman being presented at Court. When we first married this would-a been enough to send wifey into forgiving giggles.

She used to tell me I was the funniest man alive.

Now her heart is so cold you can snap off a frozen shard and cut a diamond with it.

When did I last make that woman laugh? What *decade* was that exactly? What *century*? What *millennium*?

She staring at me like I am a complete imbecile.

What I supposed to do? Walk towards the bed and risk the wrath of her forkin' fury? Curl up on the floor? Sleep in another bedroom? Put on my Derek Rose silk monogrammed pyjamas and go downstairs? The very same pair I have to hand-wash, otherwise she'll ruin them as she did my new cashmere dressing gown that was made from wool sheared from the Golden Fleece. Lady-Wife managed to shrink it three sizes in the washing machine before the month was out.

Just what the flaming heck am I supposed to do when I is too tired and blasted drunk to do anything except sleep?

Carmel rolls out of bed in that blue nylon nightie with ruffles at the cleavage that sticks to her various body parts when she walks. (*Un-for-tu-nate-ly.*)

She slips into her foamy orange slippers with bobbles on the toes and halts right up in-a my face. 'I just heard today that my papi's had a second stroke and is in hospital and I been thinking how I should-a never let you turn me against him.'

Whaaaat? That was *only* when we first married; rest of the time she did it herself. Past thirty years I been begging her to take *extended* trips back home.

'Pray, isn't this the man who pummelled your mother so often there was a bed with her name on it at the hospital?'

Morris is not the only one showing signs of dementia, clearly. For long as I known Carmel the words 'bastard' and 'daddy' been hyphenated; just as 'husband' and 'bastard' been similarly conjoined. She's a revisionist, like those Holocaust-deniers.

'That was a long time ago . . . I sure my mother has forgiven him now she's up there with the Good Lord . . . otherwise they wouldn't-a . . . let her in.'

Definitely dementia.

'He nearly a hundred years old and I've not seen him for nearly thirty of them. He asking for his little girl.'

Man had good innings, considering.

He was a big man over there, but soon as I started work for him I saw how small he really was. Broke practically every bone in her mother's body. I begged her to leave the brute, but what she tell me? 'Barry, this don't concern you.'

Too many women was like that: no matter how much beats they got, they feel say they gotta put up with it. And when they dare go the police, the police tell them a-go back to their husbands.

My own mother's mother got chopped up by her second husband so bad with a bill-hook she ended up in surgery at Holberton, and thereafter never walked again. She died from internal injuries before I born. My mother always drummed it into me, 'Treat women good, yuh hear?' And that's what I been doing, never once laying a finger on my wife and staying around to raise my children. No way was I goin' create space in my wife's bed for some shady, step-daddy character to sleep in the same house as Donna and Maxine.

No, sah, my girls was protected.

Anyways, Carmel better hotfoot it over there to secure that big house she grew up in before the will-contesters change the locks. Her father's had over eighty years to spread his seed.

She still standing up in my face with her morning breath.

'Listen to me good, Barrington. I flying home to see my father on Monday, and when I return, things is goin' change round here. I am not putting up with you putting your thing about with those trampy cows no more.'

I cut my eye at her, but she don't flinch.

Give me some freeness, woman. I am so fed up with having to face your miserable face after a night of conviviality.

'Let me tell you something, Carmel. The only cow I know is the one giving me blasted cheek when I don't deser—'

Before I can finish my sentence, she delivers a bone-crushing ba-daow across my chops.

Oh, Laaard, we have come to this, ehn? We have come to this *again*?

'God will damn you,' she says, shouldering past me.

I spin around, remembering those heavy potion jars on the dressing table are now within reach of her paws.

'You and your *narsiness*,' she says, plucking her yellowy flannelette dressing gown from the hook and wrapping herself up in it, flinging open the door.

I step out after her, repressing the overwhelming desire to help her *hooves* down those very steep stairs, all twenty-three of them.

Calm yourself down, Barry. You better than that.

I go to open my mouth instead, but it feels like I goin' retch: a projectile vomit of fifty years of deception, dis-illusionment and self-destruction hurtling down the stairs on to her back.

A bouillabaisse of vomit.

A banquet of sick.

A bucketful of shit.

Carmel . . . Carmel, *dear*, you know what? I tell you what? You right. Yes, you right. God a-damn me a-ready. Never you mind yourself, I was fast-tracked down into the Eternal Flames a long time ago. God a-damn me the day I chose to enter this hellish so-called marriage instead of following my Morris-loving, sweet-loving, full-blooded, hot-blooded, pumping-rumping, throbbing organ of an uncontainable, unrestrainable, undetainable man-loving *heart*.

2.

The Song of Sweetness

1960

. . . there you are, Carmel, swaying on the white Hollywood-style swing-seat on Papi's veranda

rocking back and forth while everybody inside sleeps off the wedding feast of

pepper pot and conch fritters, fungee and tamarind stew, papaya pie, ducana, yummy sugarcake and butterflaps

their bodies weighed down while their rum-soaked minds take flight into the night

relatives are crammed into the two spare rooms, tanties – Eudora, Beth, Mary, Ivy – the uncles – Aldwyn and Alvin – numerous spouses and cousins – Augusta, Obediah, Trevor, Adelaide, Neville, Barbara, who came from upcountry for your special day

although nobody could afford to come back from foreign – Brooklyn, Toronto, London

Mommy and Papi are in their bedrooms, east, west, so Mommy don't have to hear

the maid Loreene fornicating with Papi before sneaking back to her hut at dawn and then emerging like she all pure and innocent to cook breakfast for everyone, and not a man-eating marriage-wrecker

you could kick that girl to kingdom come – him too

you catch a whiff of the honeysuckle in the hedgerows

just below the veranda and inhale it deep, hoping its heady loveliness will make you drowsy

come morning, you goin' be smelling the yellow bell-flower just outside your bedroom

but you've hardly slept these past forty-eight hours because your mind won't stop replaying the last twelve of them when

although it was a certain Miss Carmelita Miller who walked down the aisle trying hard not to trip up on your beaded, ivory gown, it was a certain Mrs Barrington Walker who did the return trip

all grown-up and sophisticated on the arm of your handsome consort, when all you really wanted to do was a volley of cartwheels up the aisle and a little jig when you got showered with *genuine* pink and white confetti on the church steps, not that rice substitute rubbish

you a real woman now, Carmel

yes, a bona-fide lady conjoined in holy matrimony which no man can put asunder, in accordance with the instructions of the Good Lord, praise him, amen, got the ring to show for it too, gold, perfect fit on your dainty finger, goin' enjoy flashing it hither and thither to let everyone know you got a husband

you spoken for

you not goin' end up spinster now

plenty woman round here don't get husbands

they just get babies.

your *husband* – who is at this very minute spending his first night in your childhood bed, his legs dangling over the end, because he so tall and sprawling

your *husband* – who drank so much rum punch he couldn't stand straight to do any dancing and he the best male dancer in St John's, same as you the best female dancer

you don't mind: Barry's even funnier when he's drunk, you lucky to have him

all of your life Mommy's been plaiting up your hair between her knees and moaning about how

Carmel, when the day comes, you gotta find a husband who likes your inner nature. Your father picked me for my prettiness, which don't last

and she'd tug your hair so hard you'd yell and she'd dig her knuckles into your scalp to drive the point home

soon as prettiness start to fade, he was out roaming the garden, picking flowers still in full bloom

Mommy, you said when your day finally *had* come and you and Barry was engaged

don't worry about me, because Barry is a wonderful human being who makes me laugh more than anybody in the whole world and he thinks I'm sweetest girl on the whole island. You see how we get on? It's called compatibility, Mommy. Way marriages supposed to be

she shut up after that, just plaited your hair like she was a Red Indian scalping you

nobody can treat you like a child no more now you're married, not even Papi, who lost his rights over you once your husband inherited them

you goin' be a good, deserving wife too, Carmel, isn't it? you been studying the Home Economics manual from your schooldays in preparation

when your husband gets back from work, home will be *a haven of rest and order*

you goin' *touch up your make-up and put a ribbon in your hair* and have dinner ready in the oven and if he late and it gets burnt, you *not* goin' start hectoring him like some of those low-class, bad-mouthed women out there who can't keep man and end up lonely ole hag

no, you goin' ask him questions about his day in a *soft and soothing voice* and listen to his news and complaints with a pleasant smile

you not goin' blow it like Mommy, who should-a kept her lip buttoned instead of backchatting Papi, not that you exonerate his badness, and though you feel sorry for her, Mommy tests the patience of a saint, as Papi keeps telling her

no, you had a plan to catch man, and as soon as Barry started working for Papi you was ecstatic, started sneaking him the looks you'd been practising in the mirror, waiting for the right boy to come along, and then, soon as he saw you, you'd turn away with an enigmatic smile

it worked

because he started to escort you to school, standing at the end of the drive in his khaki trousers ironed like a soldier's, crisp white shirt all smart, smoothly shaven face and always teasing you

Carmel, you'd look simply goy-geous and simply mah-vellous, if it wasn't for that simply gi-normous purple pimple at the end of your nose or those two camel eyes of yours that are so crossed the only thing they can see is each other

or he'd grab your satchel and throw it in a wide, slow-motion arc into a sun-hazy field of damp tomato and cucumber plants, forcing you to chase him to get it or he'd only throw it again, or he'd do a really exaggerated Charlie Chaplin walk with a tree branch like he wasn't eight years older than you but still a schoolboy pranking around

then there was that one time when you was genuinely

annoyed with his antics, because this wasn't exactly your idea of a romantic courtship, and you tossed your head at him and shouted, *Go sling your hook, boy*

he stopped jiving around and stood still by the side of the road, head cocked, all serious, and said nothing while

Ole Pomeroy's horse and cart passed carrying a cargo of straw-hatted farm-workers and black pineapples and

Andrina rode past on her big black bicycle, balancing her small daughter on the handlebars and a baskets of yams on her head

Dr Carter's terminally ill Chevrolet juddered past so noisily it should be given its last rites and

you heard the sound of the Bagshaw tractor droning in the distance and schoolchildren's voices coming up behind you

and there was flies buzzing everywhere because of the manure in the field, but you didn't even bother wave off the one that landed on your face, watching Barry watching

you, and there he was, standing there in the rising morning heat, his sandals all dusty now, sweaty patches spreading under his arms, the sun glinting on him, and then he spoke in a tone you not heard before, *Carmel*, sniffing up his lips and nose like you stank as bad as the manure out there

Carmel . . . I know you ain't no sourpuss, really

and even though tears filled up your eyes and you tried to hold them back, you couldn't

Barry came over, looking a bit regretful, steered you to the rocky outcrop on the other side of the road by prodding you gently on the back with his hand, and you sat down, arms up against each other's, and you could feel the heat coming through his side, and he slow-punched you in the arm

But I know you a sweet girl deep down inside. Yuh see, Carmel, I am an archaeologist of the human character and I hereby declare I go help you excavate all of your sweetness

Sweet Girl – became his pet name for you, and once you knew that you was sweet deep down inside, you couldn't backchat him no more, you had to be sweet all of the time or you'd disappoint him

oh to swing higher and higher until you reach the top, because what you got?

what you got, Sweet Girl?

you got the cream of the crop, that's what

no man on this island more better-looking or got a more attractive personality than your husband, you swear it, clever too, like you used to be

at Antigua Girls' High you was top girl in your class for Latin and French, second for English and History, fourth in Classical Civilizations, fifth in the Ancient Greek Language, until you met Barry and realized he was clever enough for both of you

everybody knows you can't be too clever or you won't catch man

Mommy barely said a word to you for ages when you stopped goin' school

Papi didn't mind, all he cares about are his two Early Bird stores both ends of Scotch Row, set up by his father's family, the Millers of Antigua

whose large portraits look out from the wood-panelled walls in the hallway behind you, strangled by high-buttons and tight collars, bushy hair tamed into centre partings, moustaches slicked down with grease and twisted up at the ends, haughty busts constrained by brassières, waists strapped in by corsets

23

once you got engaged, Barry got promoted from Junior Shop Hand to Assistant Manager, but Merty said that's why he wanted to marry you, to get his hands on your family's money, but the problem with her theory is he can't stand his father-in-law because he beats Mommy

besides, you both running off to England soon

studio photographs of Mommy's side, the Gordons, are tagged at the end of the corridor

Papi calls them 'the little people' – fisher-folk, seam-stresses, coal-makers, *rum-smugglers*, staring awkwardly into the black box immortalizing them

Mommy tells you these your family too, yuh know?

she calls them *the ancestors*, thereby affording them a gravitas they only get because they dead

seems to you the longer people dead-dead, the more status they get-get

but it should be the other way round, longer they dead, the less they count, so why on earth do Mommy and Papi go on about these dead people like they matter?

all you care about is getting the catch of the century

you one lucky girl, eh?

plenty girls acted like floosies around Barry, most of the Young Ladies' Society of Antigua (membership = 4) did too

Candaisy wanted him, Drusilla as well, and she's officially the prettiest, Asseleitha's too weird to want anybody, Merty was always hitching up her skirt whenever he was in the vicinity

you never said nothing, because nobody tells Miss Merty what to do and doesn't get an ear-bashing for their effort, best friend or no best friend

at the wedding reception Drusilla told you the reason Merty caught your bridal posy was because she leapfrogged

24

on to the girls in front of her to get it and they ended up with torn stockings and scratched knees as a result

you wondered why they was scrambling all unladylike on the dusty ground when you spun back round

don't worry yourself, Miss Merty, you'll find someone, like that Clement, who's got his eye on you and seems like a nice boy and one day you'll come to England too

you all drew blood and pressed thumbs and swore that you'd never be separated for long

so here you are

swinging and kicking your bare legs out and getting a little breeze to them in the sticky heat, your nightie sticking to your underside

the moon throws a shadowy glow on to the sweet meal and rubber trees, the bougainvillaea and jacaranda, the date palms

you starting to feel a bit dozy, but you still got a hubble-bubble of new and old feelings that won't settle down and

everybody on the whole island sleeping 'cept you, and those noisy crickets and tree frogs that never shut up at night

you look up at the diamanté sky, stretching yonder into infinity

you wonder if you goin' miss it when you travel and then you correct yourself: you taking the sky with you to England, Sweet Girl, sky's not goin' nowhere you're not

you never left the island before except for trips to Barbuda next door, and that don't count and you've rarely ever left St John's, all you know is a few miles' circumference around it, your little island in the middle of the Caribbean Sea

it frightening because the world suddenly seems so huge, with all of its billions of people out there and you leaving without Mommy too, who won't leave Papi, no matter how much you and Barry beg her come with you

you start to swing slower, softer, a rhythmical lull, like the lullabies Mommy used to sing you when you was little

soon you will float back to your husband, who will stretch out his long, strong arms, all sleepy, and pull you into him – warm and safe

Mrs Barrington Walker, you not only a respectably married woman but you can't believe that just now you almost lost *it*

but he didn't put it in, just rubbed himself on top of you

asking if you was all right, then he shuddered, rolled off and turned away, curling into himself, his broad, strong, manly back glistening against the white cotton sheet

you wanted to trace the ridges of his backbone with your finger

lick off the moisture at the nape of his neck and taste him, slip yourself around his chest and see if your fingers met the other side

make him put it inside instead of being so considerate and not forcing himself, because you ready for it

but really, Mrs Walker, the question you got to ask is

is it allowed for a wife to touch her husband spontaneously or does she have to wait for him to touch her before duly responding?

you goin' ask the Young Ladies' Society about it – Merty will know

one thing is obvious: Barry's a real gentleman, unlike some of the boys round these parts, who can't keep their things in their pants and their hands away from girls' privates

Merty first did it years ago with an American diplomat

who approached her outside the cathedral after church, gave her a real American dollar

and she earned several dollars that way since, swore you to secrecy, Drusilla's done it with Maxie, her older boyfriend, Candaisy has almost done it but not quite

Barry was always play-punching and teasing, and when you danced you was all over each other physically, but he never pestered *that* way, not once, not even French kissing

Hubert had a proper feel-up once you'd been courting seven months, and he was a swot who wore spectacles and stuttered

poor Hubert, crying on the beach in full view of everybody when you finished with him, but it also annoyed and embarrassed you so much you dropped the American ice-cream he'd just bought you on to the sand and walked off without saying goodbye

you agree with Barry, who says Hubert is James Stewart, but *he* is Rock Hudson

no contest, right?

the swing stops and you glide, yes, glide, like a swan in a pond across the wooden floor in your bare feet

you pass through the corridor and ascend the wooden staircase, your bare feet avoiding the squeaky bits

there he is, asleep facing the door, you creep in and sit cross-legged on the hard wooden floor in your new, grown-up nightie, short and frilly and flirty to show off your *married woman's* cleavage

you cup your breasts in your hands, all high and nicely heavy, like two buoyant bags of water, and you wonder when he will touch them

you want him to feel how bouncy they is, because at sixteen they've not yet begun to deflate, although Mommy (the *doom monger*) has promised you it will happen soon, because you got too much weight in them and before you know it they be drooping and swaying instead of bouncing

she said it might even happen tomorrow or next week

what will it feel like to have him hold them up from behind?

he better hurry up, that's all

his mouth is slightly open.

you want to close it, because insects might get in

you almost stroke his cheek, but what if he wakes up and asks you what you doing?

his left eye twitches, which shows he dreaming about what must be uppermost in his mind now he a newly married man

yes, he dreaming about you, lady

you tiptoe around the bed and slide up beside him, careful not to touch him

you close your eyes and transmit into the back of his head what you plan to be dreaming about this night

you goin' all telepathic on him, you goin' make him dream what you dreaming

you have *magic* powers

. . . a real thatched cottage in the 'Dales' with fat cows mooing around the green hills, not the scrawny cattle you get round here

your *husband* wearing a shirt, tie, braces and smoking a pipe in the garden sunshine, sitting on a stripy deckchair doing the *Times* crossword

your children playing hide-and-seek in the apple and pear orchard with Lassie the dog

running around barking happily and

you in the kitchen prettying up your face with fresh lip-stick and a clean red-and-white-stripe pinafore over your tight-tight black pencil skirt

and on your feet, high-high heels that give you the sexy walk of Marilyn Monroe, even though you baking scones ready for a spread of real Devonshire cream with the jam you just made from fresh damson and

you goin' serve it up with real English tea in bone-china all laid out on the garden table on the crazy-paving *patio* just in front of the lawn

and you got a rockery and an herbaceous border and rob-ins, yes, robin redbreasts chirruping in the trees

and somewhere over the dales and hills and far . . . far . . . away . . . the mangrove cuckoo and the lovely yellow oriole land just now on your windowsill

the fork-tailed flycatcher hovers around the roses

the hummingbird is hovering around the orange tulips, and there, there over there, flies a brown ibis into the very English sky

you see an iguana scurry across the lawn, and a gecko darts up your rosy kitchen wallpaper, and a crocodile pokes its head into the kitchen from the garden and

you look over by the pond with water lilies and see a red-foot tortoise and a leather-back turtle emerge wearing top hats and singing *you goin' rock, rock, rock around the clock*

and you sit down to tea with a family of purple flamin-gos, and oh, oh, oh, fire, fire burning bright in the cream teas of the night

just when you think you not slept a wink with all of this activity goin' on, you wake up and feel the full blast of morning sunshine coming through the wide-open windows and on to your face and that witch Loreene is banging on the door like she goin' break it down, calling you to breakfast

    and when you open your thick, heavy, sticky eyes and turn over, you see Barry must-a got up already, because he gone

    yes, Carmel, he gone already, down to breakfast without waking you up and waiting for you so you can go down to your first breakfast together as husband and wife

3

The Art of Being Normal

Sunday, 2 May 2010

While sleep is the Great Vanquisher of an Embattled Mind, Guinness is the Great Tranquillizer of a Damaged Soul . . . and Lord knows I need it for breakfast this morning, after another round in the ring with Carmel last night.

Me and Morris are at my spacious dining table, which can comfortably seat eight people, in my capacious kitchen with its high Victorian ceiling and stately church-like window that looks out on to my amplitudinous, tree-adorned garden that stretches back over seventy flower-bedecked feet.

I am enthroned at the head of the table on my carved antique chair with tapestry upholstery that my younger girl, Maxine, bought for my fiftieth birthday from that furniture restorer's on Bradbury Street in 1986. Looks like something Henry VIII might've parked his right royal arse on.

Morris usually pops in about an hour before Sunday lunch. Not that he's ever invited. Don't need to be.

'Y'all right, Boss?' he said when I opened the door.

'Y'all right, Boss?' I replied, heading back into the kitchen.

Carmel's already gone to the Church of the Living Saints by the time I de-slumber myself. She's usually got the good sense not to start bombing Pearl Harbor the day after the night before, because she knows full well what it will lead to – the atomic fallout from my tongue.

She and me has got to sit down and talk like two grown-ups without setting off each other's trip wires.

The problem is – we reached a dead end decades ago.

The solution to that problem is a dissolution of my marriage.

I decided as soon as I got up that there comes a time when the botheration and fabrication is too much, even for a man of my considerable fortitude.

I want to spend my remaining years with Morris.

Years ago I wasn't prepared to abandon my girls, except the one time Morris's world came crumbling down over Odette . . . his wife.

He met her in England before I came over. Said he didn't think I was goin' make it over here, and he couldn't be a West Indian and not start a family – *man haf fu do wha man haf fu do*. Truth is, both of us was desperate to be anything other than what we was.

Then he had the cheek to get upset when I turned up in England with a wife of my own.

But soon after my arrival we resumed where we'd left off back home. Didn't take long. First time we got half an hour alone in his flat while Odette was out, we was back on track.

Until 1989, when the shit hit the fan. Odette had gone on one of her church retreats to Wales. As usual we took a certain *advantage*, same advantage we been taking since we was fourteen. Except this one time she travelled back to London a day early, let herself into the house quietly that night, not wanting to disturb her sleeping husband, crept upstairs and caught me and Morris trying out a *Kama Sutra* position.

Thereafter followed the Mother of All Palavers.

Morris couldn't let Odette loose in her hysterical state, so he had to bribe her. First with the house, and then, when that wouldn't shut her up, the car, and finally all of their savings.

It was touch and go a few months while the divorce was being settled. What if Odette took the ultimate revenge and ran off her mouth at everybody, including Carmel? Me and Morris was on tenterhooks, expecting to be ex-communicated from everyone we knew, including our children.

But Odette was a better woman than that. I think she was still in love with Morris. She said he was the only man she'd ever slept with. Same with Carmel: the only man she's ever slept with is me.

Odette returned to Antigua and built a spa hotel, became a rich woman over there. Kept her word too, because Morris's sons, Clarence and Laurence, never treated their father no different.

Once Morris started to recover from the drama of his divorce, he got ideas too big for the tiny, rented studio flat he'd moved into after Odette had taken him to the cleaners.

It was late afternoon.

Smoke billowed outside of the open attic window and dissolved into the sky.

The ceiling was stained from thousands of cigarettes, the wardrobe's door had a mottled mirror that made a man's face look pockmarked, the carpet was bejewelled with a galaxy of filthy gold stars.

'We middle aged now, Barry,' Morris said, as he lay in my arms smoking a Marlboro Light.

'*Youthful* middle aged,' I replied.

'What I want to suggest is,' Morris continued, suddenly unnaturally still, 'why don't we share a midlife crisis and move in together?'

I said nothing, deftly removed the cigarette from his two fingers and took a deep drag.

'We could head out to the other side of London, maybe? Get our own place. Somewhere anonymous, like Shepherd's Bush or even Hammersmith.'

Morris's tone was casual, like he didn't want to scare me, like what he was suggesting was *très ordinaire*.

'This is some doodle-bug you dropping, Morris.'

He turned his head to me.

I extended my hand.

He passed over the fag.

'Your children grown up. You got no reason to stay. Not so?'

'Move in with you?'

'Your hearing is correct, Barry.'

'Now?'

'Not in the next five minutes but maybe in the next five months.'

We lay there.

I inhaled long and slow, funnelling the fire-smoke through my nostrils.

Looked across at the open window. The autumn trees shedding their leaves.

'Morris,' I replied slowly, 'I don't know if I can jump into the great abyss of social alienation with you.'

I'd been under such pressure back home. A young man showing no interest in girls, when he could have any one of them? I was twenty-four when I married Carmel, and I'd almost left it too late for some. They was talking, and I was afraid I'd be up before a judge on some trumped-up charge of indecent exposure; or end up lying on an operating table with a bar of wood between my teeth and electric volts destroying parts of my brain for ever; or in the crazy house pumped full of drugs that would eventually drive a sane man mad.

Carmel was perfect: young, fun, naive, love-struck.

'You forgotten what happened to Horace Johnson?' I said to Morris, stubbing out the cigarette in the big glass ashtray on my lap. 'Most popular teacher in our school, lived alone, didn't have a girl, didn't mix and was accused of touching up some fella in the market. Remember the day he hanged himself in the crazy house?'

We all thought England was goin' be utopia.

This country has over fifty million citizens, whereas we didn't even have fifty thousand in the whole of Antigua and Barbuda. Folk could get lost here, be anonymous, lead they own quiet lives. In this city you can live on the same street as your neighbours for eighty years and not even say good morning unless there's a war on and you forced to share a bomb shelter. Back home everybody kept their eye on everything and everyone.

I lit another cigarette.

'This is 1980s London, Barry,' Morris said, sitting up and facing me. 'Not 1950s St John's. Why we acting so backwards? *It* is legal. *We* are legal. Nobody goin' arrest us. 'Tis we own blasted business what we do, and everybody else can keep their small-minded noses out of it.'

He put his hand on my wrist. I didn't realize it was shaking.

'This is some heavy crap we dealing with, Morris. You

35

asking me to turn my life upside down. I don't know if I can take the upheaval.'

To be honest, I didn't know what to say or think. I was a man of words for all occasions, except this one.

'Don't let me down. I depending on you.'

And with that, he leapt off the bed in one movement, like the dancer he could've been with that coiled, sprung body.

He started to get dressed while I watched.

I talked myself into it. Why shouldn't I live with Morris instead of sneaking around like a thief? I could do it. I could be brave. The whole point of a midlife crisis is to start living the life you want instead of tolerating the life you have.

It was a Sunday afternoon, early 1990, and me and Carmel was sitting at the kitchen table, drinking rosehip tea from those brown glass mugs we still got today. It was odd, because after a few years of skipping church, dressing up and socializing with her work friends, Carmel had reverted to type and started to treat church like a second home. Consequently she'd been in a bad mood for months, but this one afternoon she was filled with the post-church holiness of the Good Lord, humming a hymn, tapping the table as she read the Bible, dunking chocolate digestive biscuits into her mug, a sure sign she was getting sugar-rush happiness vibes.

I began to speak, tentatively, carefully sprinkling my softly spoken words with 'possibly', 'maybe', 'perhaps', 'trial separation' and 'It's not been right between us for a long time now, dear.'

I should-a just come right out with it and not bothered pussyfooting, because Carmel leapt out of her seat, flew over to the cutlery drawer, drew out a steak knife and *wielded* it.

'Yuh forget what yuh promised, ehn? You goin' take back

your word, ehn? Yuh think I been putting up with you all of these years to have you dump me now? Marriage is for life, you bastard, better or worse, thick or thin, sickness or health, life or *death*.'

The wife's subtle powers of persuasion did the trick. It was her first display of domestic violence. Yesterday was her second.

When I declined Morris's offer, he went into a major hump that lasted months. Wouldn't return my calls, wouldn't answer the door, and one time he walked straight past me in the street. When he did come round, it took about a year for him to really warm to me again.

Eventually he moved out of the studio flat he'd been renting and into a poky one-bedroom Ujima Housing Association flat in Stamford Hill – with the traffic thundering past day and night. We did it up. None of this flowery wallpaper, flowery carpets, fake flowers and flying ducks décor both Carmel and Odette thought the height of sophistication, but white walls, green plants, wooden floors, pine furniture.

Number of times I offered to buy him someplace bigger for himself, hand over the deeds and everything.

But that man is stubborn, *ta-rah-tid*.

'No, thank you, Mr Walker. I am perfectly capable of standing on my own two feet.'

I look over at Morris now, over two decades later in this The Year of Our Lord 2010, sitting at the table drinking hot chocolate and reading that rubbish red-top newspaper he pores over so closely you'd think it was *The Times Literary Supplement*.

We fit each other.

Always have. I goin' make him an offer of a lifetime, and then I goin' tell the wife.

'Morris, you know . . . Why don't you occupy your grey matter with something more substantial? Here, read some Shakespeare, like you said you was goin' to.'

I swipe my copy of *Shakespeare's Sonnets* over at him. He swipes it right back without looking up from his red-top. 'Not now, Barry.'

He starts drinking his hot chocolate in that slurpy-slurpy way of his, putting his head down in the mug and suctioning it up, like a horse in a trough. Morris been living alone too long. Needs someone to remind him every now and again how to behave in company. His personal hygiene is still good, though. Thank God he never gets that skanky smell of ole men who live alone. Every Christmas I buy him Acqua Di Parma's Colonia eau de Cologne. Keeps him smelling sweet the whole year.

'Morris, yuh slurping again. What happened to your brought-upsy?'

'And you breathing too often and too heavily.'

'Morris, it's bad manners, not civilized and, quite frankly, irritating.'

'Don't get me started on what is irritating about you, because I go be here all day. You too critical for a start. When's Carmel coming back? I starving.'

'Yuh see how much you listen to me? The respect I get?'

'Why do I have to respect you? Is more than respect I have for you. Yuh getting greedy now?'

'I have always had an insatiable appetite, as well you know . . .'

'Don't kid yourself, ole boy. Your virility is usually dependent on Viagra these days.'

He looks up from his rubbish red-top and gives me one of his charming-disarming smiles. The fool can still work his magic.

Me and him could rub along together under the same roof. Same as we always done. Wind each other up, then wind each other down again.

I want to broach my plan with him but, just as I've worked myself up to it, he returns to reading and I bottle out. I start thinking how this house has been my home since 1963. My feet are cemented to its foundations. Problem is, so are Carmel's. Lady-Wife won't give it up, and by rights I should relinquish it to the aggrieved party. But to leave here will be like dismantling and re-mantling myself in some strange, cold place. Houses don't turn into homes straightaway. They need years of a life lived to feel comfortable.

We got three floors: one attic, three bedrooms, two large reception rooms (front room and sitting room in the back), bathrooms, toilets – all freshly cleaned, aired and anointed with sweet-smelling pot-pourri. As well as a garage extension large enough to house my 1993 Ford Mustang, 1984 Jaguar Sovereign and 1970 Buick Coupe Convertible, which spent years rusting in the forecourt under a cover until Carmel's moaning got to me and I cleared the garage to make space for it.

Carmel goes over the house from top to bottom of a Saturday afternoon after she does the shopping. She is the Leader of the Clean World, waging her own personal war on the terror of dirt. She even empties out the bathroom and kitchen cupboards weekly, and bleaches them, as if she's back in Antigua, where deterring tropical creepy crawlies was a necessity. That woman is a lunatic with the Hoover too. I have to move fast or she will ram the damned thing into my legs. Soon as I hear its unmistakable battle roar, I know better than to stay around. I go pass the after-noon with Faruk and Morris and whoever else pops into Bodrum's, the Turkish café round the corner.

The street is nice and quiet these days too. Two months ago a whole heap of rabble-rousers moved into the house opposite, started holding parties Saturday nights and charg-ing an entrance fee, like a seventies blues. Wembley Stadium-sized sound systems was blaring hip-hop into the early Sunday hours. Boy, we did a-suffer under their bass-thumping, tin-pot dictatorship. Every time I tried to sleep it was like I was vibrating on one those reclining mas-sage chairs me and Morris try out for free on the fourth floor of Selfridges.

Lo and behold, someone firebombed the place while they was out one evening a fortnight ago. The boys in blue did their investigations but came up with nothing. I reckon it was ole Giap next door. His house is stuffed with military paraphernalia, and he talks like he still planting booby traps in the jungles of Vietnam. Good luck to him. I ain't snitching.

Since then, weekends are back to what they should be, silent and cosy, except for the whirring rumble of a distant lawn mower or the squeals of young children playing in the back gardens.

It is what I used to.

It is what I know.

It makes me feel safe.

Yet I go leave it?

Yes, I go be brave enough to do that, right?

The smell of goat curry and rice and peas in coconut milk is slow-cooking on the stove, making me salivate. A big pot that will last the week. No one can beat Carmel's culinary skills. I will miss them for sure.

One time when we was peaceably eating, I said, 'This food, my dear, is sublime. Cooking is what you was put on earth to do. Why not open up a restaurant?'

Wifey was reading the Bible. She peered over the top of her headmistressy bifocals and shot me a look that showed my disembodied head being impaled on top of a lamp-post at Dalston Junction.

Touchy . . .

She's already baked the macaroni cheese that just needs to be warmed up. Coleslaw is chilling in the fridge, all crunchy with apples and carrots to temper the spices of the curry. And when she comes back from church, she will probably fry some plantain just the way I like it: browned, crisp, slightly burnt at the edges, but soft and succulent inside.

I watch Morris. He can tell I'm watching him.

Go on, Morris, ask me what's up, man.

'What's on your mind?' he says, not even bothering to look up from his red-top, activating powers of telepathy honed by sixty years of close contact with his significant other.

'Me and Carmel.'

'She give you a hard time last night . . . or rather this morning?'

'She always give me a hard time. That woman is a fro-ward tongue-lasher, for sure.'

'You give her a hard time too, don't forget.'

'Yes, but she give me a harder time than I give her.'

'Try telling her that.'

I can't tell him Carmel slapped me and got away with it.

You can't tell another man that you've been the victim of domestic violence or that you afraid you goin' wake up one of these days tied to the bed with your foot chopped off like in that film *Misery*.

'Whose side you on, Morris?'

'My side. It the only side that don't let me down. So wha-go-wan, Barry?'

He stops reading, sits up and finally pays proper attention.

Yuh wan fu know?

'Morris, mi can't deal with all of this marital craptitude no more. There comes a point when the mask has to drop and the charade has to stop.'

Speak plain, Barry, you eedyat.

'You chose the life you have, remember? So don't go complaining now and expecting sympathy,' he says, a bit gloatified.

'I can't take no more, Morris. Look, I've decided to leave Carmel. Seriously. I decided this morning, and you'll be happy to hear that I've finally come round to your idea that we shack up together.'

I realize I'm getting a taste of how he felt all of those years ago. I am not given to jitteriness, but it's jitteriness I feeling, and *vulnerable*, like one of those annoying *emotionalists*.

But instead of joy and gratitude spreading over Morris's face at the news that I have finally come around to his way of thinking, exasperation and annoyance cloud it.

He goes into one.

'*My* idea? You referring back to the last time we had this conversation, which was on 14 September 1989 at about four o'clock in the afternoon to be exact? I was in a bad way after me and Odette had divorced, and you was a coward, Barry. I waited years for you to change your mind while I been . . .'

Morris strokes the invisible goatee that used to grow on his chin.

'You been what?'

'All on my own.'

'You been lonely? I see you practically every day.'

Morris winces. 'I prefer the word *independent*. Who cares? I used to it by now.'

He puts on his glass-half-empty face.

This is not the response I expected. What is wrong with him? Just because I been living with Carmel don't mean I've not been lonely as hell too.

'You should-a talked to me.'

'No point in talking if it can't change the situation.'

'Well, this time I've had enough of Carmel, really and truly. I don't want to live my life with this daily fretment no more. I made the wrong decision all of those years ago. Now I go make the right one.'

'You're admitting it, finally?'

His face goes from half empty to a quarter empty and therefore, mathematically speaking, three quarters full.

I keep up the pressure. 'We seventy-five years ole next year, Morris. Can you believe it? Wha' d'ya say we spend the fourth quarter of our cycle together – *discreetly*? Just like those couples you always telling me about in that rubbish red-top you reading. Those ole widowed folk who meet at bingo and get married. Or that Irish fella you told me about who rediscovered the childhood sweetheart he hadn't seen since 1935. He was ninety-two, she was ninety-one, and they finally tied the knot last year.'

C'mon, Morris. Rise up thyself, look pleased, man.

'You reckon we got another twenty-five years on this earth?' Morris says, wrinkling up his forehead. 'Is this your positive thinking nonsense again? We are two feet away from the knackers' yard, my friend.'

'I goin' be around at least another twenty years, so stop your negativity. What I keep telling you? Glass half full, my man.'

'Which means it half empty too, right? Or do I not understand the laws of chemistry and physics? Age might be relative, but, relative to anybody under the age of seventy, we nearer to death than to life.'

He's right: the inescapable truth is that it's not easy approaching your ninth decade. You look back with nostalgia on the time when the force of your piss could dislodge bricks in a wall, from two whole yards away.

You remember the time when your body moved as fast as your mind, and it didn't feel like your legs was filled with concrete when you tried to run.

You remember the time when you had hair on your head.

These days you have a little heartburn, you think you having a heart attack.

The finishing line got that much closer.

Unless you one of the lucky ones, marathon soon be done.

But I'm not telling Morris any of this. It will just make him more negative than before. Far as he's concerned, I am the greatest exponent of the Pollyanna Principle.

'As for discretion,' he continues, 'there'll be no gossip, Barry. You think folk be whispering, *Oh, look at those two horny studs goin' at it behind closed doors*? No, man. They be saying, *Oh, look at those two sweet* OAP *gentlemen keeping each other company and changing each other's bedpans*.'

Maybe this is Morris's way of saying yes.

'Which pretty much sums it up these days, not so, Morris? The whole point of leaving Carmel is to move in with you. I'd rather put up with your bickering and snickering than Carmel's sniping any day.'

'How . . . *delightful*.'

'And we can get in *staff*: a cook, housekeeper, gardener; otherwise everything will go to pot.'

'In case you hadn't noticed, my home is spotless. You see, Barry, one of us is the original domestic goddess and the other one is the original domestic slut.'

'Yes, yes, yes,' I say, waving my hand at him, warming to the possibility of freedom. 'Imagine it. We can live any-where we so-to-choose. How about Miami? I hear that place is full of pooftahs. Maybe we can live in a luxurious bunga-low in Florida with sprinklers on the lawn and half-naked butlers serving up our evening aperitif.'

Morris, who's been rocking back in his chair, slams the chair back down with such force he should be careful he don't damage his coccyx.

'This is no joke, Barry,' he says, his voice hardening. 'I'm not having you mess me around. I'm used to living on my own. Is not like I been privately suffering all of these years because I was so cruelly spurned by my paramour twenty years ago, same one now making promises he can't keep.'

'Morris, I serious,' I protest, reaching out for his arm.

Except he has gone into lockdown. Some damage limit-ation is due, and, just when I've thought of what to say to unlock him again, he bangs the table like his fist is a gavel. 'No, I'd rather things stay as they are at this late stage. You are not goin' mess me around, Barry. I can't take that. No, no, no, no, no.'

Damnation and botheration. I will show him, yes, I will show him that I am not capricious, nor fickle, cowardly or weakly. I will show him by example. Soon as Sunday lunch done, I goin' have a word with Carmel and tell her I divorcing her . . . before I chicken out.

Yes, I goin' do it.

Like the phoenix rising from the ashes of my marriage, I go spread my wings and be born anew.

4.

The Art of Sunday Lunch

Sunday, 2 May 2010

I hear voices at the door. Carmel is not alone.

How many times I told her not to bring back the 5,000 after church?

I see the cronies piling in, because we have a multi-coloured 1970s bead curtain wrapped around the frame where a kitchen door should be. Carmel is of the belief that everything you acquire should last for life – clothes, shoes, bedding, carpet, towels, furniture, *husband*.

The cronies are exalted after a three-hour church service, where they've been talking in tongues. Many moons ago, when Carmel finally managed to cajole her husband into goin' to the Pentecostal church she'd joined after she left the Baptist one we both went to in the sixties (before I realized I didn't need to go into no church to have a word in God's ear), I listened closely to this tongue-talking. Was they praying to end suffering, poverty and wars? To help the lame to walk, the deaf to hear, the blind to see? Not a bit of it. They was praying for a 'new car', 'cruise holiday', 'double-fronted fridge-freezer with water dispenser' and . . . 'Just one last thing, dear God, a new loft conversion.'

Within seconds it is the Charge of the Fright Brigade down my hallway, and they have colonized my kitchen: Miss Merty, Miss Drusilla, Miss Asselietha, Miss Candaisy.

I known them all since they was young, seeing as we all lived neck and neck in the Ovals in St John's, where everybody knew everybody else's business.

Merty and Carmel been partners in crime over sixty years, ever since Merty and her aunt moved next door to Carmel's house on Tanner Street after Merty's mother, Eunette, migrated to America and settled in the Bronx, where she raised a second family. She sent money back but never sent for Merty, as promised.

Drusilla's mother, Miss Ella, was a higgler who used to sail off to St Croix and St Thomas to buy underwear and costume jewellery to sell back in Antigua. Her father, Mr O'Neal, picked cotton on the Hermitage Estate, where he lived. *One step up from slavery, and where you'll end up for sure* was what my father used to threaten me with any time I tried to shirk my homework.

O'Neal had seventeen children by five women.

He must-a felt like a real man.

Only way he could.

Drusilla was blessed with good hair, red skin, and the kind of exaggerated appendages men in hot countries want to do things to. Soon enough the island's biggest crook, Maxie Johnson, swept her off her feet and into his palatial yard. By the time Drusilla had three pickney under the age of three, Maxie was incarcerated on another island, Rikers – courtesy of the New York City Department of Correction.

Sweetness start to sour even before she turn twenty.

Candaisy's mother, Mrs Ferguson, was the seamstress all the English women paid to copy the latest European fashions. Her daddy worked sugar in Cuba for seven years to buy a plot of land in the Ovals and returned to get work as a supervisor at the Antigua Sugar Factory. Ferguson had five boys but adored his one and only daughter, Sweet Little Miss Candaisy.

Asseleitha lived in a hut up the remote coast of Barbuda with her widowed fisherman father, two older brothers and two younger sisters. Wasn't a few hundred folk on the whole island and most of them was far away in Codrington. She came over to St John's when she was twelve, after the baby she had was sent off to New York to be raised by an aunt. Asseleitha got taken in by Candaisy's mother, who was a distant relative. Even though it meant she now had seven pickney living in a two-bedroom house.

That's the way it was: women raised each other's children and nobody expected no thanks. Wasn't no big deal. Was normal in our world.

All five cronies went to Miss Davis Primary, even Asseleitha, who was older but had catching up to do, seeing as her father had kept her off school.

Merty is wearing a dark blue dress all buttoned up to the neck, almost, but not quite, choking her (*un-for-tu-nate-ly*), a blue cardigan, grey tights, black lace-ups.

Drusilla's church attire consists of a purple dress, white shoes and matching floppy hat the size of an open parasol, which will poke you in the eye if you don't watch out.

Miss Candaisy's in a brown polka-dot dress, and she got on her 'church wig', with fluffy auburn curls rather reminiscent of Shirley Temple's.

As for Asseleitha, that woman is so thin her front and back are interchangeable, and her green beret must-a been transplanted on to her skull, because I ain't seen her without it.

Carmel's got on her church uniform of blue pleated skirt

and white blouse. She don't say any version of hello or goodbye to me these days, but I know she still vexed. None of the cronies acknowledge me when they enter. Carmel's been bad-mouthing me so long they think I am rotten egg. They all gonna hate me even more when I go leave wifey.

She nods curtly at Morris before sorting out cold drinks and pouring oil in the frying pan for the *three* plantain, which has now got to be shared between *seven*.

Meanwhile Drusilla is working off her churchified fervour by pacing up and down at the far end of the kitchen, practically swinging her black handbag that's got a brick-sized Bible sticking out of it, like a slingshot at the Highland Games.

I should be wearing a motorbike helmet in case she sends it across the room.

Merty's the Don Corleone of the church mafia, and if she'd had her way she'd-a put out a contract on me decades ago.

She sits down at the opposite end of the table, thuggish cannon balls in combat position.

'You see Annie's granddaughter just now? Tanesha?' she says, hands over stomach.

Here we go . . .

'Who told her a miniskirt was suitable attire for God's House of Worship? I blame all-a-those disgusting pop stars like that Gaga creature who wears nothing but yellow tape around her private parts. What those no-good whores should remember is . . .' She looks up at the ceiling. 'God . . . Never . . . Sleeps.'

Miss Merty, every time you open your mouth I remember why your ex, Clement, dug a tunnel underneath the perimeter wall of your house and escaped on to a passing train many decades ago. You just spent three hours in a church that's supposed to preach love, kindness, forgiveness and spiritual enlightenment, so why you come back spewing vitriol?

Used to be worse when Pastor George headed up the Church of the Living Sinners back in the 1970s. Most of them acted like lovesick teenagers around him. Me and Morris called them the Brides of Brother George. None of them questioned the fact that this Man of the Cloth was driving around in a spanking-new saloon Bentley.

Pastor did the rounds of his most sycophantic parishioners in the evenings, treated to their finest meals and finest liquor. Perks of the trade, he once told me with a wink, when I opened the door to him and all but reeled from the gale force of his cologne. Number of times Carmel came back from church spouting stuff like 'Oh, Pastor George delivered a very fine sermon this morning, Barry. All about philanderers, homosicksicals, and moral reprobates.'

She'd raise an eyebrow and give me one of her lingering looks, about which I could write a 2,000-word essay: interpretation, history, context, intention, *insinuation*.

I used to say to Morris, 'Methinks Pastor Slimeball doth protest too much.' Next thing you know, article appears in the *Hackney Gazette* about how some rent-boy's been blackmailing him – had photographic evidence. Soon after, Pastor vanished with the church funds.

I try not to mention his name *too* often in front of Carmel, especially when she's holding a Dutch pot.

She puts the food on the table, and we all circulate it, passing bowls, cutlery, condiments and plates. I make a mental note of who is taking more than their fair share.

Merty, *par exemple*, helps herself to five large slices of plantain when statistically we should each have three.

Morris notices too, and we exchange glances about what a greedy arse she is.

He usually sits quietly when the Living Sinners invade, and, because he is not a man of property, they ignore him.

The cronies compliment Carmel on her culinary skills.

'It tastes good, Carmel,' says Candaisy. Unlike Merty and Drusilla, Candaisy's not got a bad word to say about anybody. All of which makes her more likeable but also agonizingly boring. If you looking for an argument, you end up fighting with yourself.

'Yes, Ma. It bang good,' Drusilla agrees.

The doorbell rings, and my heart sinks. This lot must be the infantrymen, and it's the cavalry that's now arrived – the second, even holier-than-thou wave who clear up after church in order to suck up to their latest dreamboat, Pastor Wilkinson, who's as much a hypocrite as his predecessor.

I'm in luck. It's my elder girl, Donna, and her boy, Daniel, whom I hardly see from one year to the next these days. Donna looks well vexed that the place is busting with the cronies.

With her scraped-back hair and shiny black tracksuit she looks more like an off-duty check-out girl for Tesco than a Social Work Trainer for Tower Hamlets. She says hi-hi-hi to everyone, excluding the one male person in the room who gave her *life*. Carmel must-a been on the phone first thing.

Donna don't need much of an excuse to give me the cold shoulder anyways. She's always taken her mother's side on the bloody battlefield of animosity. I usually feel her disapproval soon as I walk into a room. She thinks I ain't got no feelings. And when I leave her mother she goin' despise me even more.

Daniel comes over to give his granddaddy a shoulder-squeeze. This is the boy I used to take to the Natural History Museum to see the dinosaurs, and to the London Aquarium to see the dolphins. Then he lost interest in trips out with Grandy. Just as well. There's a period between the Terrible Twos and the Terrible Teens when children are delightful company – after that, it's best you lock them in a basement and feed them food through a coal hole until they leave home.

Look at him now, a sixteen-year-old giant. I wonder if he'll take my side?

From the start it was obvious that Daniel's father, Frankie, wasn't goin' pay no maintenance, so I stepped in and bank-rolled his education. From the age of eleven that boy has never experienced a class size larger than twelve. Naturally he's flying on the Magic Carpet of Private Education all the way to Oxbridge Heaven. Donna has decreed he will study what they call PPE: Politrickery, Pontification and E-criminal-omics.

Far as she's concerned that boy is Obama Mark II.

He's only allowed out Saturday nights and no girlfriends until he's finished school.

She jokes she's a benevolent dictator.

I joke she should drop the 'benevolent' crap.

'Ease up, Donna. Give Daniel some freeness.'

'Dad, my son is *not* going to end up a statistic.'

And that's the problem: too many of our kids do. It can't be easy being a single mother of a growing lad, a-true.

Daniel fetches two fold-up chairs from the cupboard under the stairs. Comes and sits down next to his grandy.

That makes nine for lunch: Merty in face-off; Carmel, Candaisy and Morris to my right; Asselietha and Drusilla to my left; Big Chief and Young Chief side by side. Ain't goin' be no stew leftovers for me this week.

I savour a succulent piece of goat, and wash it down with a smooth and replenishing swallow of the Great Tranquillizer.

'Hope there's some food left,' Donna says, scanning the bowls on the table. Donna is a lazy cow. All of her life she's been eating her mother's meals, but she never reciprocates. Eats Chinese and McCrap. My daughter is most definitely a second-generation bra-burner.

'Mum, is there any wine?'

You want wine? Why didn't you bring some?

Carmel shakes her head and gets the conversation goin' again by revealing what Tryphena, one of their acquaintances, *confided* in her before church: that her eldest daughter, Melissa, has got fibroids. Now Melissa is a GP. We all know this because Tryphena's been slipping this into every conversation for the past twenty years. Not only a GP but a *senior partner* in the *Royal* Borough of Kensington and Chelsea, as if that puts Melissa and, by extension, Tryphena in direct line to the throne.

'Really? How big are they?' Drusilla asks, barely able to contain her excitement.

Best news is bad news for the media and Miss Drusilla LaFayette.

'They're inside the lining of the womb, so they can't easily be extracted. Apparently, as Melissa is menstruating three weeks out of four, she got to have hysterectomy.'

Superb Sunday lunch conversation you started up, dear, while we're all eating lumpy tendons of goat.

'She got pickney?'

'No, Drusilla, she hasn't.'

'Well, once that womb is out, no babies for her,' Drusilla states, adjusting the parasol on her head for emphasis.

Drusilla should apply to join MENSA . . . really.

'You see, these women have brought it on themselves,' she continues, waving her knife and fork in the air. 'You can't cheat nature. Woman should have baby by age twenty-five latest. That way they just pop out like golf balls.'

Merty, who don't like to be upstaged, looks sternly at Drusilla. 'You talking nonsense, Drusilla. Fifty-year-old women can have children these days.'

Lovely . . . I am witnessing a coup d'*étits* around this very table.

Yes, ladies, slug it out.

Although Drusilla is used to being slapped down by Merty, today she's determined to fight her corner.

'Yes, they can but then the pickney comes out with two heads and ten legs, though, isn't it? Anyways, how we know Melissa hasn't had abortion? This is how career women carry on. Make baby, kill baby, make baby, kill baby, make ba—'

Merty bulldozes her aside. 'Yes, but there's one person who knows everything.' She points upwards. 'Maybe he's punishing her.'

I look over at Carmel and see she is almost having a fit.

I have never understood why my very intelligent wife (in spite of her faults) remains loyal to these women.

Carmel was a late-blooming women's libber: first-generation bra-burner. Not literally, thanks be to God, because my wife's bosoms has always been supported by sturdy architectural appliances. We both encouraged our girls to get an education and have careers. Carmel herself studied part time. Got herself a degree in Business Administration and a job in Housing at the Hackney Town Hall. Became uncharacteristically political for a few years, mouthing off about the miners' strike, nuclear disarmament, even the IRA. I blamed working in a loony-left town hall. But, like all aberrations, her political period passed.

By the time she retired, wifey was a Senior Housing Manager with 2,000 properties under her jurisdiction in Hackney.

Merty's getting into her stride now; plays her trump card.

'And another thing, I hear from very good authority on the grapevine that Melissa is one of those women who lies down with women.'

Yes, you go-wan, Merty. All roads in your dutty mind lead back to sex.

'Yes, I think I heard that too . . . er . . .' Drusilla says unconvincingly, glancing nervously at Merty but determined to continue her bid for power. 'What I always say is, if woman was meant to lie down with woman, God would have given woman penis.'

Her problem is that when her mouth speaks, it don't ask her brain for permission first.

'If Melissa is one of those lesbian characters,' she adds, rising to her theme, 'it is an abomination. Does it not say in Romans that if man lies with man as he lies with woman, he will surely be put to death? Same goes with woman–woman business, and even that high and mighty pope over there in the Vatican agrees with me on this one.'

Miss Drusilla could be a professional orator for sure, a

silver-tongued politician with the power to sway millions with her mastery of the silky art of verbal persuasion.

Meanwhile, neither Drusilla nor Merty notice that Donna is grinding her back teeth. Same way she used to when I told her off as a child.

She opens her mouth.

I can't wait to hear what comes out of it.

Unlike her mother, my daughter is brave enough to nose-dive without a parachute.

Knows her Bible too, seeing as Carmel dragged her to church every Saturday and Sunday for most of her childhood.

'With respect. With *respect*, Drusilla, Merty.' She sounds like the Speaker of the House of Commons. (Ever since she's been training social workers, she's got worse.) 'God also said that eating shellfish such as shrimp and lobster is an abomination. And Leviticus has all this nonsense in it about how we shouldn't wear material woven of two kinds of cloth, and that if you curse your parents you'll be put to death, and that slavery is fine.'

Donna Walker is playing to the gallery, the city, the country, the *world*.

'Look here, we don't accept such scriptures, right? Isn't it crazy to base our opinions on arguments written in Leviticus 3,500 years ago?'

Thank you, Donna, for rescuing your father's dignity even though you don't know it.

Lovely silence.

Loaded silence.

Merty and Drusilla look down at their food like it's steaming-hot excrement.

Carmel is fingering her wedding ring like she never seen it before.

Morris is laughing inside but doing a good job of hiding it from everyone but me.

We goin' post-mortemize this later, *big time*.

Candaisy is transfixed by the sky outside.

Asselietha's head is bowed, like she praying.

I glance sideways at Daniel, who is texting under the table.

Donna continues, 'Who cares what Melissa is or isn't? It her own business. Saint Mark said we're supposed to love everyone as Christ did, unconditionally and without discrimination. My moral compass is based on various spiritual beliefs syncretized with the core values of Christ's teachings, the bits that make sense to me, at least.'

Syncretized . . . Moral compass.

Donna has inherited my super-lexical gene. Both my girls have. Not that she'd ever credit me for it.

As for her so-called 'spiritual beliefs', Carmel told me years ago that Donna is a secret 'goddess-worshipper', but she warned me not to let on I knew or Donna would be furious.

'As for some of that outrageous music out there? Buju Banton, Beenie Man and the rest with their sexist, homophobic lyrics?'

Yes, Donna. You go-wan. Far as she's concerned, all social ailments lead back to the effect of pernicious music on the youth of today.

'When I hear this child . . . this *child* of mine listening to that rubbish, I go through the roof. Really I do. Worse, it's the middle-class kids who buy this stuff, the wannabe hoodies at his school, the doctors', bankers' and lawyers' children. *They're* the bad influence.'

She shakes her head, and Daniel looks up sharply while slyly pocketing his mobile phone.

'Leave me out of it, Mum.'

'Well, I won't tolerate it.'

'I can listen to what I like.'

'Not on my watch you can't,' Donna snaps, flinging out her hand and knocking over her glass of Ribena, where it stays, spreading rather metaphorically over the white cotton tablecloth.

Merty and Drusilla, hitherto admonished, perk up at this altercation.

'So, Donna', Merty seizes the moment, 'if Daniel was one of *them,* an anti-man, you'd be happy with that?' She mimics, 'Mum, I'd like you to meet my boyfriend. He's called Giles Smythe.'

Drusilla bursts out laughing. At this point Daniel groans, scrapes back his chair and looks ready to leave the room, but something holds him back. I want to tell Donna not to answer: she's playing you, trying to assert her position as top dog. But, oh dear, Donna deflates in her chair. I can hear the air hiss out of her.

What just happened to my ball-breaker daughter? Champion of Human Rights and Political Correctness?

Problem is, Donna was raised to respect her aunties, her *elders*, especially Merty, her mother's best and most powerful friend. Somehow Merty just reduced her to feeling like an eight-year-old again..

'I've no idea if Daniel is "one of them", as you put it. If he is . . . it would be up to . . . him.'

She ain't answered the question.

'Yes, but Donna . . . would you like it? Would you approve? Would you tell your friends and skip around your house singing?'

'Of course I wouldn't jump for joy, but, as I said, it would be up to him. Most likely it would be . . . a phase. All teenagers go through *phases*.'

Donna certainly did, but I won't bring that up now.

'You wouldn't like it, then?' the Grand Inquisitor shoots back, elbows on the table, face radioactive.

Merty's the product of a lifetime of hardship, ever since she mommy left her. Everybody else gotta pay.

'The point is that people should be free to express themselves as they want to.'

'So, tell me, Donna, would you prefer it if he brought a girl home, not a boy? Honestly?'

Donna starts to mop up the spilt juice with a napkin, but she's just swirling it around on the table. 'Yes, of course, any mother would . . . I want grandchildren.'

'You can still get grandchildren, so that's no excuse. This means you wouldn't like it?'

Merty keeps her eyes trained on Donna.

My daughter looks helpless, paralysed.

But I can't get involved. How can I?

Carmel would normally intervene on behalf of her favourite child, although she don't like to stand up to Merty, but she's quieter than usual; must have her dying father on her mind.

'Look at him . . .' Merty is unable to stop her worst self running amok. 'He could become an anti-man. All his speaky-spokiness and private schooling that everyone knows is a breeding ground for sodomites.'

My grandson has had enough. He draws himself up, and, in the expensive Queen's accent that has cost me a fortune in school fees, booms, 'That's it, I've fucking had enough of this. Stop talking about me like I'm not here. Mum, I'll be outside.'

And he gone.

Is this the little boy who used to fine me tenpence for swearing or he'd report me to Donna?

A voice wades into the conversation. 'Look how you upset this young boy.'

Is this me talking?

'You should be ashamed . . . insinuating things. How you think that make him feel? And my daughter don't need to justify herself to anyone in this room.'

I just rode in on a white steed brandishing a gold-tipped sabre.

Merty blinks slowly and swivels her head away from me, as though her head is set on ball bearings and can do a 360-degree turn.

Donna offers me a grateful grimace. Daddy has redeemed himself. (It never lasts.) She stands up, picks up her bag, takes her car keys out, departs.

The two Gorgons sit there.

Pumped up. Victorious. Primed.

Candaisy, who rarely says peep anyway, keeps her eyes averted from everyone.

Asselietha's wearing that screwed-up expression she favours, like her lips are tied into a bunch with invisible string.

The whole lotta them should clear out of my house.

Carmel starts to rattle up the plates.

After such melodramatics, is time for everybody to calm down.

This is when Asselietha decides to pitch in. Why Carmel keeps company with such a nut job is beyond my reasoning.

'Those homos are rightly suffering,' she says. 'God saved us to make us holy, Mr Walker, not happy.'

This is what I truly believe happened to Asseleitha. Someone sliced off the top of her head, scooped out her brains, put them in a blender and turned on the switch. Once it was all mash-up, they poured the mixture back in through her scalp and stitched it all up.

Maybe that's why she never takes off that *narsy* ole beret.

Seeing as the Guinness has reached saturation point, I plunge in. 'What on earth you talking about, Asselietha? Everybody got a right to happiness. Why don't you mind your own business about what people do?'

Everyone freezes except Carmel, who starts making so much noise at the sink it's like the Lancaster Bombers just hit their target – a porcelain crockery factory in Dresden.

I can feel Morris willing me to shut up.

'Why you defending them?' Merty is ready to start on me now.

Thank God Asseleitha comes to my rescue with her derailed train of thought. 'The homos are suffering because suffering is part of their salvation. The Lord says they should be beaten that they mayest be better.'

Laaard. They think Daniel got a temper? It is in his genes. I will show them a temper. I am a lion and what-a lion do?

I stand up and punch the palm of one hand with the fist of another. 'Someone's goin' give you beats one of these days, you crazy lady.'

There is a communal, pantomime gasp of horror, as if I am the kind of monster to really beat a woman.

'I thanks God for your life,' Asseleitha replies, gets up and walks out of the kitchen, as if all her joints been bolted together.

Now Candaisy, who has been eating in a quiet, dignified manner, speaks for the first time.

Candaisy might not be one of the sit-and-bitchers, but she's a sit-and-listen-to-the-bitchers-kind-of-person. According to Carmel, she seeing an OPP (Other People's Property) – a married man five years younger.

Candaisy speaks with the light, breathless, girly voice of women who don't want to grow up.

'I personally . . . I personally . . . think . . .' She timidly trails off.

Right, Miss Candaisy, how the hell else is a person supposed to think except *personally*?

'I personally think we should live and let live. It's not their fault if they're –'

Boy, she brave, goin' up against Hitler and Himmler.

'You're right,' Carmel says gently, putting her hand on her arm in sisterly solidarity. 'It's not their fault they're sick, but it is their fault when they act on it. We should pray for their souls to be saved. Now what I object to, what I *really, really* object to . . .'

She unashamedly eyeballs her husband.

'. . . is the kind of married man who sticks his business in any ole smelly, venereal, baggy pussy that's had more dingle-dangles stuffed up it than I've had hot dinners. Those kind of men should be publicly flogged in the town square.'

At that, Merty's forkful of macaroni cheese, which has started the journey from her plate, can't quite travel all the way to her mouth.

I go to the fridge and fetch another Guinness, slamming the door, imagining a certain head trapped in it.

One day soon I goin' be free of all this.

Then suddenly it's all hustle and bustle and *Must be goin'*, *Carmel dear, and thank you for lunch, Carmel dear.*

'I goin' pray for your daddy, Carmel,' Merty says, hugging her.

'May he live many more years yet,' Drusilla adds, squeezing her shoulders.

What is the matter with her? The man is nearly a *hundred years old*.

'*Charles* is waiting for me,' Drusilla says unnecessarily, a triumphant dig at Merty, who ain't got no one waiting for her.

Charles is some ninety-year-old Jamaican fella been courting her. Carmel told me he owns three houses . . .

Candaisy is the only one who acknowledges me with an empathetic smile as she leaves, as if disassociating herself from the other three, as if she knows the torment within my soul, the suffering I have to endure, and any time I want to offload . . . she ready to listen.

Oh, I see, is this how you catch OPP, Candaisy?

No, Barry, don't be mean, you ole bastard. She all right.

There might be three of us left in this room, but I can still feel the presence of the other cronies as if they're still here, like . . . *Chernobyl*.

Morris is telepathically willing me to do what I said I was goin' do.

This might be my time to talk to Carmel, but is it wise when we both so worked up? Anyways, after four or five or six pints of Guinness, I feeling a bit woozy. End-of-marriage conversations should be conducted stone-cold sober and away from the kitchen knife drawer.

I will talk to her tomorrow. Monday morning is as good

as Sunday afternoon. Before she heads off for Antigua, because who knows how long she'll be gone? That makes sense – or does it? I give Morris the upwards-onwards nod, but Carmel notices. 'Barrington, you ain't goin' nowhere . . . Morris?'

Morris jumps up so fast he almost falls over. You should-a taken it slower, man. Be cool. Don't let her boss you around.

I mouth I'll catch him tomorrow, and he gets up. *Exeunt*.

Melodramatics not done yet.

Carmel wipes her hands on a tea towel and sits down in the chair Merty just vacated.

'Bar-ring-ton,' she begins, slowly, deliberately, like she's struggling to control herself, like I'm her recalcitrant child who goin' be grounded for a month after her *hecture*. 'As well you know, these mi friends, lifelong friends, best friends, most loyal friends, and I don't appreciate you threatening them. After all of this time you don't even know them properly, because you've never bothered to find out who they are deep down inside. You treat them like monsters, when they are real human people with real human feelings who've had a harder life than you'll ever understand, because you lacking in human decency, sensitivity, compassion, all-round empathy and good manners besides.'

I go to defend myself as normal, but I can only let out a croak that is thankfully more silent than not.

'Your problem is you don't go to church to get religious instruction, which is why you ain't got no morals. I'd like to remind you what I said this morning when you sneaked into my bedroom for the millionth time like the skunk you are. Things is goin' change in this house, yuh hear? Soon as I get back from seeing my daddy, we goin' get a new regime and you goin' mend your ways.'

Yes, my dear, things is goin' change beyond your current comprehension and wildest imaginings. You goin' get a new regime all right. Don't worry about that.

'No more late nights and no more no-shows or I goin' make your life hell,' she says. 'You been walking on the dark side too long, Barrington, and now I goin' drag you into the light.'

Then she makes the sign of the cross, bends her head and begins to pray for my soul.

5.

Song of Despair

1970

Carmel, what you doing at eleven o'clock on a Wednesday morning communing with your dark side, flopping about on the settee in the living room, still wearing your maternity dressing gown

the heavy damask curtains drawn but letting through a cold slice of English daylight, while you staring at the ceiling rose with the flowery lampshade hanging from it that you bought from Debenhams in the sales two years ago like

you ain't got nothing better to do with your time and ain't the mother of Donna, who's still only ten years old and needs you?

yes, she needs you to get her sleepy little head out of bed in the morning – get her ready for school *and* take her there

because this is what mothers supposed to do

whether you feel like it or not

and you should wash too, you know

whether you feel like it or not

how long you goin' wait before the dirt on your body has to be scraped off with a trowel?

or you think you don't stink renk and don't need the bubble bath Barry draws for you every evening in vain hope?

listen here, Carmel

why don't you go upstairs right now and scrub up your

filthy-new-baby-flabby-self and leave the scum behind?
whether you feel like it or not
as for Maxine?
you is a disgrace, lady
that child might choke to death any minute, she so wheezy she not been allowed outside the house since Barry brought her home from Intensive Care at Hackney Hospital, where she was tubed up for two whole weeks

but when Barry sticks that *succubus* in your arms, bawling for your teats and wriggling its fingers greedily, wanting to suck the life force out of you and you can't wait to dump her right back in the pink wooden rocking cradle that you bought from Randall's up at Stamford Hill

nor can you forget the time he popped out to the corner shop and you *dropped* her and

when he came back and saw the dark bruise starting to show

he looked at you like you was Myra Hindley

and he not left you alone with her since, but thanks God

she didn't die because baby's skulls is so fragile, thanks God

he didn't call those nosy-parker social workers who none of you like interfering in your *private* business and thanks God

Barry's the man you always thought he could be, right this minute feeding Maxine cow's milk from a bottle in the kitchen when you got a milk cart full of the stuff in your boobies that could feed a whole nursery full of babies

how can you not feed your own child, you *monster*?

like you got anything else to be getting on with?

seeing as

Merty is organizing your household after Barry told her you'd not moved from your bed in days and he was worried like when Donna was born and you went off of your head, and though

Barry calls Merty *Camp Commandant* behind her back, but at least the two of them are communicating these days

and Merty organized a rota with the Ladies' Society of Antigua to help out

so Candaisy cleans your house every Saturday afternoon, even though it has three floors that take four hours to get through because she's so meticulous, what with her now being an auxiliary nurse at Hackney Hospital

although you don't actually care no more if the floors are heaped with *dutty* clothes, or the toilet bowl is caked with shit, or the bathtub has a rim of human grime

and then Candaisy goes home and starts all over again, cleaning the two-bedroom council flat she's living in with her daughter, Paulette, and Robert (from the Bahamas), who still won't marry her

who says he loves Candaisy but y'all think she deserves better than a man who spends most of his wages down the bookies Friday evenings, and thanks God

Asseleitha treks down to Dalston to do the shopping for you at Ridley Road Market on Saturdays (she's now a cook in the staff canteen at the BBC in the Strand, so she can only afford to live in that grotty rented bedsit by Clapton Pond with damp, mildewed walls)

and she comes back weighed down with shopping bags and cooks up a big pot of stew and a big pot of rice to last the whole week, seeing as you too lazy to cook and otherwise you and Donna will have to rely on Barry's cooking capabilities, which is, basically – over-boiled potato, soggy fish fingers, lukewarm baked beans and lumpy jam sandwiches galore

and then Mondays to Fridays, Merty picks Donna up at 8.30 a.m. prompt to take her to William Patten School with her own brood of boys (aged four to ten years) trailing behind her in the snowy sludge, because Merty has five boy pickney, and all for Clement too

who's a good man, even though she calls him Mr Merty in public and you see him squirming, but at least he don't stop out nights and puts his brown pay packet unopened from British Rail on the kitchen table every Friday and

what with his wage and hers from the work cleaning rich people's houses up at Hampstead

they *finally* got a deposit for a mortgage, and to

think you used to be jealous that she had *five* pickney because you wanted more, but Barry don't have much of what they call in *Woman's Own* a 'sex drive', so your monthlies was coming regular for ten years after Donna born

and now you got the second child you said you wanted, but you acting like you don't want her

are you mad?

what is wrong with you? thanks God

Drusilla's night-cleaning shift at the office block down at Bishopsgate starts at 7 p.m. (twelve hours after her first shift runs from 7 a.m. to 10 a.m.), so she can collect Donna from school in the afternoon with her own four pickney (three by Maxie Johnson, who was gunned down in Miami, y'all heard on the Antigua grapevine) and one pickney by that Lewis who came and went) and then she takes all *ten* pickney back to her yard (Merty's five, Drusilla's own four and

70

your Donna) and makes tea for all of them, never once complaining

about you slumping around like the lady of the manor in your big living room looking out on to your big garden, when she's the one in a tiny council house that's been condemned

and Drusilla's the one to wash and plait Donna's hair and grease it with Dax to stop it getting all dried up and matted, even though the English children at school still call Donna *Sambo* in the playground

and to think you used to tell Donna she was a beautiful little girl *every day*, until you reach that point where you went

somewhere else

and you not come back yet

and now she's becoming *Daddy's Girl*

Daddy, who puts her to bed and listens to her reading her favourite book, *Ballet Shoes* by Noel Streatfeild, for the hundredth time

who got time off from work at Ford's

who's home all the time now, when before he was out all of the time

so much so that

one wintry Saturday, in the dark, early hours, you left behind your bed, your hot-water bottle and a sleeping Donna, walked downstairs into the icy hallway, and put your big brown overcoat over your thick polyester nightdress, your black winter Clarks ankle boots over your bare feet, your brown woolly hat over your mussed-up hair, and your blue woollen gloves over your rapidly freezing fingers

and you marched over to his latest property, which he

was *supposed* to be decorating on Palatine Road with Morris, and banged on the big lion head door-knocker

and when the pair of them answered, *eventually*, in their paint-spattered blue overalls with paint brushes in their hand, you still barged inside and had a look, but there was no whores in various states of undress anywhere and so

you skunked off and

felt so *chupit*

but still you worry

he up to *something*

but how can you complain when everybody was so envious of you, especially

when you bought that expensive white leather settee suite from Debenhams that's goin' last a lifetime, because you covered it in plastic and control who sits on it and anybody puts their feet on your sofa they *dead*, yes, *they dead*, plastic or no plastic, socks or no socks

and you building up your nice collection of ornaments too

and then the Ladies' Army of Antigua marched into your house a week ago and straight into the sitting room and sat lined up on the settee: Merty wearing her grey gabardine and blue hat; Drusilla wearing her beige mac with matching rain hat; Asseleitha wearing her black coat and new green beret; and Candaisy wearing the second-hand fox-fur coat Robert bought her when he won the Pools

and you faced the ladies in your armchair, sitting upright in your blue button-up maternity dressing gown with food stains down the front, trying to appear normal

and they said

Carmel, dear, you got to deal with it, same way we always had

to deal with it, life goes on no matter what you feeling, no matter
that you crying and feel
   like dying
   shape up, Carmel, shape up and look after your family and
come back to church to get some holy healing from the Good Lord
   but you can't, can you, because you is a pitiful blob
   you even forgot Donna's birthday yesterday, didn't you?
   when it's *your* job to remember, not Barry's, but when he
found her crying into her pillow in the bedroom he'd
painted all pink for her with rose stencils
   he got on the blower to Merty, who came straight over to
look after Maxine
   while Barry took Donna out for a birthday meal of fish
and chips and a bottle of Coke and strawberry ice-cream for
afters at Fruit of the Sea on Kingsland High Street
   and when she came home so happy and ran up to you,
what you do?
   you pushed her away. *Bitch*
   and Barry hugged her up and just looked at you all
sad-eyed, because you messing up your family home so bad
and he said
   he goin' make an emergency call to the doctor to take
you in before you really harm someone, but you shut him
up with
   over my dead body
   and he could see you meant it, because last time was ten
years ago, when Donna was one month old, and he found
you crying in the bath with a knife, but you was so pathetic
you didn't even leave no scars on your wrists
   the tablets worked that time, but they made you feel like
a zombie

a zombie housewife who couldn't use the brains she was
born with

and why did you leave school so young, you bloody
fooooool?

but what work can you get with no qualifications?

you twenty-six now, Carmel

practically OAP already.

ten years has passed so fast

you ruined, girl

y   o   u   r   u   i   n   e   d

no way are you going to allow a doctor to prod around
inside your mind

because whatever is going on in there, nothing can make
it right

                                                        ever.

6.

The Art of Relationships

Monday, 3 May 2010

It is the day after what I call the Sunday Horror Show and what Morris calls the Nightmare on Cazenove Road, and the wife is at this very moment shooting across the planet in a metal contraption shaped like a condor en route to Antigua. I dutifully drove her to Gatwick Airport in my 1984 Jaguar Sovereign at five o'clock this morning.

We had a very reasonable conversation in my head as we wended our way across London in the misty hour. I found the perfect words to persuade her we divorcing, and she had no choice but to accept my *fait* accomplished.

Except, in the sober light of morning, I realized my timing was completely off. How could I ask for a divorce when she was about to board a plane to be with her dying father after a thirty-year estrangement?

We barely spoke.

'Which terminal you flying from?'

'South.'

'Which airline you flying with?'

'Virgin.'

'How long you gone for?'

No answer. Great. So how long will I have to wait?

Then, at check-in, Carmel turned, looked up at me and asked, 'What happened to us, Barry?' as if we was in one of those romantic comedies she likes to watch and which, upon occasion, I am forced to sit through.

I wanted to tell her we should never-a got married.

'Life happened, Carmel.'

I watched her shuffle through the departure gate wearing one of those shapeless cardigans that reaches the knees, limping with that bad hip or back or whichever one it is, her feet in those orthopaedic-looking shoes women wear when they're not interested in trying to impress men no more. Big Mistake. Is trying to impress us that keeps them on their toes. She's getting a stoop too, because she never took the advice I doled out to our daughters to sit straight and walk tall.

I can't believe this is the sweet girl I knew back home in Antigua. What happened to her? I think England ruined her, changed her for the worse. She used to be a happy person, yes, happy-go-lucky as we used to say, and pretty too. Now look at her, the embodiment of misery.

Yet this was the girl who used to quick-step everywhere in her clickety-clicks, glancing about her like a ballerina striking a calculated pose to catch everybody with her loveliness, always beautifully attired in those flowery dresses splashed with bright colours women wore in the fifties, her hourglass figure cinched with a wide purple belt.

Women have that brief period between the ages of sixteen and twenty-one when they are naturally fresh-faced and attractive, if you like that sort of thing. After that, it's downhill all the way to the grave.

Men, on the other hand, mature nicely.

Samuel L. Jackson, Sean Connery, George Clooney, Morgan Freeman, BJW.

But oh my, Carmel was a lovely young lady. I was proud

to take her to dances after Morris left. She was a brilliant dancer. We'd practise for hours in my mother's yard.

I see her now – twirling her favourite purple satin skirt like a whirling dervish, wriggling her hips fluid as water, kicking those shapely little legs out sharply, pointing her balletic toes in those white bobby socks girls used to love to wear, letting me scoop her up, fling her taut little body into the air and then catch her, and somehow she'd get her legs around my neck and lift herself up to do a somersault over my head and then back-flip on to the floor like she made of rubber, and I'd spin around and she'd stoop down and I'd roll over her back and she'd leap on to me all aerodynamically, as fast and smooth as a swallow in flight, and all the while our legs and arms was jumping and jerking and jiving in time to the beat of 'Rock Around the Clock', and she'd be showing off her frilly, polka-dot, American knickers to all of the young fellas in St John's.

Of course we never did nothing in *that* department. Carmel might-a danced like a goer, but she was pure, even past her wedding night.

As for me, I was always trying to banish thoughts of Morris, who had abandoned me for England. Before he left we used to go to dances together, standing coolly in our short-sleeved white shirts and black ties, leaning against the bar that was usually a rickety trestle table – *surrounded*. The girls might have loved Morris, the Junior Boxing Champ of Antigua, but they was in *thrall* to the Prince of Antigua, exaggerating the roll of their hips when they saw me. Me and Morris secretly amused ourselves with the knowledge that we was both taken.

Or we'd sit in the dark on the rocks at the quay, enjoying the music away from the dance deck and the whirly-gigging teenagers pounding the floorboards, sharing a cigar we'd saved up the whole week to buy.

Couldn't sit out there the whole night, though. We'd have to join in or folk would wonder what was up.

Later, me and him would trek miles to Fort James Beach and find our hidden spot, always alert to sounds, just in case somebody chanced upon us and ruined our lives.

We'd take a plastic bottle of homemade hooch and lie on the sand, working out the constellations, listening to the wash and crash of waves, drinking in the night.

I knew Carmel from young, used to see her and the cronies-in-waiting sitting on the steps of her father's veranda in their big house in Tanner Street, eating peanut-butter snaps, peppermint sticks, black pineapple slices. As they got older and bolder, Merty used to run into the road and offer me a taste of her cane syrup poured over a lump of ice.

She was the ringleader even then.

'We nah sweet enough for you?' she'd holler, pushing up her budding titties and running down the road after me.

When I worked for Carmel's father, Miss Carmel was always around, flirting.

Evenings, Mr Francis Miller, famous scion of the Early Bird Stores, sat on his veranda filling out his big wicker chair in a pinstripe 'city-gent' suit, waistcoat, gold watch chain dangling from a pocket, tie done up tight, collar buttoned down either side and sweat running down his patchy-brown bald head.

A copy of *The Complete Works of William Shakespeare* usually open on his lap.

' "Live loathed, and long, / Most smiling, smooth, detested parasites, / Courteous destroyers, affable wolves, meek bears, /

You fools of fortune, trencher-friends, time's flies, / Cap-and-knee slaves, vapours, and minute-jacks!" '

'Where this come from, Barry? Tell me its provenance.'

What the blasted 'eck did provenance mean?

I acted as if I was on the verge of replying.

'*Timon of Athens*, of course,' he said through his nose.

Mr Miller loved throwing Shakespeare quotes at every man around him, including me, which like a ball we had to catch without dropping, knowing we all had butter fingers.

That man was a buffoon as well as a brute, but he was also my boss.

These days I know my Shakespeare, but I don't use it inflate myself.

When I asked for his daughter's hand, he was delighted, because, like most buffoons, he had no idea what I really thought of him.

Soon as we got married, we migrated to England, Carmel fell pregnant with Donna and lost her mind that first time.

Watching her disappear into Departures this morning, I wished she'd let me go all of those years ago.

If someone asks for their freedom, you got to give it to them; otherwise you become their jailer.

Soon as she's back here on dry land, I goin' serve up her papers, although how long I'll have to wait I don't yet know.

Second I fetched back home from the airport, Maxine was on the blower.

'Dad, you and I are going to talk – *this afternoon*.'

Silence.

'*Alone*.'

This is the problem with having a wife and two daughters.

I called Morris soon as I put the phone down and later we took the bus and tube to Piccadilly Circus.

'Morris,' I said, before he could get in first, 'I couldn't tell her, given her current predicament, her daddy dying and everything. How can I heap trouble upon woe?'

'You're right, Barry, I was thinking the same thing myself last night. We both got caught up with your change of heart and wasn't thinking straight. This just means you got to keep up your resolve, right? Soon as she back, you got to do the doings.'

'Without a doubt. Fear not, Morris, I ready for the showdown.'

'Don't mess me around, Barry, or you might lose me.'

'Come nah, man, you don't mean that.'

'Don't I?'

In the packed tube nearly all the passengers was fiddling with their mobile phones. As me and him was still a bit awkward, I decided to embark on a mutually harmless topic of conversation.

'Look at them. All patients showing signs of mobile-phone madness . . .'

Morris didn't reply.

'Playing childish computer games probably,' I added.

'Or listening to mobile music,' he finally responded, scanning the carriage end to end. I did a quick check too and half the patients was wearing earphones, their eyes glazed.

'Zombies,' I said, feeling we was getting back on track.

'And they get withdrawal symptoms too, Barry, if they don't get their fix. I read about it.'

'It is the beginning of the end of proper communication for the human race. Remember how back home we used to sing group songs in the evening?'

'Everybody was a singer back then, Barry. When did you last hear me sing?'

'Can't remember and, to be honest, can't say I miss your dulcet tones, dearie.'

'Uh, shut up, man.'

'I was so shocked when I came here and realized English people watched television every evening for hours without talking to each other.'

'This new generation are worse, though, Barry. All locked up inside themselves. It's like we're in a science fiction movie and they're the robots we've just cloned.'

'O brave new world, what's got such people in it,' I proclaimed, emoting and eyerolling like that hammy Laurence Olivier they all rated so much.

Morris started chuckling, which was a relief. I feel so bad when he's off with me.

I been entertaining him ever since I sat behind his goody-two-shoes self in Mr Torrington's algebra class when we was eleven. Squirted water down the back of his neck and told him it was my piss. The whole back row cracked up. He almost cried like a girl until I admitted I was kidding. He got the joke and followed me around after that.

Couldn't get rid of him.

Still can't . . .

'That novel wasn't half bad, Barry. Remember you gave it to me to read? Although I am of the opinion that *Nineteen Eighty-Four* is better.'

'One of my small victories, Mr de la Roux. Getting you reading fiction. Remember the days when people sat on the tube reading good book?'

'Not everyone's a book reader like you. A newspaper will do.'

'Not that rubbish red-top you read, Morris. Full of tittle-tattle, sensationalism, soundbiteism and nakedism.'

'Why you always pontificating? I do read books, history books and those fat biographies my sons get me for Christmas.'

'Biographies are just glorified gossip too. Novels, poetry and plays are the great investigators of the human psyche. Nothing can beat 'em. And as a *real* literature aficionado, I'm in the top 10 per cent of the Great British Public. Did I tell you about my love affair with Mr Shakespeare?'

'A thousand times a-ready.'

'Remember I told you about Dr Fleur Goldsmith in my *Taming of the Shrew* class at Birkbeck last year? First time I walked into that classroom she give me such a welcoming beam while the rest of them looked at me a bit quizzical, like maybe I should be redirected to Carnival Studies or something.'

'No . . . really? I wonder why?'

I ignore him.

'I know that play, though, Barry. Elizabeth Taylor film in the sixties. Wonder what happened to her?'

'Dr Goldsmith is an intellectual firecracker of the highest order, kind too, because she never patronized nobody, but I soon discovered that as the only man in a class full of bra-burners who thought Petruchio was a male chauvinist pig, I had to speak up for my *gender*. He'd just been given an ill-tempered vixen to handle, that's all. I empathized with him, actually.'

'You don't say . . .'

'The ladies took to me soon enough, especially Sally and Margaret, two retired lady-doctors who definitely had a crush. I wasn't surprised, especially after we went on a class trip to see *Taming of the Shrew* at the National Theatre. I met their husbands.'

Morris sniggered and put his hand to his mouth like a mischievous kid.

'Morris, I carrying my age better than most, not so?'

'Oh, yes, you a real heart throb like George Clooney or Brad Pitt.'

'A dashing and fully paid-up member of the alpha class. A reasoner and a thinker *of note*? These people down here fast becoming Epsilons, self-selecting.'

'I am Alpha too, so you can get off of your high horse.'

'Yes, but there is Alpha and Alpha *plus*.'

'You know what I like about you, Barry? You are consistent. I surprised you don't need a neck brace to hold up your head.'

'Neck brace won't do it, my man. My brain's so big my head needs special scaffolding.'

'Timber scaffold won't be strong enough, then.'

'Of course not – steel.'

'Reinforced.'

'Actually, solid adamantine, as described by Virgil in the *Aeneid*, Book 6. A generic term for a super-hard substance. *Adamantine*. Nice word. I looked it up, as *behoves* a man of my insatiable intellectual curiosity.'

'Barry?'

'What?'

'You gonna get a fat lip if you don't shut up.'

At this juncture, the train slowed into Piccadilly Circus Station, and we two retired gentlemen of the Caribbean disembarked.

*

As we make our way along Bond Street we draw curious, even, dare I say it, admiring glances. Me and Morris wearing the classic fifties suits Levinsky runs up for us and the *quintessentially* English brogues I get handmade from Foster & Son on Jermyn Street. Me and my spar can't walk up Bond Street looking like a pair of dossers.

As the sun hots up, I take off my jacket and fling it over my shoulder. Summer is in the air, and I feel myself longing for the dark days of winter to disappear.

We enter Café Zanza: dark wood panels, parquet floor, muted lighting, small round tables, flowers and, accentuating the mellow ambience, the mellifluous voice of Ella Fitzgerald effortlessly caressing the notes of 'I've Got You under My Skin'.

That woman didn't need no auto-tune to sing live.

We approach a counter with so many sugarific cakes on display a person could get diabetes just looking at them. Morris smiles at the washed-out looking barista with greasy, scraped-back hair and a slash for a mouth. 'Hello, my dear.'

She can't be bothered to smile back, let alone greet him, as if we don't belong here.

Gargoyle.

I dash her one bad look, except she don't notice and I can't keep scowling for ever. Morris, on the other hand, is too much of a gentleman and tries again, speaking with the soft, compassionate tone he uses with the aggressive, the ancient, the mentally unstable and, frequently, his lover.

Sometimes I think Morris is really too nice for his own good.

'How are you today? Feeling good? Feeling so-so? Feeling life could be a little better?'

The gargoyle can't help but react to his charm. She replies

all wistfully, 'Just tired, sir. I was out clubbing last night and I'm paying the price today. You know how it goes.'

'There is always to price to pay, isn't there?' he says, jollying her along. 'I have had one or two such days in my life too.'

Who you kidding, Morris? That is an understatement of such magnitude it falls firmly into the category of mendacitude. Your entire life has been one long hangover.

She nods her head, smiling wearily, appreciative.

'Now, what can I get you, sir?'

'I'll have a refreshing cup of peppermint tea.' Morris turns and touches my elbow. 'Barry, what you having?'

'Cool, gimme a Coke with lemon and ice. I'll get seats.'

Got to let my friend have his dignity. Man must put his hand in his pocket to feel good.

My hawk eyes see the only free spot, at the back in a corner. One table, three comfy red leather armchairs. Then I see the competition. Two ladies approaching it clumsily from the right, balancing heels, trays and bulging shopping bags. My survival skills kick into action, and I move panther-like across the room and lunge into a seat just as they arrive, pretending not to show the pain in my jolted joints. In these situations, best not to make eye contact, so I direct my attention to a poster on the wall – which implies that the grinning Italian founder of this coffee chain has all but hand-picked every single coffee bean used in his thousands of coffee bars worldwide.

The women totter off. *Adios. Arrivederci. Auf Wiedersehen*, ladies, or whatever language you speak, because I can tell you tourists.

From my vantage point I observe the *beau monde* of Bond Street. Mainly youngish, mainly female and half of them have skirts so short and heels so high they look like hookers. Every single one of them has a mobile phone either sitting on the table or being fiddled with.

Morris pootles over with the drinks.

Now . . . unless I'm *also* suffering from dementia, did he not just order a cup of peppermint tea a moment ago at the counter? So how come my spar has bought hisself a tall glass of hot chocolate stuffed with pink marshmallows, squirted with a whipped spiral of fresh cream that forms a glazed *spume*, on to which is sprinkled cinnamon powder and into which is inserted *three* chocolate flakes?

He parks his posterior next to mine, no sign of shame sweeping his face.

'Morris, seeing as you on the slippery slope downwards, have some rum in that. Overproof: it will blow your balls off.'

He needs to relax, I need to relax, and we both need to enjoy the prospect of our new life together.

But he don't respond.

I take out the silver hip flask from my inside jacket pocket and wave it in front of him. 'C'mon, don't be so boring. A little is better than nothing, ehn? Sooner or later you goin' succumb, so save yourself the aggravation.'

Morris tries to act affronted for a moment, as if he could be guilty of such weakness of will, but when I begin to pour the golden elixir into his concoction he don't try stop me.

As it makes its way down, there is a palpable sizzle.

When I pour it into my Coke, there is a hiss.

We both take our respective sips, and when it hits the spot it relaxes my still somewhat frazzled nerves after the traumatization of the past two days.

'Nothing rum can't make better,' I say, feeling my chest warm up. 'It guaranteed to dissolve the stressment.'

Morris closes his eyes as he plunges a long spoon into his drink and scoops up some rum-soaked cream.

'Feeling better?'

'Much better, thank you, Mr Walker. Teetotalism is like a bereavement. You remember all of the good times you had with a glass of something. Such good times.'

Yes, and we got even better times ahead, if I play my cards right.

We turn to face each other, both beaming the slightly idiotic, blurry smile of those starting to get tanked up.

Everything cool now, Morris. You and me always vibes good, eh?

Long time we been vibes-ing.

I look up to see Maxine wending her modelesque way towards us, black hair shaved on one side with a long, straightened fringe thing sweeping down the other, outsized sunglasses, tiny white T-shirt, what they call skinny jeans (which only merit that description if you're a beanpole like Maxine) and day-glo stilettos, of the kind usually seen on lap-dancers, I do believe.

We all present carefully selected versions of we-selves to the world at large.

She got her groove goin' on; her daddy got his. She just don't know how much yet.

Maxine clocks me and erases a flash of irritation when she sees I am not alone. She makes a beeline for Morris, whips off her shades and kisses him on both cheeks like one of those mwah-mwah-luvvie types, which she is, actually. 'A stylist to the stars.'

'How *lovely* to see you, Uncle Morris. It's been *ages*. I'm so pleased you could come too.'

The way that girl has mastered the Englishman's use of irony is re-mark-a-ble. I could write a 2,000-word essay on it: fiction, falsification, fabrication, fancification. Is not that she don't like Morris. Oh, no, she loves her godfather; it's just that she wasn't planning on a *tête-à-trois*.

'Maxie. How yuh do?' Morris asks her.

What does the cheeky madam do next? She sits down opposite him and gives me one of those middle-class English smiles that involves a wide elasticizing of the lips and nothing else.

'What about a kiss for your father?'

The father who needs his daughter's affection now more than ever.

My basso-profundo voice booms like a cannon into the flapping, squawking gathering. 'What about showing some respect for your father?'

Wings settle, feathers fluster, then float down, the room hushes.

Maxine goes stony on me, which is pretty scary if you don't know her, because she got a load of black war paint around her eyes. Both my daughters can put on that hard face our women develop to protect themselves, no matter how soft they feeling inside. Carmel too. Any time you see her on the street she looks ready to box someone.

Maxine rises to the bait. 'I am *so* pissed off with you, Dad.'

Soap opera just come to Café Zanza on Bond Street. Ears are cocked, waiting for the escalation of this dramatic scenette.

'Maxie,' Morris intervenes. He's holding a chocolate flake

to his lips, the last of the family of three to be decapitated. 'You letting yourself down. Treat your father with respect, nah?'

Yes, Morris. You go-wan. *Tell her.*

She looks sheepish, mumbles 'Sorry' at Morris, then starts rummaging in her fancy Gucci handbag that won't be a knock-off from Ridley Road Market but the real thing, paid for by Mr Credit-Card-Loan-Shark.

What I tell her? *Neither a borrower nor a lender be.* This is the problem with fathering. You have all of this armchairing, psychobabble and experientialism you wish to impart to your children, but they act like you insulting them when you try.

What is more, the so-called 'sorry' is aimed at Morris, and he thinking the same thing, because that chocolate stick don't move from its last-rites position.

'Hang on a minute,' she says, aware that me and Morris are quietly waiting for her to state whatever case she is planning on stating. 'I've just realized, I'm starving and I've got to chuck some food down in the next few minutes or I'll faint. Won't take long. Promise. Then we can conversate.'

Con-ver-sate.

'Let me get you something to eat,' Morris offers, rising. 'A sandwich?'

Don't be silly, man. Don't you know Maxine treats wheat like poison? Allergic to it, apparently, after a lifetime of eating bread.

'No, I'm fine, Uncle Morris. I've already bought something. Maybe some water, please?'

Water, water, water. What is this obsession with water these days? I come from one of the hottest countries on

89

earth, and most Antiguans never bothered much with drinking water. Was anybody dying from dehydration over there?

She takes a packet of that sushi nonsense out of her bag – popular with anorexics. She rips open the plastic cover with her black talons and pops supposedly edible objects into her mouth. I lean over and examine the contents of her 'lunch': four raw slivers of salmon on top of a thumb-sized blob of rice, a few lettuce leaves, about twenty bean-things with tails that look like human embryos, strands of grated carrot, bird seed, a few pickled slices of ginger and some slimy black leafy substance that looks like it should-a remained in the sea.

Maxine's been starving herself since she was fifteen, when someone told her she could become a model, which she did, but only during school holidays, because no daughter of mine was goin' bypass her A-levels. By the time she'd finished school she'd stopped looking like a giraffe-freak and had grown curves like a normal woman, whereupon the agency dropped her. I swear I've not seen that girl eat a proper meal since.

She could do with a hearty meal of cow-foot stew, dumplings, yam, macaroni cheese, fried spinach, green beans and a chunk of sourdough bread. The kind of food that was a source of conflict between her and Carmel when she was a kid.

At least she's moved on from her teenage idea of fine dining: a glass of white wine and a packet of cheese-and-onion crisps.

I realize I might never sit down to a meal with my wife and daughters ever again. Our fragile nuclear family is about to explode. What parental price will I have to pay? I have no doubt that from wifey and Donna's point of view, I will go from head of the family to dead in the family.

Finally, madam is ready to *con-ver-sate*.

'The thing is,' she begins, twirling her long-fringe-forelock thing, 'it's probably better if you and I have this conversation *alone* . . . Uncle Morris, it won't take long.'

Morris starts to fidget, but he's waiting for my say-so.

'Morris,' I say, tapping his knee, 'stay.'

He settles back down.

She ain't got no choice but to *con-ver-sate* on our terms.

This battle of wills lasts thirty seconds before she launches herself.

'You have really upset Mum. She can't take any more of your . . . shenanigans. I mean, coming home drunk in the middle of the night instead of going to bed at a reasonable hour with a mug of Horlicks . . . or . . . something stronger, *whatevs*.'

'Maxine,' I reply, cutting the facety wretch off, 'you love the fact that I don't act like some old codger with one foot in the grave, so don't give me any of that Horlicks crap. And you been out on the lash nuff times with me and Morris, so even *you* don't believe what you saying. Listen to me good: it is true, I am a sinner and a drinker and as the porter says to Macbeth, "Faith, Sir, we were carousing to the second *cock*."'

Morris splutters so much he practically spits out his drink.

'Dad, you are totally incorrigible,' she says, just managing to resist a laugh herself. I can always win Maxine round.

'Yes, my dear. But you know what? Your daddy still got his *joie de vivre*, and he keeping it.'

'There are limits. I am totally baffed by your behaviour.'

Baffed . . .

'What you don't seem to get is that just because Mum puts up with it, it doesn't mean she's not devastated. Do you know –'

'That's enough, Maxine.' I raise my hand. 'Your mother should get out more, which would stop her obsessing about my business and trying to contravene my basic Human Right to Freedom and a Social Life (Article 15a). Look at her: church-shops-doctors-funerals. I remember in the eighties she used to socialize with her work friends from the town hall. That Joan, Mumtaz and the other one who even came to dinner once or twice. Nice women. Carmel had plenty to chat about in those days, because she was occupied with work and therefore not banging the Bible over her head and mine. She even bothered with her appearance and smartened up for a while. A shame it didn't last.

'Do you know how many thousand times I've heard Jim Reeves crooning "Welcome to My World" out in the front room of an evening? She lucky I ain't smashed that crackly ole '78 to smithereens. I'd be relieved if she got herself a social life. She and Merty should doll themselves up and go Calypso dances. Just make sure I'm not there.'

I pull a face. Morris does too.

'Maxine, as one of the fellas said in *King Lear*, "I am too old to learn." '

'Which is unfortunate, as Mum isn't too old to be hurt.' Her voice rises dangerously near the high-decibel range again. 'As for your rudeness to Asselietha . . .'

Just then her mobile starts doing a Saint Vitus's dance on the table.

'Just a sec. Sorreeee,' she mouths, already taking the call.

I could be on my deathbed and still hear, *Sorry, Dad, I so have to take this call. Hold that breath, will you?*

I slip Morris a fiver to fetch a couple of Cokes, which I infiltrate with some more overproof.

'Sorry about that,' Maxine says when she's finished.

'Where was I? Okay . . . sure, Mum's friends can be narrow-minded, but it's not been easy for them. Actually . . . I admire them. Honestly . . . I do.'

Her eyes go all slippery-slidery.

'Mum thinks that you're, well, you're a . . . misogynist.'

Not so long ago you was throwing up baby sick all over me.

'On what grounds am I a misogynist? Pray, tell?'

I remember wiping up your mushy green poo like it was yesterday.

'The way you treat her friends.'

Wiping the snot from your nose, tears from your eyes.

'I don't like them. At least not three of them.'

Teaching you how to walk, catching you when you fell.

'You should still make the effort to be nice.'

You sucked your thumb until you was nine.

'I've held my tongue over half a century,' I finally reply.

From 0 to 12 years old I was your God.

'Your problem is that you don't understand women, Dad. You're of the post-Victorian, pre-feminist Antiguan generation that didn't form strong platonic friendships across the sexes.'

How she know? She only been to Antigua twice in her life. Last time when she was twelve. She's not interested in the place. And I was born more than thirty years *after* the Victorian era, actually.

'Maxine, dear, how many male *compañeros* your mother got?'

No answer.

'How many male friends Donna got?'

The external signs of internal squirming are starting to show.

'So don't give me this balderdash, right. Most men don't have close female friends neither.'

93

I could tell her about Philomena, but I don't have to justify myself to her. Smashing Irishwoman, secretary at Ford's, big personality, great sense of humour, said she related to coloured people because of the way she'd been treated when she first came to England and couldn't get work or lodgings. We all liked her *as a friend*. Sometimes she'd join us in the Union Bar next door for a drink or two after work. The one time I mentioned this to Carmel, I saw fire flaring down her nostrils and fangs shooting out of her mouth.

Naturally, I knew better than to tell wifey that I'd kept up my friendship with Philomena, even to this day. Since I retired, I've visited her about twice a year at her house in Walthamstow. We have a pot of tea and one of her lovely homemade cakes and catch up on Ford's *alumni* gossip, seeing as she's still in touch with half the ole workforce.

Anyways, how can I dislike women, Maxine, when I have always held you so close to my heart?

I take a lug of my rum-and-Coke liquid medicine. I just want to enjoy my daughter. She should stop being her mother's Harbinger of Grief. It don't suit her.

'Maxine, let we get one thing straight. You are not my keeper. Asseleitha deserved to be shouted down, and the others was running off their mouths so fast down the motorway they couldn't see the speeding signs.'

'You are *this* close to losing her.'

I don't even need to look at Morris to know we sharing the irony.

He emits the imperceptible cough that's been used since time immemorial to make a discreet, non-verbalized point.

But really, does Maxine honestly think she can lock horns with her father and win?

94

'I don't have to justify myself to you, so go phone your mother, duty done, you spoke to me.'

Maxine don't know what to say next, so I segue us out of the unpleasant part of our encounter into something more befitting of our usually smashing relationship that I couldn't bear to lose.

'Tell me what you been up to, my lovely daughter?'

Morris is slipping down his chair. Been off the sauce long enough to lose some immunity.

Asking Maxine how she is always works, because she always turns conversations into ring roads leading back to herself anyways.

'Gosh, where do I begin?' she says after an honourable pause.

She flicks that one-sided, fringe-forelock thing back and flops her long legs over the arm of her chair, letting those day-glo stilettos dangle.

'Begin with some rum. You want some?'

I wave my hip flask in front of her as if I'm waving a hypnotist's pendulum.

'You are *so* bad. I thought I could smell alcohol. It's still the afternoon . . . Go on, then, just a smidgeon. It's very calorific . . . I really shouldn't.'

She takes a genteel sip and beams daughterly love at me.

For all her performance of outrage, me and her get on too well for her to strip me of my fatherhood and banish me into exile.

Can't say the same about her sister.

I pour some into her empty (of course) water glass.

'There *is* something else I thought I'd talk to you about, seeing as we're here,' she says a little slyly.

'The floor is yours, my dear.'

'You *know* it's a jungle out there in the fashion world, Dad. A *jungle.*'

'You've told me enough times.'

'I've only styled two shoots in the past month, one of which was in Skegness, of *all* places, and for some disgusting *sackcloth* dresses for some awful *eco-save-the-planet* fashion line. And I'm up to my ears in debt because schmoozing with the fashion crowd bloody well doesn't come cheap unless you've got a Russian oligarch for a boyfriend, which, don't remind me, I haven't. All I attract these days are arrogant scuzzbuckets *with* money and fugly losers *without* it. And if I don't mingle, the work dries up *completely.*'

Boy, she getting pissed quickly. This is the problem when your diet consists of seaweed, grated carrot and organic air. Nothing to soak the nectar up, especially when it's 65 per cent alcohol.

I'm just glad Maxine never did drugs, especially moving in her coked-up fashion *milieu.* She promised me she'd never even try them when I gave her the lecture 'Today's Casual Marijuana Smoker is Tomorrow's Crack Addict' when she was fifteen.

'After nearly twenty years in the business *Miss Bags of Experience* is still scrabbling around for work while these trust-fund babes swan in as interns one week and a month later they're off on a paid shoot to the Maldives with Testino or Rankin. And I'll be really past it soon. Actually I *am* past it. I've been twenty-nine for eleven years already.'

I top up Maxine's glass. Must be getting thirsty with all of this ranting.

'When I left Saint Martins I thought the world would fall at my feet because my lecturers said I was a star in the making. "Pentecostal Caribbean Women's Attire on a Sunday Morning in Hackney" got me a First. Now look at me, a *stylist*. Sometimes I feel like ending it all, *really*.'

'Morris, perhaps we can advise my daughter on the options?' I suggest, scraping back my chair, stretching out my legs, disentangling my arms from behind my head. 'Poison? Drowning? Asphyxiation? What sayest thou?'

Morris starts to reassemble hisself on his chair, while Maxine reaches for her Gucci handbag like she will either storm out or land it upon my person.

'Don't mind your father,' he says. 'You and I both know *he* thinks he funny. My advice is do the thing you love; otherwise you reach my age and you swimming in a sea of regrets. I was brilliant at maths at school, so I studied it at university because my parents was determined to have a mathematician for a son. But I hated it, couldn't adapt to university life in England, so I dropped out and still ended up as a book-keeper my entire working life.'

Morris takes another sip of his rum and Coke.

'Anybody know about a wasted life? I do. Other scholarship men of my generation ended up in government as high achievers, leaders. Look at Arthur Lewis from St Lucia over there, got the Nobel Prize for Economics. What does that make me?'

'Morris,' I interject to stop him jumping off Tower Bridge into the icy Thames at midnight, 'stop it, man. Be positive, like I always telling you.'

'Yes, don't be down on yourself, Uncle Morris,' Maxine agrees, dropping her own preoccupations *miraculously*.

'I *am* a loser and a waster,' he insists. 'I should've enrolled in the Open University when the kids left home and become a history teacher, maybe for Adult Education. Unlike your father, who is something of a dilettante, I would-a pursued one subject properly, passionately.'

'Easy, man,' I tease Morris, swiping his head. 'I ain't no dilettante. I am what they call a polymath.'

'You still young, Maxie,' he says, ignoring me. 'Soon as you hit fifty you start feeling nostalgic for your forties. By the time you in your seventies you'll think people in their fifties are practically teenagers.'

'Don't get me started on that,' Maxine exclaims, deftly bringing the conversation full circle. 'I feel that way about people in their twenties, *evil* little whippersnappers. And I'm not *in* my forties yet, Uncle Morris. I've just *turned* forty.'

She undrapes her legs from the arm of her chair and I marvel at how flexible they are, like wet, twisted rope, flopping this way and that. Was I ever that supple, so unthinking about how I moved my body?

She sits forward, hugging her knees.

'*Daddy*, I was wondering if you could help me out with a little something?'

Maxine's gone all girly. Me and Morris agree that if she had kids of her own she'd stop behaving like one.

Get to the point, my dear, which, knowing you, is probably the one where you approach your father, Zeus, King of the Gods, with yuh begging bowl.

She exhales a breathy sigh befitting the yoga classes she attends over at that Peace, Love and Bellbottoms Centre in Notting Hill that's popular with celebrities and their hangers-on. She calls it networking. Oh, yes, *networking*, the latest malarkey that, I gather, involves pretentious luvvies dressing up, getting drunk and stuffing their faces with canapés, which they then have the cheek to call work.

She takes the plunge. 'Look, I've been playing around with some fashion ideas, because I agree with Morris: it's now or never. I've got to fulfil my dreams or I *really will* kill myself.'

She expels another *yogic breath*.

'Right . . . er . . . you see . . . my project might sound a bit left field, a bit *outré*, a bit *beyond* bizarre, but bear with me, guys, I have come up with something exceptional.'

We *are* bearing with you, m'dear. But look how nervous you is. You know your daddy might roar, but he don't bite.

'Okay, herewith the idea for my first fashion collection, which is . . . wait for it . . . drum-roll . . . an imaginative exploration of the relationship between fashion, food, furniture, friendship and family. I wanted to add philosophy to my list, but it's not spelt with an *f, obv*.'

She flings open her arms in a starry showbiz gesture, but drops them when Morris openly guffaws.

'*Don't* laugh, Uncle Morris.'

'I'm not.'

'Morris be-have. Maxine, you go-wan. *I'm* listening.'

'Me too, Maxie. I sorry. You know I am a philistine.' But he shrugs his shoulders in a take me or leave me gesture.

She shakes her head as if he is *beyond* help. '*As* I was saying, the plan is to encapsulate these five constituent elements into a single garment to show their interconnectedness; to show how everything is related.'

She starts rummaging in her Gucci again while Morris rolls his eyes at me like she is *beyond* bonkers. She takes out a real tapestry folder that is clearly not from W. H. Smith & Sons and extracts fancy art-paper drawings that she strokes tenderly with her elegant, fluorescent, be-taloned fingers.

'You are the first humans on earth to see these.'

I resist quipping something about other planets and galaxies and lean over the table to see her work close up, looking attentive, serious, respectful.

'Righty-ho.' Maxine points to the main drawing, an evening gown.

'Isn't it lovely? And look, the skirt will be made of leather strips that can be deconstructed into a stool. Yes, really . . . Pop-out metal rods hidden inside the seams and hey presto, it becomes a functioning stool you can actually sit on while fully dressed for the ball. How about that?'

What ball? No one goes to a ball these days except students and they can't afford no *haute* costliness.

'The buttons, lace and frills you see here will also be edible. Yep, you heard right. They'll be made out of sweets, candyfloss, popcorn, icing, glazed fruit. So my models will walk down the runway eating bits of the clothes they're wearing. *Totes* amazeballs, no?'

We nod our heads in obedient approval.

'The material of the V-shaped basque will be a collage of photographs of family and friends, and the clutch bag will be imprinted with loving quotes from letters, texts, emails. Basically, what I have is the idea that food, family and friendship equal sustenance, along with the idea that people *wear* their loved ones, dead or alive, when they go out, or can even sit on them? Bringing new meaning to the idea of community and family support? Do you see where I'm heading with this? Way deep, I know.'

Me and Morris make appreciative sounds and utterances. Her concept is a load of baloney, but we not goin' tell her that. But her designs are really bold and stunning, geometric patterns and monochromes offset against deep, rich colours. I forgot how good an artist she is.

'Furthermore and more furtherly, as you would say, Dad, when sold as *haute couture*, each garment will be *bespoke* – made from the client's personal images and quotes. The edible stuff will be replaced by regular materials, of course, but the garments can also be stripped to their core sensibility and sold off-the-peg on the high street. The basque becomes a boob tube, the petticoat becomes a gauzy little shift dress.'

Maxine is so overwhelmed at her own cleverness that her smile stretches from Soho to Shoreditch, showing off those teeth that seem to get whiter every time I see her – a blinding flash of Hollywood.

Morris is the first to speak.

'You talented, Miss Maxie. Just make sure me and Barry have front-row seats at the fashion show.'

'Maxine,' I say, tapping her knees. 'Your imagination is something to behold.'

'Gosh, *flattered*.' She's almost bouncing up and down in her seat. 'My idea *is* ground-breaking. Pure genius, really.'

Problem with flattery is some people let it go to their heads. I discovered this when both girls was little. Within minutes of getting praise, they turned into little monsters.

'Where you get your ideas from?' Morris asks.

'All I can say is, I don't just have blue-sky moments. I have a blue-sky *life*.'

She leans back in her seat and gazes at the ceiling like she's Einstein.

'I think it comes from you, Barry,' Morris pipes up. 'Look at you, man. So bloody-minded, so individualistic, so clothes-conscious and what some might call a "colourful personality", at least when they being polite. Maxie, you had eighteen years of seeing his h-ugly face every day before you managed to escape. You absorbed his personality by osmosis.'

'Perhaps he is an influence then . . . if you put it that way,' Maxine concedes, not amused, like she's not too keen on sharing credit. She starts to pack away her drawings as if she's picking up sheets of gold leaf from the table. 'I've got many more ideas. Take the unequal distribution of house-work in the marital home. Oh, where did the inspiration for *that* one come from?'

I shan't rise to the bait.

'I've got an idea for a nineteenth-century corset made out of tea towels threaded through with cutlery instead of whalebone. Men's shoes that double as a dustbin and brush. I'll give you a pair for free, Dad.'

The pair of them collapse into drunken splutterings – co-conspiratorial *colluders*.

She shifts, places her hands primly on her lap, legs pressed together, all ladylike.

'I . . . it's like . . . um . . . I'm just going to say it anyway. Look, don't ask, don't get, right?'

I register a blank face. I'm not making it easy for her.

'Dad . . . . . . *dy*, I need backing to get this show on the road.'

She speaking to the palms of her outstretched hands, studying the lines as if her future is laid out in the design of them.

'In this recession *especially,* I really need an angel to come to my rescue and you're the only one I know.'

Because she is her father's daughter she can't help adding, 'Fallen.'

Cute. Very cute. But *Dad . . . dy* ain't no pushover.

'Um . . . and I'm thinking of calling it . . . How does House of Walker sound? A sort of homage to you?'

Double cute.

Maxine starts fiddling with her mobile. She knows well enough to give me so-called 'space'. Only person knows me better is Morris.

I look past her into the café at all of those follow-fashion victims purring over their latest overpriced purchases that will be *so yesterday* by next month.

They're playing another real, ole-school chanteuse over the speakers – Sarah Vaughan's rendition of 'If You Could See Me Now' . . .

I wonder what wifey's up to? She'll have arrived over there. We've not been apart for thirty-two years, not since the last time she went home with Donna for her mother's funeral and I stayed in England to look after Maxine. I've not been back since my own mother's funeral in 1968. How many years is that? Is a long time for a man to be deracinated.

If Morris feels his life is wasted, mine has been spent in hiding: Secret Agent BJW, rumoured to have gone underground circa 1950.

My mind wanders beyond the café and out on to Bond Street on this late Monday afternoon in May. For 300 years one of the most important, most historic, most symbolic thoroughfares in one of the greatest cities on earth, with its luxurious emporia of Chanel, Prada, Versace, Armani, Burberry, Asprey, Louis Vuitton . . . House of Walker.

Walnut floors. Black lacquer walls. Crystal chandeliers.

Maxine, my younger girl. Ten years between her and Donna, who had been commandeered by Carmel, who wanted the elder one to herself. When she came along too early and too sickly, and Carmel wasn't right in the head with what we later knew to be post-natal depression, Maxine became mine.

I didn't smoke, I didn't drink, I didn't socialize, I didn't even miss it. I even took leave from work. Morris helped out; the cronies helped out too, except they wasn't hard-boiled cronies in those days but young women full of hope, expecting better things from life.

For the first eighteen months I kept Maxine alive. I attached this frail little thing to me in a sling like women back home. I never wanted to put her down, and when I did I felt pangs.

Carmel slept in the marital bed; me and Maxine slept on a mattress in the nursery.

First few months I didn't sleep for her crying. Next few months I didn't sleep for checking up on her when she wasn't crying.

In spite of Carmel's condition, I was never more content than when being a surrogate mother to Maxine.

Who'd-a thought she would grow into this giant over-the-top octopus flinging her limbs all over the place?

She right, too. She's too good to be just a stylist, although I'd never tell her. I'm glad she wants to explore her true worth. I laid the foundations for her to become a maker of art rather than an accessorizer of someone else's creativity.

'Maxine, I go chew on it.'

She's hiding it, but I can interpret everything that passes over my daughter's face. A film in slow motion would display hope, fear, excitement, pleading, the expectation of disappointment.

'Okay, okay . . . Let we sit down, put our great minds

together, one for business, one for creativity, and work out some logistics.'

Maxine knows I'm edging towards a yes, and her smile is quietly victorious. She also knows better than to grab my arms and start leading me in a waltz around the room just yet, although I wouldn't put it past her.

Morris is slumbering. He looks beatific when he sleeps. He's not snoring, although, knowing him, it's on the cards.

With my excellent peripheral I see Maxine watching me watching him.

Me and Morris have often wondered whether she suspects anything . . . especially as she spends all of her time in gay bars with her fellow fashionistas, and then keeps moaning she can't catch a fella.

As for the straight guys? Number of times she's come crying to me when she's been dumped. Last fella was called Rick, who worked in computers. When I asked what he did exactly, she exclaimed, 'How should I know? I'm not interested in computers.'

I told her that the only way she goin' keep a man is if she shows she's interested. Asks him questions and remembers the answers. 'Men like women who are interested in them, dear.'

She didn't talk to me for nearly a month.

One before that was a 'totes gorg' Argentinian who didn't speak English. She told me he didn't need to, as they communicated through the language of love . . . and something called Google Translate. It lasted ten days.

'Daddy,' she says, hunched over the table. 'If there's anything you ever want to tell me . . . You know I'm not Mum and the God Squad.'

Lord, how come she asking me this now? A colony of

ants starts crawling all over my scalp, but I'm too afraid to attack them in case she interprets my discomfort. This is too much. *Anything* is a big word that can accommodate all *things*, and every*thing*, and some*thing* that, yes, she needs to know eventually, but it ain't easy giving voice to the *love that brings shame*.

'What you want to know, that I robbed a bank?'

She shakes her head like I am *so beyond*, pretends to study the poster of the founder of this chain of cafés.

I been in a maximum-security prison too long.

He, his own affections' counsellor, is to himself . . ./ so secret and so close.

Yet me and Morris are goin' move in together. Are we really goin' do that? It sounds so definite, so final, so brave, *too* brave . . .

'Any more of that rum?' she asks, turning back, shaking it off.

'Walker's Drinking Establishment just run out of stock. Let us procure some more.'

'I know just the place where we can get the *best* Blackberry Mojito cocktails – in the bar at the Dorchester. Chambord liqueur, white rum, fresh blackberries, fresh mint, brown sugar. We'll catch a cab.'

Dorchester? Taxi? Who paying for it?

She pulls out a bulging orange make-up bag and applies red lipstick in a gold hand mirror as if she herself is a work of art. Maxine can't pass a mirror without a quick glance.

'Tom Ford Perfect Blend Lip Colour,' she informs me, as if her 74-year-old dad has the slightest interest in what cosmetic gunk she puts on her face.

'What do you think?'

She poses, cheeks sucked in, pouting, like I'm David Bailey about to shoot. Then she elevates herself in all of her sloshed, six-footed, be-heeled glory, staggers over to Morris and grabs his shoulders. 'Uncle Morris, wake up.'

He is bleary-eyed.

She plonks herself on his lap, wrapping her arms around him. 'Daddy's thinking about bankrolling my fashion venture. Don't look so surprised. He's such a darling underneath it all.'

Underneath what all?

Morris rouses himself, probably because eight stone of human being has just plonked itself on his lap and is squeezing the oxygen out of him.

'Really?' He yawns. 'About time your father did something philanthropic with his fortune.'

'I am *not* a charity case, Uncle Morris. He'll get his money back. It is a *business investment*. Go on, put in a good word for me, then.'

Morris nods obligingly. 'Barry, seeing as you're not an ancient Egyptian pharaoh who's goin' be buried with your credit card to use in the Afterlife, although you might strut around like you're a god (ahem), you might as well support Maxie's fashion venture.'

I'm not even goin' honour his slander with a rejoinder.

I been sending money back home since the seventies. Plenty of my relatives been clothed and privately schooled and housed and sent abroad through the spreading of my *lucre-lurve*, as well Morris knows. I'll sort out Daniel at university too, undergrad and postgrad, that boy will continue to benefit from my beneficence.

Never no mind, I am soused in rum and feeling quite *swell*, as those black GIs used to say who was stationed on my island back in my youth. Oh Lord, they was something else. Courtly, well groomed and with a self-assurance we colonial subjects lacked and admired. After Morris left, I engaged in some military manoeuvres with one or two or three handsomely uniformed fellas, safe in the knowledge that neither party was goin' be air-dropping propaganda leaflets about it.

As we leave, me and Morris have to prop Maxine up.

She's chatting happily away like she is seven years old again and I've just taken her to see *Herbie Goes to Monte Carlo* or *The Many Adventures of Winnie the Pooh* for the hundredth time at Holloway Odeon. We'd dissect what we'd seen as we caught the bus to Finsbury Park, cut down Blackstock Road and crossed over Green Lanes into Clissold Park. When she got tired, I put her on my shoulders.

By the time she'd started secondary school she'd been to all the museums in South Kensington. And to the Unicorn Theatre in Leicester Square, Jacksons Lane, the Tower Theatre up the road, Sadler's Wells at the Angel, the Bubble Theatre tent in Regent's Park – there wasn't a kiddie show that she didn't see. In this respect, I injected a little bit of Hampstead Bohemia into my girl's Hackney Caribbean childhood. You see, no matter how busy I was, I tried to give Maxine my Saturday afternoons. She even attended classes at Anna Scher for a couple of summers. That girl rowed the Serpentine, sailed down the Thames on tourist cruises from Charing Cross, went to the summer festivals dotted around London, the funfairs, the circus, and we even took a few day-trips to the seaside: Margate, Bournemouth, Hastings, Brighton.

It's true, I adored her, especially her combination of innocence and cheek. Young kids will tell you exactly what's on they mind without the adult filters that turns grown-ups into fakes.

Even when she was throwing a strop in the middle of the street, I couldn't stay vexed for long.

On the other hand, Maxine and her mother never really gelled. I was the buffer between them. Carmel still don't get arty-fartiness, and the only culture that interests her is the one she decimates with bleach.

I always made Maxine feel her opinions was important. I never slaughtered my child in an argument. I knew the rest of the world might do that to her, but not me, not her father.

This is when it hits me.

The world *did* do it to her.

It said, 'You, my dear, are *not* the star of our show.'

As the door of Café Zanza shuts slowly behind us, Maxine's still rabbiting on.

'Tomorrow I'm going to fast on freshly squeezed vegetable juice of spinach, cabbage, celery, fennel and, yeh, beetroot, why not? Damage limitation. Twenty-year-olds have absolutely *no idea* how lucky they are. Drink and drugs all night, then get up looking fresh and peachy the next day. I absolutely *loathe* their pert little arses.'

While we wait for an empty taxi to cruise by (and they do stop now me and Morris are OAPs, because we appear to be what we always been: *harmless*), Maxine looks up Bond Street with a Hollywood-esque triumph-over-adversity gleam in her eyes.

'From this very spot the House of Walker shall spread out across the globe to Fifth Avenue in New York,

Champs-Élysées in Paris, Causeway Bay in Hong Kong, Ostozhenka Street in Moscow . . .'

'Kingsland High Road in Hackney,' Morris interjects.

'Shuddup!' She goes to slap his arm but misses.

'When I *do* make it,' she says, pointing a disoriented finger at Morris that almost ends up squirrelling up one of his nostrils, 'I'm going to become a philanthropist. Support starving children around the world, et cetera. You certainly won't catch me wearing blood diamonds hewn from the killing fields of Sierra Leone or the Congo. Or real fur. I shall be a multimillionaire with morals. Hey, I've just invented a tongue-twister, a millionaire with . . .'

At which point she sways backwards off the kerb into the road, and I grab her just in time to avoid a collision with a cyclist who looks like he ain't about to stop for no one. I pin one of her arms to me; Morris holds the other.

'Daddy, Uncle Morris, I sense my second life is just beginning. There *is* hope. There *is* a god, and he's called my daddy.'

Yes, Maxine, some folk get only one life, which, if they fuck it up, ain't no joke, and some folk have two lives goin' on *contemporaneously*.

7

The Art of Metamorphosis

Friday, 7 May 2010

Is a somewhat temperate Friday lunchtime as I stroll down Cazenove Road to meet Morris at the Caribbean Canteen at Dalston Junction. I ain't seen that fella since the Long Night of *Expensive* Cocktails at the Dorchester, where the barman refused to serve us any more drinks and got security to evict us off of the premises.

It's all Maxine's fault. Can't take her nowhere, making a right show of herself, over-dramatizing her fashionista stories with rotating arms and ranting about celebrity so-called designers who, as she so eloquently put it, 'Don't know their bandeaux from their basques, their back yokes from their bateaux necklines and have probably never even heard of besom pockets.'

Morris was no better, egging her on, wanting to know insider gossip.

The taxi dropped madam off at her warehouse in Shoreditch, and she was last seen using her day-glos as a torch to unlock the entrance to her old warehouse building.

Soon as the carriage ejected me and the original hell-raiser at my gaff, we made for the living room to have a nightcap, and that's the last thing I remember. I don't know how that happened, because, while Morris was paralytic, I was merely on the wrong side of tipsy. By the time I woke up

Tuesday afternoon, with a sore neck from where I'd slept half on and half off an armchair, he'd already fled the scene of the crime.

Since then he's claimed a three-day hangover and has only now summoned me to lunch, for a chat. Since when do me and him *arrange* to have a chinwag?

Well, I'll soon see whether his summons is *sus*picious or *aus*picious, but I got something on my mind too – I been having second thoughts about my second chance.

Once we are *in situ* in the café, we will chow down some (good-as) home-cooked food in the absence of any left by my wife in the fridge or freezer, because (fair dues) she didn't have no time to rustle up my meals and freeze them before she left, but (shamefully) also because I'm without the kind of daughters who phone up their *poor, elderly* father and tell him they just popping around with some rice and stew because they know he needs feeding after *five days* alone.

I could be dead from starvation by the time Carmel gets back.

What happened to the idea of payback time for parents? Fatherhood's supposed to be an investment, and my daughters are defaulting on their dividends. Problem is, one of them don't cook and the other one don't eat.

As I walk down Cazenove, I join the Friday lunchtime dance of the gentlemen of the Hasidim, silently wending and criss-crossing with the gentlemen of the Mohammedeen: the former dressed in the style of pre-war Poland, with their black coats, bushy beards and long ringlets hanging down from underneath their tall black hats, as they make their way to the synagogue; the latter attired in the style of twentieth-century Pakistan, with their white skull-caps, long cotton waistcoats and *salwar kameezes*, as they also make their way to their house of spiritual sustenance, in this case the mosque.

Everybody minds they own business, which is good, because this here gentleman of the Caribbean, attired in the sharp-suited style of his early years, minds his own business too.

I can't remember when anything last kicked off, and when it does, it's because the young-bloods let their raging testosterones get the better of them.

I observe my fellow dancers, discreetly wondering, as I am wont to do, how many of these fellas are harbouring secret desires? How many of them are habitués of Abney Park Cemetery at the junction ahead? How many are leading double lives: Secret Agents K and Y?

Statistically speaking, some of them has got to be bona-fide shirt-lifters, right?

Towards the end of the road I pass Aditya's Mini-Mart, which used to be the Casablanca Club back in the eighties. Even today I still get flashbacks to what happened one Sunday morning in the early hours.

Snow had prettified the city all night, and I'd just got in from a calypso rave in Tottenham. I was drinking a mug of hot milk laced with cognac, when I heard a loud thump outside. I went to my front door and saw a car had crashed into the lamp-post opposite. Blue Datsun. Whole of its frontage mashed up like the face of an English bulldog. Without any ado, I ran out in my slippers and sank my feet deep back into my own bear prints. The driver had been shot; he was slumped back, his face a bloody mess. How he'd managed to drive forty yards up the road, as I later found out, is beyond me, because half his scalp was hanging off of the back of his head, and by the time I reach him he was, without a doubt, dead.

Then I recognized him. A Jamaican fella called Delroy Simmons, local electrician, sometimes worked for me.

I stood there, in the freezing snow, and froze.

The official story was that he'd been in a bust-up outside the Casablanca over some woman and been shot up by the gangsters who frequented it. Word on the street was he'd been cheating on his woman with a 'batty' man; she'd caught him *in flagrante delicto*, and her gangster brother took revenge on him for shaming the family.

No wonder I couldn't leave Carmel back then.

When me and Morris heard, we met at the Lord Admiral and sat bloating our emotions with pints all night, quietly contemplating the dangerous world we was living in.

Still living in.

Just last year that fella got beaten to death in Trafalgar Square by some young thugs. One of his attackers was a seventeen-year-old girl.

Soon as I land at the junction of Cazenove and Stamford Hill, I am blasted back to the present day by the bad-tempered four-wheeled kings of the road furiously honking at the daredevil motorcyclists and suicidal cyclists who weave betwixt and between them like they don't care for they lives.

I turn left and then right, taking the scenic, quieter route via Church Street, seeing as I'm in the mood for some contemplative perambulation.

So long as my legs can walk, I go walk.

I pass Queen Elizabeth's Walk, wherein reside my first three rental properties, bought in the sixties before the Great Luvvy Invasion.

I remember the exact moment when the Kingdom of Barrington was conceived.

A summer evening after work, and me and Morris was breezing off having a lager and a smoke in Clissold Park, delaying the return to our respective farmhouses until the squealing sucklings had been put to bed. We'd both taken off our sweaty shirts, partly because of the heat, partly because we was both a right pair of preening peacocks. Yes, even back then. Morris was a perfect specimen of manhood, with his polished chest and naturally pumped-up pectorals. At times like these I found it hard to keep my hands off of him in public, especially when all around us males and females of the species was engaging in extreme canoodling and groping on the grass – blatantly, unashamedly, *legally*.

At some point I found myself paying proper attention for the first time to the three slummified Victorian houses on the Walk opposite our spot. Vandalized windows, wrecked roofs, gardens being reclaimed by the forests of *Ye Olde England*. I said to Morris, 'Look how huge they is, spar. Once upon a time they must-a been built for the rich, and, you mark my words, one day the rich shall recolonize them. I, Barrington Jedidiah Walker, hereby predict the gentrification of Stoke Newington.'

Or something like that. Even if I didn't speak those words out loud to Morris *exactly*, it was on my mind.

I'd already been thinking about how I could make my mark in this country, defy the low expectations the *indigènes* had of us, exploit an economy that, compared to our poor-poor islands, was a financial paradise. I'd been thinking about how the Syrian and Lebanese immigrants back home started off their business empires by selling door to door on foot with only a suitcase, progressing to vehicles and, before you could say *ambition, resourcefulness and bloody hard work*, they was running the stores of St John's.

Mr Miller was an exception to the rule. A local Antiguan made good.

Me too. I was goin' be the exception to the rule.

Looking at those dumpy houses I could tell they'd been empty for years, which meant they had to be goin' cheap, right? So I hatched a plan to buy them and rent out. But the banks never lent us no money in those days. Soon as you stepped over the threshold of your financial future, the manager's smile *glaciered*. Didn't matter how viable your proposal, how squeaky clean your finances, how impeccable your references, how speaky-spokey you was.

I am not a man given to sourness, but I left those banks with my mouth filled with the bile of bitter gourd. I ain't no political animal neither, but, pray tell, had not our labour drip-fed plantation profits to this country for hundreds of years before manumission? Had not thousands of our young men fought in two world wars for this land? Were not we immigrants paying our taxes and making our way as good citizens of this country?

No wonder so many of us turned to the Pardner System of community lending, which became the only way to leave wage-slavery behind and get we own homes. Everybody investing and taking their turn to get a lump sum. But I didn't have time for that. I was a man on a mission before someone else got the same idea.

It took about a week of charming cajolement (in the days when *that* worked), brainwashing techniques and financial projections to convince Carmel that my plan wouldn't lead to our family's banishment to the workhouse, and to persuade her to ask her ole boy (who by this time was rapidly expanding his Early Bird empire into Montserrat, St Kitts, Barbados, Jamaica) to advance me the working capital.

It took many years to repay him, along with the 20 per cent interest that skinflint charged his very own son-in-law.

No, sah, I don't owe that man nothing. What is more and more furtherly, I hated having him bankroll me. I felt like a beggar, a real bottom-foot buckra.

I subsequently bought more broke-up houses, which I repaired and rented out. Because I never succumbed to the pressure to sell, most of those babies is now worth three hundred times what I paid for them. Yea, gramercy, I counting my ducats.

So whenever they open up another fancy delicatessen selling bite-sized lumps of cake for outsized prices, or whenever they open up one of those 'yummy-mummy' children's boutiques with no prices in the window, time soon come to put my rents up, *incrementally*.

And any time this country starts Nazifying itself and another Shitler comes to power, I can relocate somewhere safe, émigré myself and my loved ones. The youngsters don't know about Enoch Powell's Rivers of Blood speech and that movement in the seventies to send we people back to where we came from, all of that hatred we had to endure from the National Front. I ain't no historian, but any fool living long enough is witness to the history of what the mob is capable of when they rabble-roused enough by some arch manipulator.

Morris tells me I am one paranoid fella, to which I reply, 'No man, I *prepared*. Look what happened in Germany in

1933: the Jews with the money to leave, did. I might be a positive thinker, but I am also a realist. They want start something? Come on, then. I ready. I leaving.'

Except I don't want to, not now, not ever.

How did Morris expect me to abandon my manor back then when Odette left him? How did he expect me to move to the alien terra firma of another part of London – to live as man and man? We was still two thoroughbred stallions back then and people would've talked.

Truth is, I only ever lived in three houses my whole life: parental, rental, familial.

I was transplanted to Stokey over fifty years ago and I gone native.

This. My. Home.

But it took a while, because when we first arrived here the locals didn't know us, couldn't understand us, and they certainly didn't like the look of us. We had chosen to emigrate, so we expected foreignness, whereas they hadn't chosen to leave their home but all of a sudden it was full of foreigners. With the wisdom of hindsight, I now see they lost their bearings.

But some of them behaved badly – for a very long time.

Some of them behaved nicely too, especially the *trippies*.

In the sixties I witnessed the hippification of Stoke Newington, just as I was settling in. I couldn't believe the way these radicals was grabbing their freedom when I couldn't even contemplate taking mine. Some of those trippies still around today. We all veterans now. Me and my great trippy buddy Peaceman (né Rupert) sit outside the pubs in summer, we pass the time, we bemoan the younger generation (anyone under the age of sixty-five), and we usually end up talking about who has just died.

Peaceman used to own the vegetarian shop at the bottom of Stamford Hill, and I never understood how he got away with selling birdseed and rabbit food for human consumption. Used to tell him so too: 'Is a scam, man. You sell cheap pet food at quadruple the price.'

'It's brain food,' Peaceman would shoot back. 'I think you need to try some.'

Me and Peaceman was always joshing, which was rare in the seventies, when so many folk was walking around with a chip on their shoulder just waiting to be *offended*. Taking offence was very popular in those times. Oh, yes, some people made a career out of it.

Peaceman's still sporting a wispy grey goatee, a stringy grey ponytail sprouting out of his bald head and his sixties embroidered waistcoats are now patchwork. I still tell him he should be playing the banjo at country fairs in the swamplands of the Fens. He still tells me I look like I should be pimping the pros down at King's Cross or wherever they've gone to.

Boadicea (née Margaret), his common-law wife of forty-five years, still wears what look like fourteenth-century Mongolian steppe dresses.

They used to let their demented, long-haired trolls charge up and down Cazenove, getting in everyone's way. Peaceman said his kids was free spirits who would change the world, see in a new era. Of what, eating birdseed?

They became, respectively, a tax inspector, an accountant, a solicitor and a policeman.

He never got over the betrayal.

One time me and him was sitting outside the George during the period when Morris was sulking because I wouldn't leave Carmel and live with him. I must have appeared glum, because Peaceman asked me what was up. I knew I could confide in my good trippy buddy, who believed in freedom as an abiding principle, not a passing trend.

Nonetheless, every time I went to open my mouth, the bat wings of fear flew out.

Peaceman reached out across the table and squeezed my hand, said he hadn't seen me with Morris in a while.

My peripheral could tell his eyes was upon me, but mine stayed trained on the passing traffic of Church Street.

It was a . . . *moment.*

What I do?

I snatched my hand away.

What he do?

Calmly stood up, put on his red Moroccan fez cap and sauntered down Church Street in his Ali Baba shoes, his Turkish harem pants billowing.

Whenever I recall it, even today, I feel the urge to apologize.

Barry, you behaved bad, man.

A few of those natty dreads still around too – Gad, Levi, Elijah – from the Rastafication of Stoke Newington. Still wearing those massive woollen hats under which must lie a primeval forest of grey dreadlocks. These are the genuine ones for whom it was a proper religion and not what socio-babblers would call 'a transitional identity crisis solution'.

Greetings in the name of the Most High . . . they say, as we bump fists.

I been greeting some of these fellas for as long as I been in England – since they had short hair and wore zoot suits.

The socialists, feminists and workers revolutionists

descended on Stoke Newington over time as well, and some of ours went politico too, because they'd had enough of being treated like second-class citizens and wanted to put the boot into 'the system', as they called it. All of the radicals used to have Saturday demonstrations to Ban the Bomb, Burn the Bra, Support the IRA, Free Angela Davis. Then there was the Anti-Racist Alliance, the Gay Liberation Front, the Right to Work – marching up Balls Pond Road en route to Trafalgar Square; women with short hair, men with long hair, our people with balloon hair; donkey jackets, dungarees, dashikis, bovver boots of many hues; and so forthly.

All of this transformation, transmutation, transculturation. Oh, yes, I seen it all come and go.

Stoke Newington got dykeified too, and some of our women was at war with us *male chauvinist pigs*. Funny that, I'd say to Morris, because seeing as we they fathers, that make them piglets, right?

Pinkification been here a long time too, but fellas always had to be more discreet.

I should know, because Barrington Walker used to feel hungry, very hungry, *very*, *very* hungry. Some might say *greedy*, seeing as Morris was never less than obliging.

Late at night, whenever I got the urge, I used to tell Carmel I was taking my evening constitutional, or goin' down pub, or whatever, when in fact I was making excursions into Abney Park Cemetery. It was like wild countryside back then, with brambles, trees and hedges that provided camouflage for all kinds of covert negotiations.

This one night in 1977, at about ten o'clock, me and someone anonymous was getting to know each other, *quietly*, in the dark, with nobody else in our vicinity, minding we own business, when a gang of young ragamuffins came crashing in and jumped us. Big strong lads. Must-a been creeping around on the hunt. Blood sports. *Cowards*. They let the other chap run off when they saw me – a man from their father's generation.

'Batty man! Bum bandit! Poofter! Anti-Man!'

Before I could try to defend myself, I ended up in the foetal position on the ground, my hands tryin' to protect my head from several pairs of boots that each bore the poundage of a steel wrecking ball.

Any moment I expected to feel the cold blade of a knife slice into my flesh.

At some point in the proceedings, I blacked out.

When I resumed consciousness, I must-a managed to crawl home.

I told Carmel I'd been mugged. Morris never knew otherwise.

For a long time after, every time I passed some drop-foot roughneck *yout* looking ready to pick a fight, I crossed the road. The problem was, plenty of Donna's friends from Clissold School, boys and girls, used to come to her parties at our house, before they reached the hanky-panky age and I stopped them.

What if some of those boys had turned bad? What if I'd been recognized?

They was the same kind of boys who bullied any boy back home who wasn't manly enough, who wore too-bright shirts, who was a bit soft in his manner, who needed straightening out.

Up to this point I'd been somewhat *lawless*. I came to my senses after that and stopped playing in my own backyard.

I affiliated myself to the North London Association of Midnight Ramblers, Hampstead Heath Chapter.

Cruising was a craving that became an addiction that lasted quite a while, I have to say. And, even though fear had set in after my attack, it didn't stop me none.

The summer of 1977 was also the Summer of Donna, who turned against me big time – losing herself in the throes of rebelment. Not against Saint Carmel, of course, but against the man who allegedly made her mother suffer. The man who'd committed crimes worse than Papa Doc, Baby Doc and Pol Pot. She couldn't be in my company five minutes without storming out.

Then she met some boy called Shumba at the 73 bus stop on Albion Road. Shumba meant lion, she told us, and he was an English Rasta, she added, a malicious gleam in her eyes as she watched us digest this particular piece of unsavoury information.

Fast-forward to the end of the first week of courtship, by which time she'd twisted her hair into rat's tails that she'd superglued together. 'Instant dreadlocks,' she snapped, when I inquired about the gelatinous substance all over her head.

By the end of the second week she'd taken to wearing a maxi African wrapper, declaring it was her religion to keep her legs covered.

Third week arrived and the rat's tails had disappeared inside a headscarf, which was no bad thing.

Then she asked me if this Shumba person could visit her at home, because his squat in Stockwell was overcrowded. I'd always been a liberal kind of fella, and, as I knew my elder daughter hated me and as I wanted to repair the relationship, I agreed.

The look on Maxine's face when this *embalmed cadaver* walked through my front door, straight out of a horror movie, a-true. The fella had spaced-out black pupils in manically bright blue eyes, dutty blond dreadlocks in clumps and a coat swamping him that was last worn in the Russian Revolution.

He entered our nice, clean kitchen . . . polluting it.

Carmel started stirring pots that didn't need no stirring, splashing chicken curry on to the floor, laying the table like she was skimming stones on the pond at Clissold Park.

Little Maxine couldn't take her eyes off this *monster*, as she described him to me later.

I remained calm and extended my hand forthwith to this creature, who smelt like he'd never heard of soap or shampoo and who looked like he'd never used a nail file or a toothbrush.

'Greetings and salutations, Mr Walker,' he said, clasping my hand in both of his. He sat down without being asked, and spread his long legs out widthways and lengthways. I was surprised he didn't put his boots on the table, he looked so relaxed, like he owned the joint. From his coat he extracted a pouch holding a rusty tin of tobacco and a packet of Rizlas; then he started rolling up, without asking permission first.

I kept my lips buttoned tight. I was not goin' give my daughter an excuse to storm out. So I resorted to the English thing and commented on how the summer was shaping up nicely so far, but it wasn't as hot as last year, which was sweltering by English standards but came nowhere near the heat of the tropics.

'You know Bob Marley is living in London, right?' he said, interrupting me. 'Mi and mi bredren aren't impressed. He's a coconut who only appeals to the Babylonians who don't understand real reggae, the real *roots* reggae.'

I wanted to slap this fool and send him packing. Instead, I plied him with Guinness and started my interrogation. Turned out his father, a lord something or other, owned 3,000 acres of Northumberland.

'I man couldn't deal with *dat*,' he said, shovelling yam, green banana, dumplings and chicken curry down his throat with all the finesse of a pig at a trough.

'Really?' I replied, wondering how on earth anyone could *not* deal with 3,000 acres.

'Nah, man,' he said. 'I don't take a penny off-a mi fader. Mi can't deal with all-a-that hereditary, capitalist bullshit becorse I is re-varrrrr-looo-shan-arrrr-eeeee . . .'

At which point I realized this boy was as high as a kite. Completely off his trolley.

My hitherto feisty daughter, Donna the Daft, sat meekly, mutely, at his side, gazing in adoration as if this eedyat was Mahatma Gandhi.

Next day I cornered her (before my 'pre-hysterical' three minutes was up). Turned out his real name was Hugo, he'd been to Eton, and he stood to inherit the family title *and* the estate.

I joked, 'Go to Gretna Green. Get a quickie. Start a family and I'll find a good lawyer to represent you in the "acrimony and alimony" proceedings.'

'No way, Dad. Marriage is a vehicle for female oppression,' she retorted, flaring up. 'No way am I going to end up like . . .'

Donna never had no sense of humour then, and she never acquired one along the way.

I hoped the dreadlocks would pass as soon as the boyfriend did.

She cut them off the day he dumped her for another *sistren* who was a better cook (fair dues).

She left those disembodied rat's tails on the bathroom floor while she bawled her heart out in her bedroom.

'Go away! I hate you!' she screamed when I knocked on the door to offer fatherly succour.

After that she started bringing home boyfriends her mother would like. Actually, Carmel really *did* like some of them. Oh, yes, she would flick the fringe of her wig and flirt, which made Donna squirm.

Then one of these boyfriends cheated on Donna with her best friend or somesuch teenage soap opera, and Donna went hardcore, in tandem with the times.

Turned up for breakfast with her head shorn like a boy, wearing green combats, an oversized army sweater – riddled with what looked like bullet holes – and what they used to call 'bovver boots'.

Oh my days.

Carmel went to object but I put a finger to my lips.

Not having the desired effect must-a vexed Donna real bad. She took a couple of spoonfuls of the cornmeal Carmel had prepared for her, slung an original gas-mask khaki bag over her shoulder (just in case of Hiroshima II), flicked away the multicultural curtain beads of the kitchen door and shuffled down the hall.

Soon thereafter I took a one-day 'Introduction to Feminism' course at Hackney Adult Education in order to better understand my elder daughter. I listened respectfully to the teacher lecturing us about the perpetuation of patriarchy and the oppression of women, until I couldn't take no more of being treated like a punch bag.

'Excuse me, mzzzzz,' I said, rising up myself. 'Pray, did

not the greatest philosopher of ancient times, Mr Aristotle, declare that the female is a female by virtue of a certain lack of qualities; that we should regard the female nature as afflicted with a natural defectiveness?'

Well, the whole class went into uproar at that, especially the teacher, who said it was Simone de Beauvoir who'd exposed exactly those kinds of offensive attitudes. The two wimpy men in the class joined in the onslaught on their brother too. I got their number, sucking up to the women to get into their practical, black, oversized panties.

Nonetheless, I'd paid my money and I wasn't leaving without having had my say.

'The female problem is twofold,' I continued, overriding their cacophonous offendedness. 'First, they menstruate twelve times a year, or, as I like to say, "mentalate", which incapacitates them physically and psychically. Second, they are charged with bringing forth new life, which likewise incapacitates them for nine months and thereafter for eighteen years of motherhood. Anyways, anyone thinking women are oppressed should meet some of the bush women from my part of the world. Trust me, if they could get away with it, they'd cut off a fella's balls, pluck them, chop them, marinate them, stew them, serve them up on a plate with rice and peas and present the fella with the bill.'

Mzzzzz recovered enough to banish me from her class forthwith. I told her she had *nuff issues* as I left, suggesting she get some of that new-fangled therapy to deal with them.

What happened to the idea of free speech in this so-called democracy, by the way?

Needless to say, relations with Donna continued to deteriorate. She'd buy her clothes at this Laurence Corner army-surplus store up by Euston Station. Soon as she got home, she'd rip the garment up, only to put it back together with safety-pins, no doubt influenced by those punk rockers. Selfsame ones who'd also descended on Stokey and who, *one* might say, if *one* were writing an essay on Deconstruction for a cultural-studies class, 'turned the quotidian safety-pin into the quintessence of subversive fashion'.

During this sociopathic late-teen period, Donna was the Princess of Metamorphosis. A shape-shifter straight out of Greek myth, a-true. One day she was a moody but nonetheless feminine girl dressed all flowery; next, she was all rat's tails and African wraps; then she swiftly mutated into this war-veteran hobo character. What had happened to the girl who just two years earlier had pleaded with me to take her to that pretty Laura Ashley shop on Regent Street for her fifteenth birthday, where she'd picked out floaty frocks that mothers, aunties and grandmothers would approve of?

Then the plot thickened.

One evening she brought home a girl whom she whisked upstairs to her bedroom. Well, the girl looked more like a skinny teenage boy than a girl. Morning time, Donna came down to take tea and toast upstairs to her new 'friend', who later escaped out of the door without coming into the kitchen to greet the master of the house.

As she didn't need no permission to bring her girlie friends home, I couldn't say nothing.

Over the next couple of weeks I saw flashes of the mysterious friend, who always appeared and disappeared without being introduced. So I suggested (mildly, smilingly, non-antagonistically) to Donna that we meet her. Carmel agreed. I could tell she didn't have a clue. Carmel's naivety is and was a thing to behold. Most things go over her bewigged head. (Just as well.)

Still, Donna managed to elude the parental introduction.

Eventually I caught them sitting on the doorstep one hot Saturday night when I was returning home from a splurge with Morris at a drinking hole down by London Fields. They was sharing a cigarette and a can of lager on the front steps of the house, wearing matching men's vests and boxer shorts. Soon as I appeared in the driveway, Donna jumped up and tried to drag the girl inside, but her friend was having none of it.

'Hello, Mr Walker,' she said, a bit wary but pleasant enough.

I parked myself on the wall of the stoop, ignoring Donna, who'd bundled her knees up to her chest and buried her head.

It transpired the girl's name was Merle, she worked in a so-called 'women's print collective' down in Dalston, she was eighteen, was born in Montserrat and . . . she halted . . . before blurting out that she was 'a lesbian and proud of it'.

Donna's head shot up and her eyes nearly popped out in that hereditary, genealogical way passed down through the maternal line. I was caught off guard, but Merle stayed transfixed on me with an openness that was prepared for either a negative or a positive response.

What a brave little girl she was.

'Merle,' I said. 'That's fine by me. You do what you want, because I ain't no bigot. You girls have my blessing, but I can't speak for the wife,' I added, gesturing towards the upper floors of the house. Me and Merle shared a chuckle.

Donna was furious. She'd wanted to thrash her head

129

against a concrete wall, only to discover there wasn't no wall there.

'You're really cool,' Merle said, slipping Donna a glance that said I wasn't quite living up to the image of the mass murderer she'd expected. 'I wish I had a dad like you. Mine kicked me out a year ago when he caught me with my ex. I had to move into a hostel.'

'You love and support your children no matter what,' I replied, feeling rather sanctimonious: the Good Understanding Kind of Father. 'Where yuh mother?'

'Back in Montserrat. They divorced when I was young.'

'Well, far as I'm concerned, you girls do as you please. So long as my daughter happy, so am I.'

We fell silent, me and her quite comfortably, quite naturally.

That night, that faraway night, with its deep-blue-summer-night-star-filled sky.

With the street lamps giving off a fuzzy yellow light.

That lovely warm summer night, with no cars revving or roaring, no buses rumbling in the distance, or horns honking, and no people walking and talking, or dogs barking, or planes soaring.

That night, that long-ago-in-the-past-of-my-life night, with Carmel and Maxine safely asleep inside the big house that Barrington Walker had bought for his family.

In that moment, I wanted to tell this stranger, this Merle, this girl from the tiny island of Montserrat, that I had *commensurate preferences* too, but I couldn't be a brave warrior like her.

I wanted to tell her about Morris.

I wanted to sing his name out into the night.

His name is Morris. He is my Morris and he always been my Morris. He's a good-hearted man, a special man, a sexy man, a history-loving man, a loyal man, a man who appreciates good joke, a man of many moods, a drinking man and a man with whom I can be myself *completely*.

Yes, I was in the throes of a Malibu-and-Coke-soaked madness, a madness that could lead to the demise of my life as I'd hitherto known it. But I was on the *verge*.

Donna would finally know who her father really was, behind the façade – the dissembler, the impostor.

It was the right moment. It was the right place. It was the right time. And maybe my daughter would consider me a kindred spirit and stop hating me, because, even though she wasn't my favourite, I still loved her, my first child. I would still kill for her, my first child.

(Actually, looking back, I don't know if I'd really-a killed for her. We parents say these things and I'm sure it applies when they're innocent babies, but as soon as they start backchatting you, I'm not so sure we'd be so fast to dive into the swirling rapids after them. Upon occasion we might even be tempted to give them a shove in.)

'Merle,' I said, beginning my speech of a lifetime, 'lemme tell you something. I really admire your courage. Most folk pretend they just the same as everybody else because they afraid of negative reaction. But you now, you stay true to who you are, and few from our community is brave enough to do that. However.' I paused. 'There comes a time when even the biggest cowards got to . . .'

At which point Donna cut me off.

'Don't be so bloody patronizing and spare us the lecture, Dad. I don't need your approval or permission. I'm old enough to do as I please. Who do you think you are, acting the big patriarch? And another thing, I'm not a *girl*, I'm a woman. Merle, let's go inside. We need to *talk*.'

She heaved little Merley up by her arms, but Merle managed to mouth an apologetic 'Sorry' before she was propelled into the house.

Lord, but your children can be the most vicious little gits. They think they own the copyright on human feeling and that you don't have none.

I was left in the dark, in the fug, in the moonlight and the *moon pon stick* light, waiting for the morning, watching smoke spiral from the cigarettes they'd left behind.

That was the first and last time I had the slightest urge to spill the beans about who I really was.

Soon afterwards, Merle dumped my daughter, which came as no big surprise. Actually, if I was an Agony Aunt, I'd have advised it. Next thing you know, Donna re-feminized herself and brought a boyfriend home. Thank goodness I'd not confided nothing to her that night, because for sure it would have been related verbatim to her mother as soon as those two became thieving-thick again.

As it was, I got used to entering a room and the conversation goin' dead.

I would-a lost little Maxine and everything and, if Carmel went full out for revenge, my reputation too.

Cock of the Hackney Walk no more. I might as well have worn a placard with HOMO painted on it. Donna never apologized. She don't even remember it. A couple of years back she told Daniel off for being rude to her and said she'd never have spoken to her parents like that. She wouldn't-a been able to get away with it.

About a year later I bumped into Merle, sitting on the

pavement outside that radical Centerprise Bookshop on Kingsland High Street, begging. I took her inside the café to feed her some of that radical cow-feed they liked to serve up in there. Turned out she was homeless, had no money, no one to turn to, nowhere to go.

Little Merley couldn't help herself no more.

That very afternoon I moved her into a one-bedroom flat I'd just put on the rental market in Lordship Lane. I stocked up the fridge, sorted her out with some cash and took her down the dole office to sign on. I never told no one, not even Morris. She stayed there eleven years at peppercorn rent, picked up the education she lost when her father kicked her out, did a degree in so-called 'Women's Studies' (I never said nothing) and now teaches it at the London Metropolitan University.

She only moved out of the flat when she met Hennie from Amsterdam nineteen years ago and they bought a flat together in De Beauvoir Square.

I see them both from time to time when they pop down Ridley Road Market to buy bread and buns and Jamaican patties from Tom's Bakery – best bakery in London. Except Little Merley is Mama Merley these days, positively matronly, wearing skirts and make-up and everything. They are two chubby, happy women in their prime, and they still humour me when I greet them with 'Hello, Merley from Monsterrat; hello, Hennie from Holland'.

Any time I'm not with Morris, Merle asks after him.

No one need spell nothing out.

Maxine also went through a milder, non-psychotic version of Donna's coming-of-rage period, and I came to understand (admittedly years after the fact) that it was the nature of adolescence and not to take it too personally. But by the time I worked out that, in order to become them-selves, children have got to disengage from their parents, I'd already been wounded.

Carmel was let off lightly because she played the 'victim card'.

Donna, in particular, stored up all her beshittery for her father – who was beshat upon from a great height.

This is what happens when 75 per cent of your life is in the past. Each step forwards triggers a step backwards. All of these memories haunting me but they are also the making of me, here, in Hackney.

My perambulatory reverie has taken me from the quiet backstreets of Stokey to Newington Green, and I end up in the middle of Kingsland High Street, with its clamorous throng and traffic forcing me into the present tense.

Folk nod at me through the crowds, same way they done since Noah set sail with two of everything.

They think they know me:

Husband of Carmel.

Father of Donna and Maxine.

Grandfather to Daniel.

Retired engine-fitter.

Man of property.

Man of style.

Buggerer of men . . . How I go live with that?

And if I live with Morris, folk will work it out.

This is what's been stirring inside of me all week while I've been alone. The thought of what I'm about to do feels like climbing Kilimanjaro with no clothes, crampons, rope, pick or SOS flare.

Maybe things should stay as they are.

The Caribbean Canteen is all sunshine-yellow walls, Trif-fidian parlour palms and posters of clichéd golden beaches with aquamarine seas. Morris is huddled at the corner wooden table that faces the window. He shouldn't slouch; it ages him. He must-a watched me cut a distinguished, broad-shouldered swathe through the lumpenproletariat of Dalston.

'Y'all right, Boss?'

'Y'all right, Boss?'

Morris is always waiting for me. Story of his life. He is of the belief that it's better to be half an hour early than ten minutes late. Very noble, but I'd rather be half an hour late than ten minutes early. I can tell he's disgruntled. I can spot his mood soon as I see him, even from a distance. When you've known somebody this long, you can read their body language. It's the same on the telephone: soon as he speaks, sometimes in the split second before he greets me, I know his state of mind.

He's wearing his Andy Capp tweed hat, even though he's inside an eating establishment, but I'm not goin' pull him up on the correct etiquette today. I am his lover, not his father.

The canteen is filled with the yuppies who've been colonizing Dalston since they built the tube extension and the rip-off rabbit-hutch development next to it. Years ago only Caribbean people touched Caribbean food. Now even English people realize that the seemingly rotten, decomposing plantain is actually the ripest, sweetest vegetable on earth. We both opt for the Breadfruit Casserole with slices of buttered hard dough: a lovely thick broth bobbing with meaty and wheaty things.

I decide to warm him up with some harmless conversation

about the past. This is one of the pleasures of a lifelong friendship: so many of your memories are shared.

I launch myself . . .

'I been thinking about those young radicals who used to hang out here in the sixties and seventies. Remember that Shumba-boy Donna was seeing in 1977? *That* type, yuh know, so up they own arses they need an enema to get themselves down again. I bet him and some of those radical dropouts ended up as investment bankers grouse shooting on the moors with their fellow aristos, and some of those young *feministas* ended up as housewives in places like Cheltenham and the *shires*.'

'Why you goin' on about that now? What they done to you?'

'Because it's on my mind, and, as you my friend, I thought it might be interesting to discourse it with you,' I reply in a *reasonable* manner.

'You so critical, Barry.' Morris sticks his spoon into his casserole and leaves it there. 'It's fine to be angry when young, but people can't stay angry for ever. Soon as they start having children they want a good job and house in a safe area that is child-friendly with good schools. You should be glad those radicals fought those battles, because it meant we didn't have to.' He stops and scans the room surreptitiously before whispering, 'Like those gay liberationists trying to make life better for our lot.'

'Why you bringing them up? You know we don't business with this gay-liberation stuff.' I stick my spoon in my casserole and leave it there too. 'To be quite frank with you,' I add, humouring him by whispering too (even though nobody is close enough to eavesdrop and, like I always say, why the hell would they want to?), 'I didn't really appreciate all of that attention-seeking behaviour of those *gay* liberationists. They should-a kept the noise down a bit. As well you know, I believe in discretion.'

Morris shakes his head. 'Yuh talking nonsense again, Barry. I believe in discretion too, but society don't become more equal unless some brave folk get up on their soapboxes and start revolutions, like in Russia, Mexico, China, France. You see, unlike you, who seems to think you are superior to most people, I believe in equality. I never did like discrimination of any kind.'

Wha rong wit yuh, Morris? Right. Is fight you want? Is fight you get. Morris has got the hump bad. He knows full well I am an anti-discriminatory person.

'You better watch out, Morris,' I joke, still trying to lighten the proceedings, dipping my bread into my casserole again like he not getting to me. 'You starting to sound like a communist, one of those reds under the bed.'

He shakes his head *again*, as if I am completely beyond his help. 'You will recall the book and telly drama called *The Naked Civil Servant* in 1975. The one about that real-life gay fella who used to wear make-up and prance around the streets of London from the 1930s onwards? Quentin Crisp? I told you about him, remember?'

How could I forget? Morris talked about him for years. Oh Quentin this and Quentin that, like they was best friends.

'You mean that eccentric pooftah with blue-rinse hair?'

I will wind Morris up bad-bad. I will wind him up so much he'll regret being unreasonable with me when I was trying to discourse pleasantly.

'This is your problem, Barry. He was the same as me and you. So that makes you a pooftah too.'

'I, for one, do not wear make-up, dye my hair, or do the

mince-walk like that Larry Grayson in *The Generation Game* or Frankie Howerd in *Up Pompeii*, although, to be honest, Howerd was funny as hell. Morris, when did you ever see me flapping about with limp wrists and squealing like a constipated castrato?'

'I don't understand you, Barry,' Morris says, continuing his moralistic crusade. 'You hate it when Merty and that lot chat homophobic nonsense, but look at yourself.'

'Morris, I am an individual, specific, not generic. I am no more a pooftah than I am a homo, buller or anti-man.' I start to quietly hum 'I am What I am'.

'You homosexual, Barry,' he says, goin' po-faced on me. 'We established that fact a long time ago.'

'Morris, dear. I ain't no homosexual, I am a . . . Barrysexual!'

I won't have nobody sticking me in a box and labelling it.

'Great, well . . . shut up now and let me finish my story,' he says. 'So me, Odette and the boys began to watch *The Naked Civil Servant*, not realizing what it was goin' be about. Soon as the boys realized, you should-a heard them sounding off about how that "pansy" should be shot dead. Yes, *shot dead*. Worse, Barry, I was so afraid of implicating myself, I agreed with them. I was *a quisling*, Barry. I felt so bad I never ever told you about it.'

Morris has gone all moist-eyed.

'So what, we all been quislings at some point or other, Morris.'

'You see, Barry, I didn't approve of the way Mr Crisp went about things either, all that make-up and mincing, but I really admired the way he stood up for himself. He used to get beaten up all of the time. Now that takes a courage neither of us has had . . . until now.'

No 'until now' about it, my friend. Seriously, though, what 74-year-ole man divorces his wife and moves in with his long-term male lover?

He which hath no stomach to this fight / Let him depart.

'I didn't sleep good for weeks afterwards,' Morris says. 'This is why I appreciate what these gay liberationists been doing all of these years. They been educating the masses and getting us our freedom . . . *should* we choose to take it.'

For the first time since I arrived, Morris lightens up. He takes off his hat and puts it on his lap. He stares warmly, *lovingly*, at me.

What . . . is . . . he . . . up . . . to?

'Today we even got civil partnerships,' he says, weighing his words carefully, like he wants to make sure the scales balance.

Morris, don't you dare even suggest it.

'Seeing as you say you're divorcing Carmel, and seeing as I'm *chupit* enough to half believe you . . .' He grins, tipping his head sideways. 'Why don't we go the whole hog? I've looked into Chelsea Town Hall, which has a tiny register room for four persons. We can drag two witnesses off the street. Judy Garland got married there, you know. Boss, I feel ready now, again. Wanna join me?'

All of my hunger has gone. The smell from my stew is noxious and making me nauseous.

Now I know why he had the hump when I came in. Whenever Morris wants something badly, he expects a negative response and acts like he's already got it. Which, in this instance, is foresight.

What kind of tomfoolery preposterous proposal is this, I ask you?

'You know I said you was suffering from dementia the

other night at the dance?' I tell him, straight-faced. 'Okay, I meant it as a joke, only now I'm not so su—'

Before I finish my sentence he's up from his chair and he gone.

Lord ha mercy . . . I blown it now. Should I pursue him? Tell him I was only jesting, in the way people do when what they've said backfires.

I leave the canteen too and start walking home, barging into any bastard who don't get out of my way.

This is one holy mess. I have really upset Morris, but I was goin' do that anyway, wasn't I? Thing is, I can't change the way I am for nobody. The development of an individual's personality stops at the age of eleven. I don't care what the psycho-tricksters say. Any half-brained person seeing me wearing a Homburg and wide-lapelled 1950s suit will understand I am a fella not big on change. I ain't never worn a pair of jeans in my life, and I like my socks gartered, which says it all.

I never told Morris I wanted to get a civilian partnership or whatever they call it. He's jumping the gun in wanting to jump the proverbial broom. We are not Elton John and David Furnish. I said I would leave Carmel and that we would move in together, *eventually* . . . *probably*. But, given my current state of mind, what seemed like a great idea last Sunday now feels *improbable*.

How can I take the upheaval of telling Carmel I divorcing her?

Fact is, I am too used to being in a prison of my own making: judge, jailer and jackass cellmate.

Once inside my *empty* house, I take off my brogues and socks and leave them on the carpet by the front door, because Carmel's not here to cuss me off and, seeing as there is already a certain *accumulation* of discarded garments – shirts, trousers, underwear – I making it easier for her to lift it all up and walk ten yards to the washing machine in the kitchen instead of hauling the bundle downstairs from the bedroom or bathroom with her dodgy joints.

What I goin' do now, ehn? I can't stand it when I've upset Morris, or, rather, when Morris *gets* upset. Not now, Morris, of all times. How I goin' cope?

First, I will have a little siesta to de-stress myself.

After that I will pick up *The Siege of Krishnapur* by Mr J. G. Farrell to bring the repression of the Indian Mutiny into my living room and transport me back in time, away from the trials and tribulations of the mutinous Morris.

Third, I will help myself to some Bacardi and Lemon, Bacardi and Coke, Bacardi and Soda, Bacardi and Bacardi . . . to help ease the terrible sufferance in my heart.

Eventually, I will make the slow journey towards the household site of human somnambulation.

I will therefore ascend the thick, carpeted stairs and I will thenceforth descend into my bed.

On my own – *emotionally*.

Nothing new there.

8.

Song of Prayer

1980

. . . on your own again, isn't it, Carmel?

late this night, praying up against your bed, waiting for him to come home, knowing he might not come home at all, but you can't help yourself, can you, acting like a right mug, as the English people say

waiting, waiting, always waiting . . .

can't help thinking back on the past neither, and wondering what the future goin' bring you, remembering how your first ten years in this country was spent in a haze and a daze, wasn't it, Carmel?

1960–1970 – you barely left Hackney, raising Donna, goin' church, goin' home to Antigua only two times, taking Donna, who hated the heat, missing dear Mommy (now dearly departed)

Barry never came with you because he said he had to supervise building work on his properties during his holidays from Ford's

and you believed him

then

after Maxine born in 1970 you was sunk so deep into the swamp-a madness you temporarily lost your belief in Our Lord even to this day you don't understand what happened to you

just as well Barry didn't believe in sending nobody to the crazy house, *You see how quickly they put us in those places, Carmel? Getting us sectioned? Well, it's not happening to the mother of my children*

which is why he let you ride your madness out

that's why he agreed not to let the doctor see you until you was showing signs of improvement, which you did after eighteen mad months

but in the end it was Our Lord who raised you up, wasn't it? Soon as you started goin' church again, your spirits lifted and it was like you was

bathed in Holy Light and was blessed by His Hand and you glowed with His Love from deep within

even though Barry said the reason you felt better was because of the Valium prescribed by Dr Sampson (typical heathen speak)

oh, but you'll never forget that September evening in 1971 when Barry came home from work, sleeves rolled up as usual, showing off his strong forearms, canvas satchel slung over his shoulder, and he stood handsomely, broadly, a Hollywood heart-throb in the doorway, with his fine moustache and sexy eyes and thick head of hair, and he looked so *shock* that you wasn't the usual catatonic wreck with madwoman hair in a scruffy dressing gown slumped on the settee barely managing to greet him

no, you was wearing a new pair of cream nylon slacks and a cream nylon blouse with orange frills down the front, and you'd got your hair straightened into a lovely bob, and you had on a touch of foundation and peachy lipstick, and you and Donna was playing Snap! around the kitchen table collapsing into a fit of giggles while Maxine was sleeping in her cot by the fridge

and then Barry announced theatrically

I see the God-Pill of Mood Upliftment seems to have done the trick, wifey

and you realized it was the first time since Maxine born that he wasn't looking at you like you was standing on the window ledge of a skyscraper about to jump

best thing about that time is how Barry stood right by you

but soon as you was back in the swing of things, he started forgetting that *decent* men come straight home after work, except Fridays, when they allowed to go down the pub with their mates

or that *decent* men actually *do* come home every night; otherwise their wives get upset and end up crying themselves to sleep

Merty says all men is dogs and that he'll never change – even though Clement never spent a single night apart from her until he decided never to spend another day *with* her – running off with that whore-bitch Janet from church

Drusilla says you got to make your man jealous, let him know he got rivals, more the merrier

she should know, falling for all of those sweet-talking charmers who only need tell her how beautiful she is for her to drop her girdled panties whenever they feel like popping round for dinner and a quick one

she should learn to keep her fanny hole bolted until good husband material show up instead of *this* one in the front door and *that* one out the back door

Merty says if Drusilla started charging she'd be a millionaire in no time

Merty's been getting more and more bitter since Clement left her and her eldest boy went to prison for 'resisting arrest and aggravated assault', when he was the one the notorious Stoke Newington police assaulted by beating him up in a Black Maria underneath a blanket so it wouldn't show

and now Merty holds prayer meetings four evenings a week in her sitting room, and she's still got that cleaning job, but she don't own her own home, because the mortgage plan fell through on her meagre salary alone when Clement left her

and Candaisy says you got to give husbands time to appreciate you (as if twenty years of marriage to Barry is not long enough?)

she's a charge nurse up at the Whittington, which y'all agree has a better class of patient than Hackney Hospital, where she was for seventeen years previous, and Robert don't gamble no more so they bought their own house on Amhurst Road

even Asseleitha's a proper chef now for the BBC, with a mortgage on a one-bedroom flat in Shacklewell Lane, also known as the Front Line, but the louts down there stopped *sssssssing* her every time she walked past (in blatant disrespect of such a good, churchgoing woman), ever since she started standing at the corner of Shacklewell and Kingsland and preaching from the Bible with a loudspeaker

which even you thought was a bit much but

who else you ladies goin' turn to?

Asseleitha says God will sort Barry out if you ask him nicely, and you tend to agree with Sister Asseleitha, who's no nun but should be

Barry calls her the Patron Saint of Celibacy . . . like you'd find *that* funny, since you've not been getting *no conjugals* since Maxine conceived over ten years ago now

in the meantime, you enrolled on an access course at Hackney Adult Education, and before six years was up you'd got yourself a 2.1 in Business Administration from the Open University at the grand ole age of thirty-four

you, Carmelita Walker, née Miller – has got a *degree*

you, lady, are finally fulfilling your *potential*

Barry was proud of you when you collected your diploma in your gown and mortar board at the graduation ceremony all the way over in Milton Keynes, showing his better nature, even though it gave you the 'academical advantage', which, as he put it, can't be easy for such a vain, egotistical man

his problem is he's not got enough staying power to study for his Achilles heel – *a degree*

Barry's a dibbler-dabbler who hides his flimsy knowledge behind an intellectual self-aggrandizement that is plainly *showing off*, but woe betide anybody who tells him that to his face

he can dish it out but he can't take it

thick ego, thin skin – that's him

and then what happen, Carmel?

the Lord came to your assistance, that's what happen

only two weeks after graduation in 1978 he found you a job with prospects: Housing Assistant for Hackney Council, sharing an office with

Theresa from Barnet, who is twenty-five and engaged

Joan from Manchester, who is twenty-six and never getting married

Mumtaz from Leicester, who is twenty-eight and happily

single, so long as she stays in hiding from her *entire extended family* and

you can't wait to get into the office in the morning and start cracking jokes with your new friends

some lunchtimes you even enjoy a sneaky half of lager-and-lime with a ploughman's at the Queen Eleanor

although you'd prefer hard dough with your Cheddar, and you even sometimes have a sneaky fag afterwards too, which don't make you feel as light-headed as the sneaky spliff Joan persuades y'all to smoke behind the bushes in the summertime in London Fields

see, Barry's not the only one with secrets

got a photograph of him on your desk to show everybody what you got, the one from Maxine's birthday party, when she was blowing out candles and Barry leant over and kissed you on the cheek and you thought he was goin' say *I love you, wifey*

for the first time *ever*, but instead he whispered, *Thank you for bringing me Maxine*

and you wanted to slap him

as for Maxine, she got too much personality for she own damned good

since when do children get to rule the roost?

needs a good beating, but Barry won't allow it, because he's a pussy when it come to corporal punishment, treats her like his little princess, stuffing her bedroom with dolls and toys, allowing her to scrawl with crayon all over its walls and indulging her sulks, which just makes your job harder

Maxine looks like him too, with her long-long legs and pretty-pretty face, prettier than Donna, but more of a handful than Donna was at her age

Maxine might be ten years old now, but she still fights like mad when you give her a cup of senna tea to clear her out Saturday mornings

still won't do housework without a fight

as if you would allow her to be the first West Indian girl in the world to get away with not knowing how to look after a household?

Barry lets her think she has a choice about things, when you know better – children should do what they told

her finicky eating drives you mad too, and it's Barry's fault because he indulges her

don't like soursop, don't like tamarind jam, don't like sugarcake, don't like ginger beer, sorrel, guineps, dates, dumps, stinking toe, saltfish, don't like anything cooked in fat meat, don't like stew fish, don't like white yam, pumpkin, cassava, don't like condensed milk in her tea

what she like?

Coke, doughnuts, crisps, burgers

this is the problem with raising children away from their homeland

as for Donna, thanks God she comes back every other weekend, even though she brings all of her laundry home for you to do

and because you taught her to never wear nothing twice without washing it, it's a *lot*

she living in halls at Birmingham University, and in seventeen months' time she will graduate in Social Science and then train to become a social worker, which you don't really approve of, but Donna is too strong-headed to listen to your objections and even so – a degree is a *degree*

you already planning your outfit for her graduation

and after Maxine has been dragged to bed, you and Donna curl up on the settee to catch up, you with a cup of camomile tea and her with a bottle of wine, which she almost empties (you notice)

and you should never-a told her the number of nights you couldn't sleep for weeping about Barry, even today, because now she's always on at you to divorce him on the grounds of *twenty years of patriarchal oppression*

she says black women been oppressed so long they forgotten what it is to be free, it's all *black* this and *black* that since Donna went to university

As a black woman I think . . . As a black woman I believe . . . As a black woman I object . . .

Yes, Donna, you told her when she'd said it for the umpteenth time, *you don't need to keep reminding me you is a black woman, seeing as you talking to the woman who gave birth to you*

just as well you've always hidden those Barbara Cartland novels in the front room that you and the Ladies' Society of Antigua been passing around ever since you arrived in England (Barry thinks you in there reading the Bible)

it's like an addiction because those books give you such a high that you

can feel your heart pounding through your ribcage like the heroines in the stories

unlike that book Donna gave you a while back called *The Women's Room*

Mum, this is what you need to be reading

but it was so depressing you didn't even get past the first chapter

Donna's always doing the Bob Marley *stand up for your*

rights talk, but every time she got a new boyfriend, and the latest is some Lesroy who's been two-timing her, she goes all mushy and you're the one who ends up consoling her

you just hope Donna gets married to a good man who is worthy of her, soon as she graduates is best, and then gives you grandchildren to babysit

she won't be complete until she does – no woman is.

until then, she knows nothing about marriage, so you don't heed her advice

Pastor George, on the other hand, *does*, he's been married twenty-three years and preaches *Marriage is for ever and for ever is not finite, it is in-finite*

he also says that people who are at it like bunnies goin' be dining with Lucifer, and as for the homos, they goin' end up raped by Lucifer himself, and they won't get no kicks from it either, because his scorching hot rod's so big it will go in one end and come out the other . . .

half the congregation goes quiet when he says stuff like that

the other half, including you, holler right back, because you ain't got nothing to hide

you might as well be married to yourself, seeing as Barry don't touch you, and to think you thought that bastard had a low sex drive

girl, you was *hoodwinked*

like you care anyway, because the longer you go without getting any, the more righteous you becoming, not sullying your mind or your body with craven desires for a man who's still too damned sexy for his own good

keeping yourself clean for Him

you not bitter about Barry, because you got equanimity,

which comes from reaching out to Our Lord with a pure and open heart

a whole hour every night Reaching Out to Him

the worn patch on the carpet is visual proof of your Dedication to Him

you always denied yourself the comfort of a cushion because praying is not supposed to be a picnic, but Candaisy told you just the other day the knees are the first to go in the elderly, and, seeing as you about to hit the big 4-0 in four years' time

you goin' get a shag pile soon, in the Continued Service of Our Lord

got your eye on a luxurious creamy one in Debenhams

and so you give thanks for the future shag pile upon which you shall contemplate the meaning of His Life and reflect on how you can make yourself worthy of Him and Humbly Walk in Jesus' name

Pastor George says you got to give thanks for your good fortunes as a way to happiness or you goin' end up mean-spirited and get cancer

so stop feeling sorry for yourself and see what you got to give thanks for, Carmel

what you got, girl?

what you got this night while you been reflecting and cogitating on the meaning of your life?

you give thanks for your two daughters, that's what, and your lovely degree, your lovely job, your lovely big house that is the envy of everyone you know

you trying to give thanks for your husband too, even though it's now past midnight and you still waiting

you close your eyes to pray, but it hurts so much after all of these years that they spring open again you goin' try, though, isn't it?

you give thanks for Barry, even though you know in your bones that he is an *adulterer*

and then you feel rage surging through you, and you find yourself *slaying* instead of praying –

may disease stop his heart, O Lord!

may a high-speed train cut him in two where it hurts, O Lord!

may he die in agony, O Lord!

may he die alone, O Lord!

may he die begging forgiveness, O Lord!

then you think, hold your horses, Carmel, yuh hearing yourself, woman?

what did Jesus preach?

love or hate?

and what is love?

Love is Patient and Kind! Love is Pure and Holy! Love is Bountiful and Unconditional!

love is not vengeful or vicious! It does not envy or boast! It is not arrogant or rude!

let us love one another, for love is from God and

God is Love and Whosoever Loves God has been Born of God and Knows God!

who is always here?   He is!

who listens?   He does!

who is loyal?   He is!

who is kind?   He is!

very good, Carmel, now every time you feel yourself goin' astray, you got to rein yourself in, and exercise self-control, which is the only way you goin' survive this marriage – for the *rest of your life*, even though you can't help shouting at that bastard through any door he chooses to slam in your face or you choose to slam in his

but hold up, Carmel, hold up, dear

now . . . what is forgiveness?

forgiveness is a purification of the heart, you accept forgiveness for your sins, for your faults and failings, and you forgive the sins of others . . . like, for example, a certain husband *who has not come home to his bed for two nights and counting . . .*

ease up, lady, ease up, you having a tough time of it tonight, isn't it?

your good side says one thing, but your dark side keeps overpowering it

don't give in to the dark, Carmel, be Filled with Goodness, be Filled with Light

so . . . let's start again

give thanks, Carmel, give thanks that he actually comes home at all, same day or next day or next-next day

least you still married

meanwhile . . . keep looking for hard, factual evidence of his misdemeanours – in his wallet, his pockets, sniffing his clothes, eavesdropping on his calls and conversations, opening his mail, following him every now and again, and generally trying to disentangle lies from truth, because you goin' catch him off guard one of these days and then Armageddon goin' rain down pestilence on him

like you need evidence? Only one reason man don't come home – is because he out there fornicating with some bitch hag

don't need no private detective charging fortune to work that one out don't need a human judge in a human courtroom to sentence him to eternal damnation

someone else go do that when he dies – the Boss Judge, Judge of Judges, Judge Most High

even so . . . even *so* . . . you letting yourself down tonight, *lady*

you deviating from the path of righteousness, *lady*

fill your heart with love, Carmel

it's not that you don't love your husband

it's just that at the age of thirty-six you been waiting twenty years for him to love you

9.

The Art of Being a Man

Saturday, 8 May 2010

Next morning I wade through the fog of sleep to the landing and pick up the telephone.

I already guess the news it will bring.

Carmel's weeping as she tells me her daddy dead. I feel for her. Don't need to love someone to be compassionate. Don't matter what your parents are like, nothing compares to losing them, whatever age it happen. Only thing worse must be losing one of your children.

'He wasn't a bad man, Barry. He just had a bad temper, that's all. I'm sure he felt guilty about what he did to Mommy.'

Easy to feel guilty after the fact.

'My papi's with the angels now.'

'Yes, my dear, he with the angels now.'

The fallen ones burnin' alongside him. You see, Carmel? Your grief don't change what he was, a *narsy* man, but I ain't goin over that ground with her right now.

'Mi feel like an orphan, Barry.'

'I sorry, Carmel.'

And I *am*. For her.

'When you coming for the funeral, Barry?' Carmel's voice is heavy with hope.

'You know I don't business with funerals.'

'Yes, but this mi papi.'

'I sorry, Carmel. I sorry . . . but I just can't.'

Sigh.

Click.

I stand there a while before I put the phone back in its socket, and then I sit down in the chair next to the phone and catch myself. I recognize what I feeling. The cycle of grief, the way hearing about a person's death, let alone my own father-in-law's, resurrects old pain.

My own father dead before I reach my sixteenth. Mr Patmore Walker, Esq. – son of Mr Gideon Walker, Esq., son of Mr Jesse Walker, Esq., son of Solomon, son of Caesar, son of Congo Bob – worked as a junior clerk in the court house. He was the first in his family to go to school but not quite first in class so he didn't get the single island scholarship to a British university available to my people in 1929.

He wanted to be a teacher, so he should-a started his own school with kids sitting on mats. I would-a advised him so, if he'd lived long enough. Making my way in England, I learnt that when the fortress draws up its ramparts, you gotta start building your own empire. Don't wait for nobody give it you.

But he was a passive, placid man, except where he and his wife was concerned. My mother might-a been a lowly maid for the Pattersons, but she had high ambitions that her husband never met, with his highly intelligent mind but lowly job at the court house. Theirs was not one of those marriages of everyone else's inconvenience, which was rare in the Ovals, but they nonetheless quietly, consistently, bickered.

My father was home after work, every evening on the dot; he didn't disappear without no explanation, didn't spend hours over at the rum bar, didn't lie, didn't cheat, didn't beat.

His favourite pastime was reading the Agatha Christie novels his pen friend sent him from England, transporting himself to the land of the British who'd brought us there, who still ruled over us and in whose power it was to give us, or not, medicine, education, employment, electricity, running water and, for those who could sell a few cows to pay for it, the right to passage on a steamship ploughing a watery furrow all the way to the centre of the world.

This one evening my father was washing hisself down in the yard from the huge barrel of water that it was me and my older brother Larry's job to fill to the brim every morning from the tap, carrying two pails, each balanced on a shoulder rod.

I heard him singing his favourite Roaring Lion calypso, which my mother hated, which was why he was always singing it.

'If you want to be happy and live a king's life, / never make a pretty woman your wife.'

One moment my mother was shelling peas out back; the coal pot was cooking up something aromatic to satisfy my wolfish teenage appetite while I was (half-heartedly) doing homework on my bed; and Larry was over at his girl Ellorice's – and the next, my father had collapsed.

His heart had stopped and couldn't be kick-started into action again, no matter how hard we and the neighbours tried. It was only when his ribs started to crack that we gave up.

He was thirty-three years younger than I am now.

I never heard my father sing again. Never had him to guide me through life, although that meant I was also spared the fear of his disapproval because at this stage me and Morris was already hanky-pankying.

He died at a point in the father–son relationship when I'd had enough of him telling me to work harder at school, enough of carrying the weight of his expectations, when I hadn't worked out what I wanted for myself yet. I'd become a sullen, monosyllabic arse.

I didn't understand then that when your people come from nothing, each subsequent generation is supposed to supersede the achievements of its parents. My father had escaped the fields of his predecessors, and he wanted me getting letters after my name and a career worthy of my intelligence. Bettering ourselves was no joke when we was only a few generations away from the hold of the SS *Business Enterprise* out of Africa. Especially when back home change came slow. The colonial overlords ran *tings*, and the red-skinned Antiguans from 'good' families in St John's was next, followed by the redskins, who didn't come from families of note but who had the appropriate doses of alchemically advantageous admixture for a certain degree of success in the island's pigmentory hierarchy. Lastly was we darkies.

This is why my father had been saving to RSVP a Yes to the British Colonial Office ever since they first sent embossed, gilt-edged invitations to all the citizens of the Caribbean.

He knew we all had to leave to get on. And we wasn't like those badass, kamikaze Jamaicans full of the blood of Yoruba warriors living on an island twenty-six times larger than ours. No, sah, and we was cut off from each other on remote plantations and villages. The Jamaicans had massive mountain ranges to escape to. What we have? *Volcanic mounds.*

How was we supposed to rise up? And do what? End up back in the sea again? Yuh mad? We didn't even get universal suffrage until 1951. For most of his adult life, my father couldn't vote. How that make him feel?

Maybe that explains me to myself too. I don't like to buck the so-called 'system', like those gay exhibitionists Morris loves so much. I like to infiltrate the system and benefit from it. Same goes with my marriage. I don't like being an outsider.

Yes, I am my father's son.

If only I could bring him back and get reacquainted. Ask him how he escaped the curse of we people by being a good husband and father. The curse Carmel's father carried all of his life – a wife-cheater and a wife-beater.

As for my mother, news reached me in 1968 that she was laid up with a cancer that had worked itself into all of her organs without her even realizing what it was. That woman never gave in to no illness, because people couldn't afford to back then. They soldiered on using teas, herbs and compresses.

I got the telegram early one Sunday morning and caught the first boat home with Larry, which didn't leave for three days and took two weeks.

By the time mi reach Antigua, mi mother gone.

Like with mi father, I didn't get to say goodbye. To this day, mi feel it deep inside and I *cyan't* talk about it to nobody – not Morris, not Maxine, not nobody.

How many times I told Carmel I don't do funerals. She don't listen.

Last one I attended was 1979, after Larry smoked himself to an early appointment with Saint Peter at the Celestial Gates.

Forty Embassy Filters a day for twenty-five years did the trick. Back then the cigarette companies never said they was selling cancer sticks. Didn't even have warnings on the packets. Smokers got hooked on something they thought gave them harmless pleasure.

Towards the end, Larry had a room in St Joseph's Hospice on Mare Street, run by the Angels of St Joseph's. He was the first of many to enter what we came to call the Place of No Return. Larry was unconscious most of the time, but when he did come to there was a certain peace and acceptance in his eyes as he prepared himself for the great journey ahead, with the assistance of a morphine drip.

Larrington Emmanuel Walker was older than me and came to England before I did. He started off a ticket-collector and ended up a train-driver for National Rail, based at Liverpool Street.

When we was kids he used to put me on the handlebars of the big black bicycle the Pattersons had given my mother for us and we'd freewheel hell-for-leather downhill. Nobody worried about so-called 'health and safety' in those days. Makes me laugh when I see children today cycling on the pavement wearing helmets. They too damn cosseted. Childhood is about getting knocked about here and there. You supposed to acquire a few scars that will last the rest of your life. Number of times I came off that bike. Number of times Larry put me back on it again.

Me and Larry was sent out several times a day to the shops on Temple Street to get food for our meals. Bread from Dickie Lake's for breakfast; flour for dumplings and saltfish from Mr and Mrs Ho's for lunch; maybe one ounce of cheese and one ounce of butter from Mrs Connor's for evening tea to go with the leftover bread. When Larry got a job waiting tables over at a hotel in town and caught himself a wage and some tips, we'd go down to the harbour and enjoy a secret tot or two of smuggled rum from the fishermen, acclimatizing my inexperienced palate to the one good thing to come out of the history of sugar cane.

As I got older, Larry showed me how to sweet-talk the girls, which I went along with, hoping it might cure me.

He was also the first one who taught me the power of secrets and silence, long before the Odette débâcle.

Me and Morris was at my house one afternoon when we was seventeen, school had finished early, and no one was around. It was raining heavily and muggy-hot, steaming, the windows was open, fan palms all wet and dripping outside, and we had been on fire all day the way only teenagers can be, feelin' like we was goin' *explode*. Soon as we got inside we was all over each other, while the rain hammered on to the corrugated-tin roof of the bungalow.

Larry, who should-a been at work but for some reason wasn't, suddenly threw the door open in a hurry to get out of the rain and caught us right there on the floor by the door.

He reeled like someone had just fired a gunshot into his chest, staggered backwards and was gone – the light wooden doorframe with torn mosquito netting swinging back and forth like something from an outback horror movie.

Me and Morris scrambled up from the wooden floor, re-aligned our arms and legs, and returned our school shirts and shorts to their rightful places.

Morris didn't want to leave me alone in case something bad went down when Larry returned, so he stayed with me while my mother came home and cooked dinner for us, asking why we boys was so quiet when normally she couldn't shut us up.

When the rain stopped, we sat on the stoop and waited for Larry to come back. I remember thinking I might end up like Horace Johnson – suicided on the end of a rope.

Larry finally appeared out of the shadows, unsteady, which meant he'd been drinking homemade hooch at some rum shack down in St John's. I braced myself for whatever onslaught was goin' be the beginning of the end of my life as I'd known it.

Instead, Larry squeezed my shoulder as he passed me to go inside.

'You two *chupit* boys is damned *rass* lucky it was me. Watch yourselves, you right pair of *eedyots*.'

Five years older.

A hundred years wiser.

Full of kindness.

That was my brother.

All of this happened in 1953, a year after *The Diary of Anne Frank* reached Antigua and every boy in school was reading it. I remember thinking that Larry was the kind of man who would-a harboured people like her in his attic, people being persecuted.

He never said a word about it afterwards, even though sometimes I'd see him watching me and Morris like he sensed we was still carrying on with all of our stuff, even in late 1970s London.

Occasionally, me and him would be sitting alone somewhere, and our conversation would quieten, and I knew we was both thinking about it, but neither of us knew how to start talking about it.

I could tell that Larry didn't approve of it, didn't understand it, and I was pretty sure he didn't like it, but he accepted it because I was his little brother.

He was a good man, a true man of God.

So . . . some of us was gathered in his room at St Joseph's Hospice, singing hymns, and his nineteen-year-old twin sons, Dudley (law student) and Eddie (apprentice BT engineer), was sitting on both sides of my brother, holding his hands, still the sweet boys who used to come visit us on Sunday afternoons. Larry was a good father to them, raising them alone after Ellorice passed when they was nippers, but it hit them hard, especially Melvin, the eldest, who had six years on the twins and got derailed.

All of a sudden, the door burst open and none other than Melvin barged in, fired up with drugs.

'I hear you've been bad-talking me, saying I don't deserve nothing from Dad's will because I am a useless junkie,' he shouted at his brothers. 'I want what's rightfully mine, a third of everything, and if anybody gives me any beef, they'll end with a hook for a hand. *Guaranteed.*'

I looked over and saw that Larry had not only opened his eyes but that he seemed more alert than he had been for days. But his face had drained of whatever colour was left and I could see his heart was breaking.

When Melvin noticed Larry was awake, he had two choices: beg forgiveness or storm back out.

Sadly, he was too wired up to shift gear.

Later that day Larry left his body with only two of his sons to watch his spirit pass.

At the funeral my three young nephews was so tall and dignified in their new black suits, even Melvin. The sun was brightening up a wintry sky, and everybody was singing 'How Sweet Thou Art' with the kind of churchified sound that is moving, in spite of the fact that as usual the loudest singers was those who can't even hold a tune. Then, just as my brother's coffin was being lowered into the grave, Melvin kicked off again and all three of them began brawling. All-a-we elders dived in. I held Melvin's arms behind him, even though it was like trying to hold back a raging bull.

Once order been restored, the burial resumed.

Soon as the men began shovelling earth over Larry, that point in funerals when even the hardest nut got to crack, Melvin fell to his knees and went to pieces.

That's when my legs buckled.

My only brother was being ferried across the swampy River Acheron, what the Ancient Greeks called the River of Pain.

I was at the shore, keeled over, clutching my stomach, head thrown back, howling.

'Tis in my memory locked.

I wasn't just grieving for Larry but for my parents as well, because I'd not allowed myself that luxury when they'd passed. Grieving for three loved ones at once is a Major Incident motorway pile-up.

As for Melvin? Never did get his act together. Ended up caught in what I call the 'revolving door for recidivists' – at Her Majesty's Pleasure.

Last saw him early nineties. Dudley told me a few weeks back that one of Melvin's pickney was killed by a gang. Boy called Jerome, known as JJ, fourteen years young, lived with his mother, last name Cole-Wilson. We'd not known he existed and apparently Melvin ain't seen his chile in over ten years.

He failed him. No excuses. He did.

Dudley is a criminal lawyer specializing in corporate

fraud. Eddie runs his own IT company with a staff of 350, most of them based over in India.

One out of three's not so bad, Larry.

Some parents get worse statistics.

If you listening up there, somewhere?

Lord, I really need to talk to Morris about all of this.

The phone rings again just as I am heating up my morning porridge in the microwave, with water because there ain't no milk left.

I know exactly who it is, Carmel's Rottweiler, Miss Donna. I really don't want to answer it because by the time she done with me I'll have burns requiring a skin transplant in my right ear. My daughter can curse like a fishwife when she ready. Except she knows I'm at home because her mother just told her so, and, as I don't believe in answering-machines – ever since an indiscreet 'aquaintance' from the days when I was in the directory looked me up and left a message which, thankfully, I got to first – I've no choice but to pick it up.

We speak, or rather, she does.

I am *heartless-unsupportive-thoughtless* and, in case I don't get the message, *unfeeling*.

'I'm flying out to Antigua this afternoon,' she finally declares, having expectorated all over me until she ain't got no more phlegm left. 'Maxine can't, or rather *won't*, get out of a work commitment. Some silly fashion shoot or other. It's left to me to represent the family.'

No comment. I'm taking the Fifth.

'I will drop Daniel off at yours at around midday. Yes, Dad, you can look after him. He's got this week off to revise for his mocks, so don't let him go out *anywhere* or have any friends over, okay? Nor will you be introducing my son to any alcohol. I've kept him teetotal until now and away from the drugs they all seem to take these days. I should know. Honestly, twelve-year-olds on a detox programme. And definitely no girls in the house. I'm relying on you to behave yourself this coming week, to set an example. Do you understand?'

Silence.

Welcome to Planet Donna Deluded.

'I said, *Do-you-understand?*'

Who the hell she think she talking to?

'Am I making myself clear, *Dad*?' she repeats, like a parent issuing a final warning to a naughty child.

Alles klar, mein Führer.

'Clear as crystal, dear,' I reply.

'Good. I think it's time you got to know your grandson.'

Daniel staying here? Oh my days. This is too much. (a) Morris has got the hump with me; (b) I'm letting my inner coward dominate my outer bravura; (c) Carmel feels I'm letting her down (and she don't know the half of it); (d) Donna thinks I'm even more evil than previously thought; and (e) now I've got a teenage lodger, so to speak.

What I goin' do with him? We have not been alone together for years, it is true. Probably since I took him to Chessington Zoo when he was, what, twelve? If only Morris was around in case the lad turns out uncommunicative. Morris has this socially *adroit* way of engaging others in mindless chit-chat, which can come in useful sometimes.

I am not usually given to panic, but first thing I do is start collecting the numerous empty cartons, bottles and wrappers deposited on the various surfaces in the kitchen. (How they get there?)

Soon as I open the bin, the stink of decomposing food nearly knocks me out. Actually, I been noticing the kitchen smells a bit renk. Now I know why.

Next I take the bag out the front to dump in the rubbish bins on wheels: one black, one green. I do believe one is for that 'loony-liberal' recycling nonsense and the other is for general rubbish – but, as Carmel's not bothered to tell me which is for which, I put everything in the green one.

Back in the kitchen, I decide to wash the crockery piled up in the sink, although quite how you remove encrusted food from a plate without resorting to a hammer and chisel is beyond me. Also beyond my particular area of domestic expertise is how you remove tea and coffee stains from mugs. Those stains is so engrained no amount of wiping with a dishcloth can shift them. Carmel must have a special cleaning procedure she inherited from her mother. Women have these skills they pass down through the generations, like secret rites, like how to give birth to children and how to give men grief.

I look in bewilderment at the dishwasher Carmel bought in 1998, but, seeing as she's never bothered to show me how to operate it, it's no flaming use, ehn?

My stomach tells me I not filled it yet, so I reheat the porridge again in the microwave and, when it's done, try to eat what looks like congealed sick and tastes like glue paste. I bring down the coffee jar for my morning coffee and see it's empty, but luckily I do espy a half-full cup of black coffee from a few days ago hiding behind the kettle, just waiting to be discovered at this very opportune moment. As there's no mould on it, I stick it in the microwave.

I have to say, it don't taste too bad.

Right, Barrington will have to make an expedition to

Sainsbury's to stock up on provisions for a growing lad, because Mother Hubbard's cupboards are bare. Can't remember when I last wandered down the hallowed aisles of a supermarket for a major shop. Maybe ten years ago? Surely it wasn't in the nineties or even the eighties? To be quite frank, I suffer from an allergy to them. Supermarkets are for the *ladies*. They love them, talk about them, even dress up to go to them. Carmel always makes sure she puts on her second-best wig when she goes shopping. One time she even went to Waitrose up at Stamford Hill but came back moaning about how everyone looked down they noses at her because she wasn't dressed to go to a Buckingham Palace tea party.

But Sainsbury's now. Carmel makes a weekly trip Friday morning to avoid the weekend crowds and gets a taxi home because she don't drive. Says I'm the reason she don't drive on account of me telling her years ago she'd never be able to because she don't know her right from her left, which she still don't. Women are wired differently to men. Oh, yes, they can put on an emotional performance when it suits them, but they're not so hot when it comes to technical things. She usually comes back from Sainsbury's with six boxes of chocolates saying that, as they're part of some 3-for-the-price-of-2 deal, she saving money rather than spending it. I nod my head in agreement. How many times she pinged the elastic waistband on her nylon trousers and blamed her metabolism or a thyroid problem? Those chocolates are escorted under her armed guard to the front room, where she hides them. She'll get through the whole lot in the week while listening to Jim Reeves.

I methodically compile a comprehensive shopping list for my imminent 'house guest'.

1. Rum (for Daniel to experience his cultural traditions)
2. Whiskey (I running out)
3. Soda water, Coke & ginger ale (mixers)
4. Salted peanuts & cashews (to go with the drinks)
5. Maxwell House coffee x 2 (forward planning)
6. Cakes (children like them)
7. Curly Wurlys (my girls used to love those)
8. Jumbo multi-pack of crisps (Walkers, of course!)
9. Coco Pops (his breakfast)
10. Hot chocolate drink (his bedtime)
11. Biscuit assortment (snacks)
12. Jam doughnuts (for me, he can keep his flaming hands off of them)
13. Milk (essential protein for growing bones)
14. Nice loaf of sliced white bread (none of this rip-off *wholemeal* la-di-da)
15. Orange Juice (vitamin C – one of his '5-a-day')
16. Frozen pizza x 7 (carbs, protein, several '5-a-days', etc.)
17. Tinned baked beans (Emergency Supplies No. 1)
18. Tinned spaghetti Bolognese (Emergency Supplies No. 2)
19. Tinned tomato soup (Emergency Supplies No. 3 & another of his '5-a-day')
20. Ribena (vitamins – last one of his '5-a-day')
21. Guinness (to fortify the blood)

I drive to the aircraft-hangar masquerading as a super-market and wander through the maze of aisles, fighting the soporific music trying to manipulate me into an overspend-ing trance.

Oh my days, I can't believe my eyes because the place stuffed with so many permutations of every kind of food and drink it's confusing. I count thirty-two different brands, types and sizes of frozen pizzas and fifteen types of so-called fresh pizza. I no lie. Ten different tins and packets of tomato soup. As for biscuits? Two rows of them, hundreds of different varieties. I get dizzy trying to second-guess what Daniel would and wouldn't like. How does he like his milk, *par exemple*? Whole milk, full fat with cream, full fat without cream, skimmed, semi-skimmed, fat-free, organic? Oat milk? Almond milk? Jesus, when did folk get so faddish?

I spend at least ninety minutes traipsing through the maze, and by the time I get home I am well and truly ready for my siesta. But it is not to be. Soon as I put everything away, the doorbell rings.

Daniel's on the doorstep, wearing jeans and a black T-shirt with PUMA written across the front in gold. He stands there taller than last Sunday. Must-a grown an inch, at least. Get a whiff of pungent aftershave too, pretending he's shaving in spite of his baby cheeks saying otherwise. I see Donna peering from her car to make sure I open the door, but she drives off without so much as a hello-goodbye-and-I-hate-you (by-the-way) wave.

A whole week with Daniel? Just me and him? A whole week filled with awkwardity? Or maybe it's my last chance for me and him to get to know each other again before I upset his mother and grandmother so much they turn him against me and forbid him ever to see his evil grandfather again.

'Hello, Grandy,' he says, all big smiles and showing off his strong, masculine, toothpaste-advert Walker teeth. He walks inside laden with sports bags strapped over his broad Walker shoulders.

'Hello, Danny-Boy,' I reply, all smiles too, slapping his back hard in the male version of a hug that is actually an assertion of masculine prowess.

I notice the pile of shoes and clothes by the front door and surreptitiously kick them to one side, but Lord, he's sharp.

'The bachelor life is it, Grandy?' he says in his uptown Queen's. I notice he's got my chuckle, somewhat spiced with derision. Funny how things pass down, until one day you realize we all morphed into each other. His voice is deeper than I thought, a classy baritone. 'Mum said you'd turn this place into a dump within a week,' he says, raising one bemused eyebrow in a manner much too snide for his years.

Don't hold back, boy . . .

'Really?' I reply, emitting a mischievous, grandfatherly twinkle. 'And what else did my delightful daughter say about me?'

He gives me a looks that says, *I don't think you really want to know, do you?*

'I tell you what. You go upstairs and offload your stuff, and then we can have a natter about what slanderous things are being said about innocent people. Which room you want? Your mother's or your auntie's?'

'Eurgh, not Mum's. I'll have nightmares.'

I can see me and him is goin' bond.

'Fine, I'll put the kettle on, or would you prefer something a little stronger?'

'Grandy, it's only, like, half eleven in the *morning*.'

God knows why I just invited my grandson to a pre-lunch

booze-up. Must be nerves. Nonetheless, it's a proven fact that drink breaks down barriers. A little drink or two won't harm the boy.

'You're right, laddie. Maybe you ain't had no breakfast yet? Can't drink on an empty stomach. I got some Coco Pops for you.'

He gives me a funny look that I can't quite *deconstruct* and takes the stairs, leapfrogging over several steps with his long, springy legs.

By the time he's hurdled back down, I got the bar set up.

A bottle of Chivas Regal Scotch, Captain Morgan, English Harbour Three-Year-Old Rum, Bacardi Gold. Glengoyne, Jack Daniel's, Wild Turkey, mixers, ice bucket, cut-crystal spirit tumblers.

'Welcome to Barry's Bar,' I announce, rubbing my hands together, as he bounds into the kitchen all sprinter-just-off-the-blocks-high-voltage.

'I'm not sure I should,' he says, faltering, startled at the party-style display on the table, yet gulping in front of all of that mouth-watering temptation. 'Wow, Mum would be livid.'

'You're right. Maybe you should stick to Ribena.'

That does the trick.

'Gimme one glass of Wild Turkey 'cos I is a rude bwoy,' he says, imitating what he thinks is my accent but sounding Jamaican. He picks up the bottle and reads the label, declaring, 'An' mi wan' it on de rocks, Grampops.'

'What? Yuh making fun of your grandfather, is it?'

'No, not at all,' he grins, switching back to Queen's. 'It's just I wish I could talk patois like you, but Mum forbade it. She got really pissed off when I used to come back from here sounding like you.'

I'm discovering one thing about my grandson – he can talk. Donna right. Our kids get confused and mash up standard English with patois and cockney without realizing the difference when it counts, like in an exam or at a job interview.

'Danny-Boy, lemme tell you something.'

He's had one kind of education and now he needs another.

'Speaking one tongue don't preclude excellence in another. But you got to treat patois as a separate language that you slip into when it's socially acceptable to do so. I can speak the Queen's when I feel like it. But most of the time I just do me own thing. Fear thee not, though, I know my syntax from my semiotics, my homographs from my homophones, and don't even get me started on my dangling participles.'

I stop myself just in time from getting smutty. Is Daniel I talking to here, not Morris.

'Wow, really?' His eyes are wide, impressed.

'Oh, yes, back home I'd get beats at school if didn't know my grammar.'

'I know my grammar too, but we're in the minority, Grandy. You should see how people write on Facebook, barely literate with an *egregious* misuse of capitals, apostrophes and full stops.'

'That's right,' I agree. 'The world-renowned, centuries-old full stop exists for a reason, and it's all about *meaning*.'

I can't believe me and him is actually having a mutually enthusiastic conversation about grammar.

'By the way, what is this Facebook thing that's bandied about all over the place? Is it part of that silly networking business or one of those book-reading groups?'

He gives me that drop-face 'doh' look the youngsters affect these days, so I give him an exaggerated 'doh' look back, and he laughs. 'It's part of online social media. I'll show it to you sometime.' He pauses before adding, 'You *have* heard of the internet, right?'

'Don't worry thyself, you can leave me out of all this new-fangled-dangled nonsense. I know how to switch on a computer and write a letter or two. That's enough.'

'You're missing out, Grandy. The internet brings the world into your sitting room.'

'I don't want the whole world making noise in my yard, Danny-Boy. I got enough troublemakers in my life a-ready. Man has survived a few hundred thousand years without the internet thus far, I do believe?'

I hand him a tumbler of whiskey, recalling how not so long ago it would-a been a glass of milk.

'I prefer Courvoisier myself,' he says. 'It's my poison of choice, Grandy.'

Of choice . . .

'Any other secrets you keeping from your mother? You know she thinks you are totally teetotalized?'

'And *you* think I eat Coco Pops.'

Lord, Daniel-a cocky bugger. Is this the same boy who used to run screaming with joy into my arms when he visited, who held my hand everywhere we went, who believed every single thing I told him?

'What I meant to say,' he says, clearing his throat, looking a bit abashed, 'is that I'm not the little boy you used to take to the swings in the park.'

'In which case let's talk, man to man,' I say, humouring him, while pouring myself some Wild Turkey, and, to show who the real man is, I go hardball – neat and knocked back in one. 'And you don't have to stand on no ceremony with me,' I add, rather redundantly, because so far he's not exactly been falling over himself to be respectful. 'I want you to be yourself so we can get to know each other. So let's cut to the chase, ehn? What your mother been saying about me?'

I take my rightful place on the throne while he turns in his seat to face me in the morning light of the kitchen window behind me. I can't work out which bits of him look like me. He a handsome boy, I think, which is a good start, got my intelligent eyes, and good thick, dark eyebrows in the tradition of all Walker men. Folk underestimate eyebrows, they can make or break a face. Even under the ruthless glare of daylight he's got unblemished skin with no bitter-and-twistedness seeping into his features from a lifetime of disappointment and resentment. Yet I can't look at youngsters these days without imagining them further down the line of life. What kind of person my grandson goin' become?

'Do you really want to know?' he asks, like Donna been slagging me off bad-bad.

'What she saying? What's my dear daughter been saying?'

He adopts a pensive frown, like I just asked him to explain how the universe was created and he finding the right words. Then he sips some whiskey and swills it rather exaggeratedly around in his mouth, as if he's having a post-dinner drink in an English gentlemen's club circa 1920.

Take your time, laddie . . .

'She doesn't hate you. She hates herself and transfers it on to others,' he finally declares with the supreme confidence of the young.

'You know what they call that?' I interject. 'Freudian Projection. It's –'

'Yes of course. I know,' he retorts like a bullish politician being interrogated by Jeremy Paxman. 'I studied it for my Psychology GCSE. It's a psychological defence mechanism whereby someone unconsciously denies his or her own attributes, thoughts and emotions, which are then projected on to others, such as a convenient alternative target.'

Was I ever such a smug know-it-all? Only problem is, he sounds like he's reciting it from a textbook.

'Mum's a classic case. Whatever she accuses anyone of, she's guilty of herself. Take you: *selfish, unrea*—'

He stops himself, but not in time. Is this what he thinks of me too?

'Like I . . . said,' he adds, scrutinizing me so carefully I feel *microscoped*. Most children don't study adults like this. They too busy looking inwards.

'It's not about *you*; it's about her. Most of the time she thinks you're a lovable old rogue. Really she does . . . *really*.'

He might be a smart arse, but, yes, he can be a sensitive smart arse.

'Actually, Grandy. Living with Mum is like living in an insane asylum. Auntie Maxine's mad too but in a creative way, which is allowed. Whereas Mum is non-creatively mad. Not officially diagnosed, but it's only a matter of time . . .'

He takes another swig of his drink and grimaces in a distasteful manner.

'Why you think she mad?' I realize I actually have absolutely no idea what goes on inside this boy's head.

I help myself to a sizeable refill.

'You wouldn't believe it.' He waves his tumbler at Jeeves for a top-up. 'What I have to put up with. For a start she's got an altar to herself in her bedroom with candles, incense, photos and notes scrawled with sayings about how much she loves herself! How sectionable is that? And even though she's been going to therapy every week since for ever, it doesn't cure her. She still blames Dad for everything, when I know for a fact she was a right bitch to him and forced him to leave.'

'Hey, hold up, that's my daughter you calling a bitch.'

'And *my* mother.'

(Well, at least I tried . . .)

'Tell me, how you know what went on when he left before you was born?'

'He told me.'

'Yuh mean you see your father? Yuh see Frankie?'

'No, I commune telepathically with him.'

He catches himself again, probably because my face is showing what my mouth ain't saying: that he needs a good slap upside-a his head.

'What I mean is . . . I found him on Facebook when I was thirteen. I can really talk to him, you know? We understand each other. He's had a really hard life, but now he's got a job doing something with recycling for Haringey Council.'

Euphemism for rubbish collector . . .

'You telling me you been seeing Frankie three years already?'

'Four,' he replies, shaking his head like I am beyond help. 'I'm *eighteen* next birthday.'

Eighteen? Time's been passing quicker than I thought.

'Your mother don't know about Frankie, right?'

'She'd go even more mental.'

How can I tell him the night he born I was chasing around London trying to find Frankie, who was Donna's wutliss live-in boyfriend? When I did, he was partying at his brother's house and said he was too busy to come to the hospital to witness the birth of his son. His excuse when I pressed him? He couldn't 'handle being a parent'.

Donna knew he was bad news, but, as she confided to Carmel, she 'couldn't help loving him'.

That man must have a dick of supernatural proportions and properties to have reduced my ball-breaking thirty-something daughter to a quivering, love-struck teenager.

It was only when she heard he'd had another son three months before Daniel born that she threatened to kick him out, whereupon he kicked off, literally, right in front of the baby. Donna ended up in Hackney Hospital with a cracked jaw and fractured ribs. Me and Morris paid Frankie a visit he'll never forget, and one she'll never know about, unless he wants another knock on his door at midnight.

'Can I have another one?' Daniel's waving his glass at me again.

'Here, it's about time you try some rum. Is your cultural heritage.'

'Grandy, I *have* drunk rum before, you know?'

I pass him his drink.

'I'd better be careful or I'll end up like Mum, a total alky.'

'Except Donna's not a big drinker, Danny-Boy.'

'You're kidding me, right? She drinks like it's orange juice and then has the cheek to tell me I'm not allowed to drink. How insane is that? Then she'll spend drunken hours on the phone to her girlfriends, crying about how lonely she is because she's on the shelf.'

Donna lonely? I never thought she was lonely.

'You don't seem to feel much sympathy for Donna,' I tell him. 'Is hard being a single mother.'

'How can I? She says she wants a nice, respectable man to

178

marry, so this is how she goes about it. Posts a really old photo of herself on those dating sites, pretends she's thirty-five instead of fifty, and then wonders why her dates run off after the first drink. What did she think? They weren't expecting a woman to turn up who could be their *mother*? She even asked me to go on a date with her, and *believe*, I was about to call Social Services when she said seeing a film or eating out together was 'special time' between us. She said parents went on dates with their children these days. First I've heard of it.

'Now get this. Say she asks me how I am and I reply "Fine", or she asks me if I've got any homework to do and I reply "Yes." Next thing you know she loses her temper and shouts that if it wasn't for her I'd not have been born. Yes, she really did say that. Or she buys these celebrity cookbooks but doesn't even open them. I was raised on junk food, which should be classed as a form of child abuse. She can't even rinse lettuce under a tap, has to buy it ready-washed. I taught myself to cook. You'd be proud of me. I'd go organic if I could afford it. I'll cook for you this week, you'll see.'

Daniel waves his empty glass at me for a fourth time. 'Any more where that came from?'

I beckon for him to pass his glass over to me. He swipes it over and it ends up smashing on the kitchen tiles.

Danny-Boy, I want to tell him, unlike you flawless teenagers, we adults can be contradictory fools. We fuck up. Sorry to fall off the Pedestal of Perfection, Sonny-Jim, but all we trying a-do is stop you from fucking up too.

I feel sorry for Donna, though. It never entered my mind she was a lonely lush. Sorry for Maxine too. You can't reach forty and still be unwillingly single and not feel it.

Sorry for their father too, who's been trapped in the loneliest-ownliest marriage in the world.

Who alone suffers, suffers most i' the mind.

It is time to detour the conversation.

'I hear you've got to revise for your exams this week, right? How you getting on with all of that?'

'Cool. I've been revising for months now, unbeknownst to *her*.'

All of Daniel's conversations lead back to his mother, same way all Maxine's conversations lead back to herself.

Daniel raps his skull with his knuckles. 'The data is all lodged up in this hard drive of mine. I'm leaving nothing to chance. After Oxford I'm setting my sights on Harvard. One degree's not enough these days, but there's too much competition ahead of me, Grandy. Only one person can be Britain's first black PM. I'm running out of time.'

He has plenty of time to get on with it. What a shame it's only when you got practically a whole century behind you that you can appreciate that fact.

'Mr Lowry, head of Sixth Form, says I'm the "shining star" of the school. He also said I had nice legs when he passed me in the corridor on my way to play rugger last year.'

He emits a derisory snort and runs a hand over his cropped head.

'As he went to Oxford himself and is friends with half the dons there, he reckons I'm a shoo-in. It's the game, Grandy. It's all about *who* you know, not what you know. I've read about it.'

If only life was so straightforward. That university's only got a handful of our black British kids out of some twenty thousand. I been reading about *that*, Danny-Boy. He's got the advantage of acting just like them, so maybe he'll get through the interview when hidden prejudices come into play. Daniel's got to be the exception. Same way Obama proved everyone wrong.

'Danny-Boy,' I say, breaking my unspoken rule not to give advice to anyone under the age of twenty-five because they get insulted when you dare imply they don't know everything, 'the real test of success is how you manage failure. You got to be prepared to improvise.'

'I've got plenty of experience improvising when my plans go tits up. Like, do you think that when I was in the womb, planning my future, I knew I'd be born to a madwoman?'

Maybe the boy has a sense of humour after all. I been wondering . . .

Maybe he right to be cocky, too. All-a-we people need more self-belief. I seen how we talk ourselves out of our ambitions and then complain we can't get on. I talked myself into buying properties, same way I could-a talked myself out of it.

'Yuh ready for something to nyam?'

Pizza has got to be safe, right? All children, even seventeen-year-old boy-men, like pizza, don't they?

'I got pizza?'

'Yep, Mum said it would be junk food. See what I mean about her?'

Don't suppose he likes Curly Wurlys or drinks hot chocolate either. What the hell do I know?

'How about beans on toast, then?'

You can't go wrong with that.

'Brown or white bread?'

'White.'

'Wholemeal's better, but, what the hell, I'm sure the beans aren't sugar-free either.'

Whoever heard of sugar-free baked beans? This boy is as absurd as his auntie.

I set to cooking, and we fall into relaxed, boozed-up quietude.

'I like being here, Grandy,' Daniel says drowsily, beaming sweetly the way he used to before he became a fancy-pants-know-it-all.

'Where's your partner-in-crime?' he asks, as I dollop beans on to his toast.

'I take it you mean *Uncle* Morris? He busy right now.'

My tone signals an end to this particular conversational *thread*.

'Aha, so you had a lover's tiff?' he says, smirking.

Where the hell did *that* come from?

'What you say?' I reply, sounding sharper than I intended.

'It's Mum's joke. She says you and Morris should have married each other, because you're inseparable.'

What am I supposed to say to that, ehn?

Danny-Boy, let me tell you something you don't know. Me and Uncle Morris been lovers since we was younger than you are now. So what you got to say about that?

If one thing go make him speechless, it go be that, right?

That night I sit up in bed contemplating how those Ancient Greek eggheads came up with four categories of love: Agape is unconditional love; Eros – intimate; Philia – brotherly; and Storge – a deep, familial affection. Eliminating Eros and Philia, was I feeling unconditional, familial love for my grandson? Yet how can you distinguish between an *obligation* to love and the real thing? I'm not sure I even like him. Am I merely feeling a residual affection for the memory of the adorable grandson who seems to have turned into a bit of an arrogant prat?

Lord, where is that *rass* mood-merchant when I need him? All of my life I been able to discourse things with Mr Mary-Mary-Quite-Contrary, and there's nothing like someone disagreeing with everything you say as a way to clarify your own opinions. I need to talk to him about Carmel, about Daniel, about my conversation with Donna, about the inner turmoil I suffering.

Morris, you obstreperous ole fart, seeing as you're usually so telepathic, why don't you be the one to eat humble pie and just call me now, in the middle of the night, help me straighten out my thoughts?

10

The Art of Losing It

Saturday, 15 May 2010

The Prince of Poshness usually stumbles all groggy into the kitchen about four hours after I have arisen. As anyone over fifty knows, longer you live, less sleep you need. In his disorientated state, I even get him eating Coco Pops for breakfast, a victory that generates a succession of grandfatherly smirks, *internalized*.

He spends the day revising in Carmel's hallowed Front Room, where there's no telly to distract him and no grandfather wanting to creep in and watch it.

It is a week after I was made his *de facto* guardian, and he's been in there over four hours without a pee break, not even mucking about with his mobile phone, because he leaves it in his room every day. I know. I check. Lord knows what I'd-a become with his self-discipline. At his age all I wanted to do was fool around with my Antiguan Valentino, who had all of my attention when with me, and all of my attention when not. Yes, it's true, I had the chance to bust mi balls studying, but I was too preoccupied with emptying them instead.

I go outside and stretch my arms up to the sky. I can feel all the cricks popping in my joints, but when I try to bend over I barely reach my thighs. I try to roll my shoulders, but they won't rotate. Am I the fella who used to do cartwheels and backflips with Morris on the beach just for the sake of it?

I sit down on the front steps to catch the late-spring sun, fully cognizant of the fact that Carmel wouldn't approve.

'Why you acting like you don't have a sixty-foot back garden?'

'And why *you* acting like you didn't grow up in a communal culture where everybody sat out front come rain or shine?'

That woman acts really English when she feel like it.

Nonetheless, I should try to enjoy the calm before the (butt-butter) storm. But how can I? Way I see it, I have three options. Maintain the status quo? Divorce Carmel and live alone? Divorce Carmel and move in with Morris?

Yes, I'm a scaredy-cat, Morris. The idea of telling Carmel that I'm taking her on a journey towards her *decree-absolutely-no-turning-back* . . . It's only when you about to enter a Conflict Zone that you realize how entrenched you are in your so-called Comfort Zone.

I put my sleeves at half mast, release my braces and unbutton my shirt, discreetly, seeing as I got one or two grey weeds sprouting there these days.

Then I indulge in one of the greatest stress-busters known to mankind, a hand-rolled Montecristo Habana straight off the paddle-steamer from Cuba.

I notice my hands all dry-up and realize I didn't moisturize them with Vaseline Intensive Care this morning. Yuh slipping, Barry. This is what happen when everybody gives you a hard time, including the wife *and* the mistress.

I know I should call, but I got Daniel on my hands, right?

Eventually I decide to ask Laddie-O what he wants to eat tonight, and offer some tea and biscuits at the same time as a mid-afternoon stop gap. PG for me and Fairtrade Organic Earl Grey for him (I ask you), forcing me to break my boycott of the wholefood shop, seeing as I couldn't be bothered to go all the way to Sainsbury's.

I knock on the door, and Daniel complains he's had a headache for hours. I tell him he should ease up with the studyfying, fetch him some aspirin and a glass of water, and bring in the tray containing our respective teas and ginger biscuits artfully arranged on a plate, all nice and civilized.

He says he'll be with me in a minute because he's just finishing off.

I watch him in his green khaki pants and grey shirt with REASONABLE DOUBT splashed across it in black Gothic print, all sprawled on Carmel's white leather sofa (still covered in plastic wrapping forty years after she bought it . . .), with his textbooks and laptop and one leg bent under the other.

How the hell do you sit on your own leg and not feel it snap?

As my gaze wanders around the room, I realize I've not looked at it properly in years. Furniture, décor, wife – after a few decades you might look, but you don't see what you looking at, right?

I don't know how he sticks it out in a room stuffed with the very same *objets tat* that sealed wifey's reputation as a Madame Arriviste back in the sixties. Could write a cultural-studies essay about *that* particular phenomenon: 'Coming from sparsely furnished homes, the women of the West Indies went goggle-eyed at the veritable cornucopia of colourful fripperies on sale in the Land of Hope and Affordable Ornaments.' *Easy.*

I confront the concentric, psychedelic and positively hallucinogenic orange discs masquerading as wallpaper and realize nobody need bother with LSD no more. No wonder Daniel got a headache. I should line up the local junkies and charge them to look at this wall.

Superimposed on said walls are sentimental reproductions of tearful Victorian urchins and gilt-edged photographs of the various Walker and Miller generations. The carpet is thick Persian, and the embroidered drapes more suited to a medieval castle. Lace antimacassars are placed on armrests, a glass coffee table is adorned with silk flowers in a vase, its stem wrapped in a red, frilly *thing* (why?), a glass cabinet is filled with every type of gold-rimmed drinking vessel, even though the sole drinker resident in this house is not allowed to use them except on special occasions. A trolley features her pineapple ice bucket, the radiogram in the corner is what they call vintage these days, and another cupboard must be where she locks up her chocolate stash and whatever else. Add to this ceramic dogs and cats, glass fishes, birds, crochet dolls with flouncy flamenco skirts and a wooden clock above the gas fireplace doubling as a giant map of Antigua, and it's safe to say wifey is the Goddess of Bad Taste.

If Mr Socrates was right when he said, 'Let all my external possessions be in friendly harmony with what is within', then this room is a worrying reflection of my wife's state of mind.

Salvador Dalí would-a loved it, though. Maxine thinks it is '*beyond* kitsch' and keeps threatening to steal in one night, dismantle the whole room and reassemble it as an art installation. I always objected to its rather trashy OTT-ness, even back in the day when I could be forgiven for not knowing no better. After I took my History of Art course, I could barely come in here.

Donna used to plead with Carmel to strip the front room down to plain white walls, trendy Habitat furniture and bare floorboards. Wifey too smart for that. No way was she giving up sovereignty.

History of Art, Birkbeck, one evening a week from 1984 to 1986. I loved that course. Come to think of it, wonder what happened to that fella Stephen Swindon or Swinthorne or whatever it was. Not thought about him in years. I was forty-eight, he was about ten years younger and, from the way he used to ogle me in class, totally up for a taste of Antiguan masculinity. We fellas don't need to spell nothing out. We got vibe language. Don't need to spend money courting and being polite and telling a girl how pretty she is for weeks, either, before we allowed to get our cocks out either.

Stephen could've walked out of *Brideshead Revisited*, with his foppish blond fringe and rah-rah vowels. Lived in a loft over at Canary Wharf. Old spice warehouse, acres of scarred floorboards, brick walls and wharf windows with no curtains, because, what the heck, nobody could see in except the seagulls circling the Thames. Still with the same hoists outside that used to haul up barrels of cinnamon and turmeric, saffron and cumin – when the spoils of Empire flowed upriver.

Had a Chinese emperor's brass bed at one end, with the kind of black satin sheets so slippery one could spin on one's own buttocks, if one was so inclined. At the other end was a wrecked trestle table with rusty iron legs as some kind of fashion *statement*. In the vast atrium in between there was a black leather chair and a sofa, a big modern telly, sound system and sliced tree trunks masquerading as coffee tables. His wardrobe was a clothes rack with all of his flashy, colour-coded barrister suits and shirts on show; a regiment of John Lobb shoes stood smartly to attention just underneath.

I'd never been in a home like it before, and it opened my eyes to the possibility of a lifestyle for *real men*: wood and metal, leather and brick.

I grew rather fond of being seen to while leaning out of a window, waving at the unsuspecting tourists passing by on pleasure boats . . . I have to say.

Me and Stephen amused ourselves for a while, exotic beasts to one another, until he started getting ideas and wanting more than I could give him – a proper relationship.

How did he think that was goin' work out?

He left the class thereafter.

Wonder what became of him? He wanted to become an art collector.

Years later, when Maxine was eighteen, I bought that huge Shoreditch loft apartment for her when she passed her exams with a royal line-up of four As – wishing it was me moving into a place like that. She painted the brick walls white, the concrete floor yellow, put a futon in one corner, a copper bath she'd found in a skip in another, placed a fridge she painted pink by the stone sink, and turned the last corner of the room into her 'studio' – cluttered up with easels, oils, fabrics and other signs of artistic intent.

How can she think she's so different from those posh interns out there, backed to the hilt by their parents?

Anyways . . . so where will I live after this possible, potential divorce, then?

Divorce: such a spiteful-sounding word – but such an appealing concept.

Marriage: such a softly seductive word – but such a spiteful reality.

So who goin' get the house? Okay, what about if (if it comes to it) I let Carmel take away the front room, brick by brick?

I get the rest, 'cos I ain't moving. No, sah. Problem is, wifey will put up a fight. That woman is too *she own way*.

'What you want for dinner tonight, Danny-Boy?' I ask him, as I resurface from the country I visit most frequently, the past. He looks up slightly dazed from deep concentration.

'You want Chinese, Indian, Caribbean, Chippian or Kebabian?'

Experience has taught me I need to get enough food for four, because, like the Tasmanian Devil, teenage boys can eat 40 per cent of their body weight in one sitting and still have those flat stomachs most men over twenty envy, most men over thirty try to get back, and most men over forty remember with fond yet melancholic nostalgia.

'How about the traditional man-on-the-street English chippie tonight?' he replies, as if it would be *simply* the most exciting adventure into the lifestyle of the working classes. 'Haddock, chips and mushy peas for me, guv.'

'Cool, then, and I'll get some pies for tomorrow's lunch.'

The tea is pepping him up, enabling the swift transition from study mode to social interaction mode.

'Hey-up, I thought you was goin' cook for me this week,' I remind him, calling his bluff. 'I still waiting.'

'Um, yes . . . I'll make amends soon.' He pauses, thinking. 'How about a warm salad, Grandy?'

Oh, lovely. Can't wait. Boiled lettuce? Microwaved cucumber? Toasted celery?

'I've brought a recipe that I got in a Sunday supplement

that I've been waiting to try out,' he says over-enthusiastically, to compensate for my obvious lack of it.

Yes, sah, I blame those newspaper supplements. All of them food-obsessed. Same with the telly, and then everybody's wondering why the whole country getting fatty.

'I'm not sure my imagination can stretch to all of that,' I reply honestly. 'You know I is a rice-and-stew man at heart.'

'Or,' he says, unfazed, grabbing a handful of ginger biscuits and raising them to his biscuit-crunching machinery, 'how about a soup that's, like, entirely locally sourced?'

You know, Donna's biggest fear since Daniel born is that he will end up a statistic: gangs, stabbings, shootings and all of that stuff they do in the inner cities – stuff that would make Martin Luther King and those Civil Rights activists turn in their once segregated graves at how the enemy from without has become the enemy within; how murder by racialist thugs has been superseded by internecine fratricide; how if you live in certain parts of this country you fret your son won't reach adulthood.

Take Young JJ, Jerome Cole-Wilson, now buried in the Tomb of the Unknown Relative. He was one-a we, one of our family. Daniel could-a been a role model for him.

As for Daniel, Donna really needn't worry. If her son is a statistic, he's in an elite category of *one*.

'Locally sourced?' I quip back. 'You mean baked rat, or fried cat, or how about worm sandwiches, or spring onions marinated in pigeon excrement?'

Daniel looks up from his drink and shakes his head in a blatantly metaphorical tut-tut.

Where's the boy's sense of humour?

Later, after we've eaten our fish and chips, I'm looking

forward to another evening sitting with him watching the CSI crime dramas with all of those forensics experts dressed like glamorous supermodels instead of like scientists who have to scrape blood off walls. He gets up and starts to clear the table, then declares out of the blue that he goin' party at some school friends', will be back late and I shouldn't stay up for him.

My gut reaction is to tell him he can't go in case, well, in case he ends up *dead*.

'You want me come pick you up when you done?'

'No, thanks, my friend's got a car.'

I refrain from snapping, *Your friend got a name?*

'You got a girlfriend, Daniel?' I ask, all innocent, like I ain't been dying to ask him this since he arrived.

'Don't tell Mum, but, yes, Sharmilla. She's really hot but really clever too. Doing her A-Levels at Woodford County High a year early, but she's at a wedding this week in Coventry.'

'Well, you go and enjoy yourself, because you need to blow off some steam, ehn? Strike some poses on the dancefloor.'

Boy, you really sucking up to him. But is it 'strike some poses' or 'shape some dance moves'?

'Exactly! I knew you'd understand,' he says, scraping a pot with what looks like a hairbrush. I always wondered what that was for. 'Mum asks me a million questions whenever I want to go out at night and does everything she can to dissuade me. She wants me to be a boring swot with no social life. I'm surprised I haven't ended up with serious mental health issues *myself* living with her.' He purses his lips. 'I *tell* you, Grandy . . .'

You've *told* me, Danny . . .

He starts to do the dishes, as he does every evening, a whole day's worth. Mrs Morris, the Original Domestic Goddess, would approve.

Sometime later he is upstairs changing when the doorbell rings. Before I'm off my chair, he vaults downstairs at such a speed that I don't think he actually touches them.

I stand in the hallway hoping I can get a peep at his friends. Daniel turns round to say goodbye, quite transformed from the slouching, studious scruff he's been all week. He's wearing a *pink* polo shirt, cream chinos, loafers, and two fake, I assume, diamond studs in each ear. It might well be fashion, but if it's not effeminate, you could-a fooled me.

As he hurries out, I hurry to the window in the front room, hoping to see who's in the car, a Toyota Cruiser. All I can see is him edging himself into the back seat, and I want to fling open the window and shout out, 'Don't look at any roughnecks the wrong way, Danny-Boy, or they might shoot you!'

I was never sorry I only had daughters. And I *do* like the females, so long as they're not mentalating or Mother Superiors.

Donna's gone to extremes to protect her son, but, as Mr Socrates himself acknowledged, 'Of all animals, the boy is the most unmanageable.'

With Daniel gone, I shorten a long evening by entertaining my good friends Mr Whisky and Mr Rum, who, I have to say, are exceptionally demanding company tonight, while all the while I try to memorize some sonnets, until the words start to bleed into each other, and the pages begin to pulsate in my hands like beating hearts.

Several times I think I hear the phone about to brrring. When it don't, I go into the hallway to check it's not off the hook, because maybe the police are trying to get through about Daniel, who might be goin' cold on a mortuary slab with marbling skin and a single slash across his throat. Or Morris might be calling, sobbing, distraught, regretful, threatening to throw himself under a train if I don't forgive him.

Eventually I crawl up to bed, because for some reason mi legs won't hold me up.

But I keep listening for the sound of Daniel shutting the front door behind him.

I must-a nodded off eventually, because the rumble of a train vibrating underneath my bedroom wakes me up. I put on my reading glasses and look at the extra-large illuminated numbers on my digital bedside clock. It is 2.37 a.m. *precisely*.

I listen again as my still woozy mind tries to focus itself and says in my ear, 'Barry, you don't live above a tube line so is not a train you hearing, yuh know?'

Once out on the landing I recognize that ragga music, loud enough to vibrate on my chest. Giap next door must at this very minute be assembling another firebomb.

I stagger on to the landing, and the acrid stink of sensi gusts up my nose; at the same time I hear lyrics thumping out of the front room: something about killing a nasty batty boy.

Oh, Lord, it's party time in Carmel's precious inner sanctum, and that Buju Banton fella is being played inside *my* house?

My house . . .

I try to dash down the stairs but almost end up flying headlong, so I take it slowly, and once I reach solid ground I pause to restabilize myself. How much I drink? Must be, what, five or six solid hours of companionship with the *spirits*? You eedyat, Barry. How you goin' manage this situation when you still off of your face, ehn?

I open the door carefully. What is this? Three youths plus Daniel laid out on the sofa sleeping.

The room is a fug of sensi so thick it chokes me up. One of those iPod things plugged into portable speakers is playing on the mantelpiece, and Carmel's beloved ornaments are all messed up. I feel outraged on her behalf, surprising myself.

One of the youths is doing some kind of arm dancing while lying down with his feet up on the glass coffee table.

Another one is lolling about in an armchair, holding my bottle of Captain Morgan, eyes closed, spliff in his mouth, head nodding.

Another one is doing some kind of hip-hop gyrating in the corner next to the radiogram, except he ain't no hoodie but looks like a skinny public-school weed trying to copy cool dance moves he's seen on that MTV or whatever it is.

All three of them are Justin-and-Crispin types, with their hair spiked up, and attired in Daniel's gay-golfer style. The gyrating one sees me enter and greets me with a stoned nod, like everything's normal, then does a double-take.

The one on the coffee table sees me, freezes.

I stumble over to Daniel and shake him. He don't stir. I shake him again, then walk over to the mantelpiece, extract the iPod from its base, throw it on the ground and try to grind the damned thing into the carpet.

At this point the armchair one must-a opened his eyes, because he jumps up all rugby-sized, like he ready to knock my blocks off. Let him try, though. *Let him try.* They might be young bulls but mi no care. I go take them on.

Kamikaze Barry kicks in, the one I ain't felt since Frankie got a thrashing. If these hooligans want start something, this time I go finish it. This my home. I no outlaw lurking in the municipal bushes this time. No, sah. This . . . *my* . . . *home.*

'What yuh think you doing here?' I shout angrily, with the arm movements to match. 'You in my house uninvited, smoking it up, trashing it. You trespassers get the fuck out of *my yard right now!*'

The armchair one pushes hisself into my face. 'How dare you damage *my* personal property?' he says, like *I'm* the burglar. 'We have every right to be here. Dan *invited* us.'

He can't even stand up straight with his posturing.

'Daniel don't own this house; I do.' I thrust my head forwards, ready to take him on. 'Now get out and take your . . . *homo* . . . *homophobic* music with you . . .'

Even as I speak, I regret it.

'Excuse me?' he says, taken aback, blowing his boozy breath into my face. 'So why would that bother you . . . unless . . .'

He's off his head, but, even so, I see a subtle shift in his eyes, his body language, some kind of recognition, like he can *tell*, in his drunken madness, that in my drunken fury my face just admitted something.

'You *are*, aren't you?' he says quietly, sinisterly.

Something in me snaps, the way it does when folk hold things in so long that they start acting beyond common sense, beyond reason.

'Yes, I am a cock-sucker,' I reply, just as quietly, just as sinisterly, not quite knowing how those words exited my mouth.

'Granddad.' I hear Daniel, urgent, close by.

The armchair thug is gob-smacked; his mouth opens and closes, but nothing comes out of it. This is even better than giving him a box-down.

'Yes, it's true,' I say, directing my attention to Daniel, who is now right next to me, his face humiliated, disbelieving. Then I swing back to the frat-boy thug. 'I am a *cocksucker*.'

He looks so scared it's laughable, like I goin' throw him on the floor and stick my cock-fucking cock into his cock-sized hole.

Daniel approaches closer. 'You *are* joking, right, Grandy?'

'Do I look like I making joke?'

I feel like one of those gangbanger lifers rioting in one of those hell-hole maximum-security prisons in America or South America that they always voyeurizing on TV. *Deranged*.

I will disembowel the next person who crosses me, with my *bare hands*.

'But you're disrespecting me,' Daniel pleads faintly, like we don't have a rapt audience with perfect hearing listening.

'All of you youths go on about being disrespected all of the time because you pussies. Acting all tough on the outside and saying batty man *have to dead* when inside you is pussies. Pure and simple. *Pussies*.'

'You're shaming me, Grandy.'

'And *you* have shamed me, you *rass* punk. Now take your friends out of my yard. Go on, get out. *Gwarn, no! Gwarn, no!* Y'all leave *now*, because I calling the police. *Aryou goo way!*'

His friends exit fast like I just got my cock out and started chasing them. Daniel hovers in the hallway.

'My things, I need my things.'

He's up the stairs and down again in no time.

I slam the door behind him.

Goo way, bwoy. You as rotten as your daddy, you a loser like the rest of *dem*, bringing all of this badness into the home of your 74-year-old grandfather, who's been looking after you nicely.

Then I collapse on to the hallway carpet and lose myself.

Song of Desire

1990

you started losing your old self and gaining a new one in 1985, when you *finally* started noticing what Joan, Theresa and Mumtaz been telling you for years

that among Hackney Council's thousands of employees there was plenty of attractive middle-aged fellas (even the English ones)

who was polite, single, *educated* and perfectly decent specimens of mankind

such as, in no particular order

Elroy from Planning and Development; Norbert from Environmental Health and Consumers; Mathew from Parks and Open Spaces; Christopher from Arts and Entertainment; Julian and Mike from Street Trading and Licensing; Winston from Leisure Services; Ahren from Social Services; Elroy from Baths; Luciano from Finance . . . to name but a few

except you'd been blind to them all in the seven years you been there

and one Friday night in the Queen Eleanor after work

after Joan had been boasting about her latest conquest – a *dancer* (no less) in *Starlight Express*

and after Theresa was telling y'all she loved her husband so much she dreaded him goin' out of the house in case he had a car accident and didn't come back after Mumtaz was swooning over her *chartered accountant* boyfriend who took her off on weekend breaks to Lisbon, West Berlin, Madrid, Brussels . . .

you then confided the awful state of your marriage, but they just shook their heads sagely and Joan said, *Carm, did you think we didn't know? We've been waiting for you to open up*

and after you had a little cry you complained how you was an invisible frump compared to the womanly curves of Joan, say, poured into black sheath dresses designed for career women with style

and they all shouted you down

You are a very attractive woman, Carm, but you must stop wearing clothes two sizes too big and put on some lippy, love

and so you traipsed to Marks & Spencer up at Angel next Saturday morning and bought yourself your first underwire brassière and you began to

unbutton your blouse just before entering the town hall in the morning to show off

what Mumtaz (who'd started a poetry-writing evening class at Chats Palace) christened your

shimmery melted-chocolate cleavage

that Joan said any man would be happy to *bury his head in and slurp up*, which would-a shocked you only a few years earlier, but you was used to her bawdiness by now

knowing the Ladies' Society of Antigua would never approve of your boisterous, fun-loving mates

especially Merty, still stuck in a rotten cleaning job with her grown-up sons now getting into police trouble and badgering you all the time to get her transferred to a better council house, even though you told her it was corrupt

and what with Drusilla working sixty-hour weeks to pay

for the house she'd finally bought on Rectory Road on one person's salary

and Asseleitha's breakdown during a talking-in-tongues session at church when she started shouting about how she daddy raped her from when was little and took her baby girl away four days after she born – *Clarice*

the baby she thought about every day since 1956

Clarice

who would be a middle-aged woman in her fifties now

and y'all had to hold her back from running out into the road and throwing herself under a No. 30 bus on Mare Street

and, terrible as it was, none of you know how to raise it with her, so she's disappeared even deeper inside herself

but thanks God Candaisy was okay, because Robert was good to her and she had a nice house, good job, nice daughter, Paulette (and a good son-in law and three nice grandchildren), but even so you wouldn't tell Miss Candaisy about your heathen friends

under whose influence your work shoes got a tad higher, your tights got a tad darker, your black skirts slightly tighter, your walk got a wiggle and a waggle

and when you freed your hair from the scraped-back bun and got it relaxed and conditioned on a regular basis instead of yearly at Justine's on Dalston Lane

the girls decided your transformation was complete, and one Friday night in the Goring Arms after work Mumtaz officially declared you

sassy yet sophisticated, voluptuous yet with an air of virtuousness

which y'all toasted with another bottle of Beaujolais Nouveau and already you'd begun to notice the waves of desire you created among the grey suits in the corridors of local government, parting like the Red Sea at your approach, for you was now a town-hall vamp at the grand ole age of forty-one, wasn't you, Carmel?

not that you was planning on becoming a cheating scumbag like Barry, no matter how many times he denied he was seeing other women

but then the girls started teasing you that Reuben Balázs from Town Planning (divorced, thirty-six, raised in Barnet after fleeing the Hungarian Revolution in 1956)

had a *major crush* on you, because they'd all noticed he was a leftie loudmouth in the staff canteen selling copies of the *Socialist Worker*, but when you joined the table he became uncharacteristically awkward

when you spoke, letting people know they wasn't the only ones with *opinions*, because you could be quite vociferous in the workplace yourself these days (especially since your promotion from Housing Assistant to Housing *Officer*)

Reuben listened, mutely

and Mumtaz said if you was both in a cartoon there'd be *a trail of little red hearts pumping out of him to you*

which made you notice him *differently*, but, still, he was one big hairy bear who needed to shave off his beard, trim his great bush of Sephardic locks and generally smarten up to compete with the others who'd caught your eye

but it was Reuben who kept popping into your new *Single Occupancy Manager's Office*, asking if you was all right, staring at you like you was the most gorgeous woman in the whole world

and he bought for you (over a nine-month period) a Swiss cheese plant, rubber plant, spider plant, yucca tree and money tree, which you put on the window ledge to catch the sunlight in the afternoon

in between the gold-framed photographs of Donna in her graduation gown and the one from four years ago of Maxine beaming on her first day at the Skinners' Company's School for Girls, which you was so relieved she got into rather than that dreadful Kingsland School

and he bought you so many boxes of Milk Tray you joked he should arrive by helicopter next time and parachute in through your office window like in the adverts

and slowly over time you

started looking forward to his presence, the way he spoke so nicely to you, his big-bearness, the way he was so obviously charmed by you, and you was surprised by your confident argy-bargy debates with him about Maggie Thatcher the *Milk Snatcher*, who you quite admired in a funny way, actually, not her policies but as a woman in power giving those public-school toffs in the Cabinet what for

although he argued she wasn't a champion of women's rights

you replied no, she wasn't, but she was still a role model, showing how a woman could have it all

surprised you wasn't intimidated by a man who'd studied Politics at Leeds (only getting a Third, because he said he preferred the student union to attending lectures, thereby ruining his chances of a research job in Parliament)

and you couldn't help wondering what it would be like to kiss a leftie heathen Englishman with a beard and when he said *Hello there, Carmel*, you started hearing

I want to make love to you, Carmel

when you teased him about shaving, he did

when you teased he should buy a smarter suit, he did

when he turned up in leather lace-ups without prompting (instead of scuffed Jesus Creepers)

you knew there was no turning back

even the idea of a pinkish-olivey (what colour would it be?) willy became quite attractive, though the idea of stroking such a *strange object* filled you with excited terror

and he was in your mind when you woke up, his bear hands caressing your thighs, when

you showered he was soaping your breasts and buttocks with your patchouli bath oil

so that by the time it was lunchtime at work you couldn't wait for him to slip into your office for a cup of tea and eateries

rolling the sugared wheat of *marrow cake . . . mango sponge . . . coconut-and-lime cheesecake*

around your tongue until it dissolved

inside your warm, salivary and tea-wet mouth

and you was *grateful*, so grateful, that there was your massive desk as a barrier between him and you

with your brand-new Smith-Corona Typetronic Typewriter plonked in the middle of the desk

and an erect regiment of foolscap lever-arch files lined up on the front line

to protect your moral decency

along with bound sheaves of the Housing Committee minutes piled up

with directives from the Chief Executive's office, ramming home the points about the Council's

problems, solutions, strategies, statements, assessments, internal audits

and Council pamphlets on policy

thick reference books with hard knobbly spines to run your fingers down

a dictionary overwhelming you with *temptation* . . . *seduction* . . . *betrayal of your wedding vows*

and . . . *God never sleeps*

your address book, its silky red-padded cover

so touchable

your fingertips like palpitating pads, feeling so tactile

the tray of letters to your right, waiting to be replied to

solid metal of the staple gun, shooting out staples with a masculine ferocity

and when even the hole puncher assumed erotic overtones you knew you was done for, *Lady*

what with the bundle of brown manila envelopes licked down and lapped up by your moist tongue

aroused ready to be *ffffffffranked* in the post room

your big black diary, two pages spread

wantonly widely open

every single nerve sensitized

and you was truly beyond help when the *fffffffax* machine suddenly whirrrrrred into action

blatantly, orally, outrageously, orgasmically disgorging

incoming data and statistics from Finance

insistently splurging endless liquid streams of white paper into the room

without decency or restraint, without decorum

and you knew you had to switch it off or lose all self-control

under his steady, knowing, warm gaze

not letting up, because, after nine months' patience

he wasn't making no bones about what he wanted no more

so you tried

you tried really hard to concentrate on the *harmless* insipid grey notebook

the bland and *harmless* grey index-box

the old-fashioned metal sharpener

screwed on . . . *fastened*

to the desk's lip

two boxes of boring harmless Tipp-Ex

dotted over your breasts by his hands like Aboriginal art

the way he was looking you was wondering if your nipples was showing beneath your blouse

your gold Jesus on the cross (died for you to do this?), dipping on a chain just above your

melted chocolate cleeeeeee vahhhhhge

knowing you'd switched the Panasonic telephone-with-answering machine to mute

you fiddling nervously with the pens and pencils in your Charles and Diana commemoration wedding mug, which you'd good-naturedly defended from his republican barbs when he first started popping in

and when he got up and went to the door and turned the key slowly

listened for a second to voices passing in the hallway outside

you was thinking of starting up that argument again, about how you won't have nobody slandering Diana, who is such a sweet, beautiful, well-mannered lady and very good for the Royal Family too, and Charles was lucky to get her

but before you knew it he was touching you *there* and *there* and then everywhere

and you felt your

self becoming someone else

someone you'd never been
your self
you was *carnivorous*, you was *omnivorous*, you was *rapacious, ravishing, ravaged*
feeling the nape of your neck, your earlobes ticklish, underarms, belly, belly button, armpits, behind your knees, spine, your magic triangle, clavicle
his bites
the meat of your large womanly hips kneaded
and *there, Reuben, here . . . Reuben, here, Reuben, here and there*
against the filing cabinet with the legs of the spider plant hanging off the top of it
up against the Sasco wall planner – 1985 . . . *1986, 1987, 1988, 1989*
on the regulation heavy-duty grey-ribbed carpet used throughout the town hall and all municipal offices borough-wide
there, on your front, on your back, on your side
and you
was
a   n   i   m   a   l

12

The Art of Family

Maxine a sight to sober up even the biggest booze-head, as I feel myself returning to the human race, having spent X days in the animal kingdom.

She is towering over me, wearing some kind of extravagant head tie, spider's legs instead of eyelashes, and she must be wearing heels so high they give her ten feet of giraffe-osity.

'Dad, wake up!' she's shouting like a lunatic.

I become aware I'm in the bath with all of my clothes on, same ones I was wearing when Daniel departed this abode.

I feel myself returning to the human race.

A can of Dragon Stout is floating on top of the scum, along with bloated slippers resembling dead fish and a cigar unravelling back to its first incarnation as tobacco leaves.

Maxine helps me out of the bath, strips me down, pushes me into the walk-in shower and shoves me naked on to the stool.

Now . . . this is what I call *shame*, Danny-Boy.

As the warm water hits my legs, they start to reactivate themselves.

I realize I must have befouled myself by what I see disappearing down the drain as she hoses her father clean.

All I can hear coming from her is 'I don't believe it' and 'Oh Christ!' and 'Trust *you.*'

She bundles me up in a big white towel that is positively, welcomely, *wombic* and leads me to my bedroom to get dressed.

I want to tell her I can dress myself without anyone's help, thank you, seeing as I been doing it for the past seventy-odd years, but my mental–verbal connection a-dead. Maybe she can read my mind, because she goes to leave but not before she lets out a groan, pulls the sheets and pillowcases off of the bed, bundles them up, holds them at arm's length in front of her and leaves the room with an expression of gross distaste.

Once dressed and decent, I ease my way down the stairs, one foot at a time, and walk into a maelstrom of arms and legs in the kitchen – washing up, clearing up sick, hurling things in the bin.

'What day is it?' I ask, clearing my throat, a stranger to myself.

'I don't *believe* it. *Tuesday.*' She shakes her head.

I am so fed up with people shaking their head at me.

'What time is it?'

She looks at her big black designer watch with a picture of Minnie Mouse on the face that is age-appropriate to a five-year-old.

'Eight thirty.'

'Eight thirty?'

She stands behind me, steering my head and shoulders towards the window.

'Yes, eight thirty in the morning. Look! See! Daylight!'

'Oh, yes.'

It is indeed a beautiful spring day – clear sky, getting sunny a-ready.

'Sit,' she orders.

Maxine fills a jug of water and tries to funnel it down my throat.

I desist; she insists.

'You must be dangerously dehydrated, you idiot,' she yells, welling up.

'Put the damned water in a glass, then. I am not a pot plant. And mind your manners, I am still your father,' I croak back, tears in my eyes too.

'When did you last eat?'

What does the Seaweed Queen know about eating?

I screw up my face up as if trying to remember . . .

She starts rummaging in the fridge and cupboards.

'I don't believe this . . . cardboard pizzas, tinned crap, *biscuits*. Ever heard of fruit and vegetables?'

She heats up a tin of Heinz tomato soup, butters cream crackers, puts chunks of cheese on them, fills up a tall glass of milk.

'Now *feed*. I'll get some proper food for you later.'

She sits down while I start to eat, taking it slowly.

'You've got to tell me why you've been on a bender, Dad? You could have died and where would that have left me? Over the edge, *mos def*. I mean it's not like you to lose the plot *completely*, although you did get so off your face at the Dorchester they threw us out, if you remember?'

Me? She blaming me?

'I thought something was up *then*. And why haven't you been answering the phone? Donna's been ringing too.

Yep, you'd better batten down the hatches. Miss *Thang* is back.'

She watches me eat. 'Right, then, now that I've just saved you from death by dehydration, I'm going to wake up Little Lord Fakeleroy. Donna put money on it for him to text her and apparently he didn't do it, not once. Nor has he, or *you*, answered the phone all week. *Surely* he's not starting to undergo a belated teenage rebellion?'

Maxine arises herself, but I rest my hand on her arm.

'Maxine, don't bother. He not here.'

'Where is he, then?'

I look at her.

'At a friend's? The shops? Where?'

'Mi no-no.'

'What do you mean you don't know?'

'He gone, Maxine. He gone.'

I can feel the waterworks getting ready to sprinkle again.

'Yes-but-where-has-he-gone?' she replies, talking to me like I am a retard or a foreigner.

I reply in kind: 'Like-I-said, I-don't-know.'

'Try again. *Not* good enough. What happened?'

Seeing as I don't know where to begin, I . . . don't.

She sits back, cross-legged, cross-armed. 'You'd better come up with some answers soon, because if you look at my face, you won't see a happy clown smile painted on it.'

She does this circling thing around her face like a mime artist.

How old am I?

Then she starts spasming her crossed-over left foot, shod in monstrous wooden clog stilts that must weigh more than her skinny-jeaned legs.

'It's not just you, Dad. Before she left Donna asked me to

check up on you and the son she infantilizes, but I've been rushed off my feet with networking.'

She gazes up at the sky through the window. 'Come to think of it, wouldn't it be brilliant if we could stop time when we felt like it, catch up on stuff and then slip back into it?'

I work my way through the crackers.

'Yes, you carry on eating and I'll speak for both of us.'

She thrums one set of black tiger claws on the wooden table.

'Did you see me in *ES* magazine last Friday? Almost standing next to Anna Wintour at a party? No, I didn't think so. Don't worry, I picked up twenty copies outside Bond Street Station.'

I carry on eating, feeling better with each bite.

'Whatevs.' She shrugs. 'Anyway, when Donna rolls up, we can expect a scene of Jerry Springer proportions. Are you ready for that, or do you want to tell me where Golden Boy is, so that I can mollify her before she arrives?'

One thing at a time. She told me to eat. First things first.

She sits there twitching, staring at her nails. Then she gets a brainwave.

'Hang on a minute: how do you *know* he's not here?' She levers herself up and stands, wobbling on stilts. 'You've been out of it since Godknowswhen. Have you actually been into his room?'

Before I can stop her, she's clambering up the stairs, yomping in and out of bedrooms with as much noise as a battalion of soldiers before stomping back down again.

She appears back in the hallway and, before I can stop her, opens the door to the front room, freezing as she surveys the carnage inside, tantamount to the Sistine Chapel being spray-painted with railway graffiti.

I ain't been in there since the Night of Satanic Boys.

It is a dark, dangerous monster's lair.

Before she can storm back into the kitchen and wrestle me to the ground, forcing me to admit to having murdered Daniel, the doorbell rings, a key turns and Miss Donna steps over the threshold.

Hang on a minute: who gave these girls keys to my house?

Donna stands in the hallway with an expression befitting a Soviet commandant in deepest Siberia who's walked into a hushed, terrified dormitory of prisoners.

She clocks *me* first, down the end of the passage sitting not too regally on my throne.

Actually, I could probably be mistaken for a long-term resident of the asylum in *One Flew Over the Cuckoo's Nest*.

Miss *Thang*-awanga swivels her head to her left and locks on to Maxine in the act of slowly closing the front-room door while trying to look as if she's really pleased to see her elder sister.

'Where's Daniel?' she asks Maxine, who turns helplessly to me, as if I am the font of that particular piece of wisdom.

Donna swoops her concentration-camp searchlight beam on to me, but I have escaped into the forest and am pathetically trying to hide behind a thin birch tree.

She puts one foot on the stairs and screeches 'Danyellll!', the way some parents do, calling their children like dogs. I never shouted at my daughters like that. Carmel neither. Donna became autocratic the day Daniel born, and she realized she had absolute power over another human being. In a few hours she went from being a daughter to a parent, a status some folk let go to their heads.

'Where is my son?' she asks again, her voice splintering, as if it dawning on her that we been waiting to tell her face to face about a terrible tragedy that has befallen her only child.

'I don't know,' Maxine replies, swallowing her words. 'I've just got here myself. Dad doesn't know either.'

Donna leans against the wall, rolls her head against it and closes her eyes, like she's trying to stop herself from fainting.

'What have you done with him?' I can hear the beginning of a whine. 'Is he dead? Is my baby boy dead?'

Well, she certainly acting like he is already.

Maxine follows Donna as she barrels down the hallway in a red velvet tracksuit and hair still spiky and mussed up from the flight.

'You have to tell me what's going on,' she says, standing right over me like she goin' lunge.

I am so fed up with people about to lunge at me.

Long, short and tall of it, I have no choice but to tell my daughters about the events leading up to Daniel's departure, conveniently omitting certain key elements.

Even talking about it makes me want to lubricate my vocal cords again. But if I did that, Maxine would bash me over the head with the bottle.

Soon as I reach the dénouement, Donna is on her mobile speaking to some woman called Margot, asking for some boy called Eddie, who gives her the number of some boy called Benedict, who's out with Ash, who passes her on to Steven, with whom, she soon discovers, Daniel is staying.

Next thing I know she's cooing down the phone, asking how her 'little soldier' is feeling and wanting to hear his side of the story, because 'You know what *he's* like.'

'I know it wasn't your fault, Babycakes,' she whimpers, crawling right up his arse. 'At least you realize now that alcohol is bad for you.'

Pause.

'Is that a "Yes, Mum" I hear?'

Pause.

'*Good* boy.'

Maxine can't believe what she's hearing either. Keeps making faces at me.

'All right, then, Pumpkin. I'll be over to collect you when you're ready. Just give me a call.' Donna snaps her phone shut like a castanet.

'Thank *God* my son is alive,' she booms, like she making a public announcement over a tannoy system. 'No thanks to either of you, especially *you*.'

I look over my shoulder, because surely she's not talking to her father so rudely.

'Typical male behaviour. Mum leaves you alone for a few minutes and everything goes to pot. Daniel was deeply hurt that you threw him out on to the street to fend for himself. He could have ended up sleeping rough with drug addicts or become a rent-boy. He's explained it all to me, and yes, he got a bit tipsy, silly boy, but we all made mistakes at his age. He's still so young and understandably very upset at your overreaction, but he'll get over it. I know my son.'

Oh no you don't.

'The poor lamb really missed me. I can sense it.' She dismounts from her war horse and slumps into a chair. 'He sounded so miserable on the phone. I think he's realized how much he needs me.'

Yet again me and Maxine bounce eyeballs off each other.

At least one thing is apparent: Daniel did not spill the beans.

Maybe he biding his time.

'I'm shattered. Couldn't sleep on the flight back, because of the squealing piglet next to me. Planes should have a soundproofed compartment for little children, or the hold will do. Max, put the kettle on, I'm dying for a cup of coffee.'

Maxine does an eyebrow shuffle at me, but I give her a quiet nod to do as her sister says.

She makes the coffee and slams it down, which Donna don't even notice.

'Our primary objective now is to spare Mum this nonsense about Daniel. She's just buried her father, and the last thing she needs is to return home to a stressful situation. The funeral was bloody awful, by the way. All these money-grabbers turned up posing as his children. Mum's lawyer saw them off and hired a security firm to patrol the property, because as soon as Mum leaves, they'll be trying to squat it. It's just as well *one of us* was there to help Mum project-manage everything.'

Me and Maxine exchange another set of glances.

'She needs our support more than ever. Max, pass the sugar, will you?'

Maxine don't move from where she's leaning against the sideboard. Her mission has always been to assert herself by opposing her elder sister. If Donna had become an artist, Maxine would-a become a solicitor. Some folk have to react against something: parents, siblings, government, society. They think they have free will, when all they doing is *wilfully opposing*. Oh, yes, I should write a thesis about that too.

Donna's always envied Maxine's free spirit, personality and imagination, whereas Maxine's always envied Donna her steady career trajectory, annual salary and pension plan.

Donna gets up and snatches the bowl of sugar from the sideboard.

Donna resented Maxine for taking me away from her those first few years when Carmel wasn't coping. Two pickney is not a good number. Children in larger families learn pretty sharpish that they only goin' get a percentage of everything, a quarter, sixth of conversation, affection, treats. When you only got two kids, they can't relinquish the hope that they might just get *everything*.

While Donna takes herself to the shops, me and Maxine brave the front room, Carmel's ancient treasures scattered on the floor amongst cans, bottles, spliff and ciggie stubs.

When Maxine opens the windows, a breeze ushers in fresh air to decimate the foul vapours.

She starts wind-milling.

'The biggest problem is putting things back in their rightful place,' she says, holding a porcelain milkmaid in one hand and a crocheted dolphin in the other. 'I don't suppose you have any idea where these dreadful things go?'

I don't answer, because a surge of nausea has come over me. I sit down on the settee while Maxine whizzes around.

Eventually she notices and levers herself down on the coffee table directly opposite.

'You're still feeling rough, Daddy?'

'My dear, I have never felt rougher.'

'You'd better lay off the booze. Let this be a warning. You are *way* too old to be caning it.'

Thanks.

'You're lucky you've got away with it. The Grim Reaper usually comes knocking for profligates like you in their late fifties.'

'That's *not* what I'm talking about.'

I have a faint cold fear thrills through my veins, / That almost freezes up the heat of life.

'Then what *are* you talking about?'

Be not afraid of shadows . . .

'I feel . . . *psychosomatically* rough.'

'Really? Okay, explain how you feel *psychosomatically rough*, using words of fewer than seven syllables preferably. Deal?'

I stare at her and see her clear brown eyes holding me in: steady, strong, warm, almost grown-up.

I can feel myself welling up again, so I avert.

This is the problem with succumbing to the tyranny of tears: once you let them out, they start to abuse your vulnerability.

You tremble and look pale . . .

'What really happened here?' she asks. 'I would suggest more than you've said.'

I sink down into the settee.

'You were absolutely petrified when Donna was on the phone.'

How the hell she notice?

'I *totally* know something's up.'

I hear cars pass outside. I never usually do.

'I mean, it's not like Uncle Morris not to be nipping at your ankles either. Where is he and why haven't you mentioned him? He wouldn't let you go off the rails.'

The rest of the house is silent. Is funny how you don't notice silence most of the time. But silence is a sound in itself, a-true. Silence is the humming absence of a tangible sound that you can ascribe to something. Actually, you only really experience silence when you dead, although that theory is hypothetical and not one I'd like to put to the test.

A bluebottle comes in through the window and zooms annoying around the room, before exiting again. How can something so tiny aggravate the hell out of the human race?

Maxine comes and nudges herself up next to me.

'You could have killed yourself.'

No, I only wanted to numb myself.

'*Goneril* will be back with the shopping soon, so tell me what I need to know before she does.'

All of this Spanish Inquisitiveness. Why do women always feel the need to go prying into other people's feelings?

'Maxine, get on with tidying up and leave your father be.'

I raise myself.

'No!' She grips my arm tight and forces me back down. 'Tell me what happened, or I'll have to get on the blower to your grandson.'

Pray you now, forget and forgive. I am old and foolish.

'I'm deadly serious. Talk to me.'

And somehow, when the pressure becomes unbearable, I do. I tell her about me and Morris since way back in St John's and how we been carrying on ever since like agents in post-war West Berlin. I tell her he's got the hump. I can't tell her I leaving her mother.

Maxine is quiet for once, and when she speaks she picks her words carefully.

'Daddy, do you really think I never knew about you and Uncle Morris?' She takes my hand in both of hers. I feel her soft, silky, skinny fingers – so light and warm. 'Nothing gets past my gaydar, and you are *beyond* camp. Have you looked at yourself in the mirror lately?'

Laaard, this girl is a dark horse.

'I first suspected when I was a teenager. By the time I was twenty-one and going to gay bars, I was pretty sure you and

Uncle Morris were an "item", but I never felt able to raise it with you. You're my *dad*.'

'What about Donna?'

'Daddy, watch my lips: we-do-not-tell-Donna, okay?'

'Maxine, I supposed to shock you, but it is me who is a-shock.'

'I'd say you haven't been thinking straight for a very long time. You've been trapped inside yourself, which can lead to a very distorted view of things. My advice to you is to join a gay pensioners' club for support, where you can share experiences with fellow old-timers over a gentle game of table tennis or croquet.'

Oh, lovely, dribbling in a wheelchair with mi tongue lolling out and a patch on mi pants where I keep wetting meself.

'Seriously, though.' The mischievous imp grins. 'You've got to start acting your age.'

Like you?

'To be honest,' she continues with increasing gusto, relishing her Agony Auntie role, 'your biggest problem is that you don't always notice what's really going on with other people, if you don't mind my saying.'

So now *I'm* the solipsist?

'If you'd been paying attention, it would have been obvious I'd be totally cool with your homosexuality.'

The only homo I am is sapiens, dearie, but I hold my tongue. I ain't got the energy to start up that particular debate.

'What I *do* have a problem with, *how-evs,* is that you've been cheating on Mum all this time. It's been bugging me for twenty years.'

'It's not really cheating –'

'Shuddup, Daddy. It is cheating and, from a feminist perspective, totally out of order.'

'You got a feminist perspective? Since when?'

'All my life, but not in the dungarees, hairy armpits and doughnuts-for-breakfast kind of way, *obv*.'

'Right.'

'Okay, getting back on point . . .'

She realizes she's been totally off point? A miracle.

'I can see you're feeling rotten, so I want to take this opportunity to thank you for being you, to make you feel better. Morris was right: you raised me to express myself. And you led by example too. No way was Mr Barrington Walker going to disappear into the bland sea of homogeneity. You told me never to get hung up on racial discrimination but to turn a negative into a positive; otherwise I'd develop a victim mentality. You encouraged me to break through the "tiled roof", as you put it.

'The thing is, Mum will never know about you and Morris so long as Daniel zips it. And a word of caution about Golden Boy: you might want to consider buying his silence?'

Increasingly Maxine turns a sentence into a question by inflection. It is the Californian Cheerleader Disease.

'I took him to Brighton when he was nine, bumped into an old mate and lost him for over an hour. Had to fork out for a new BMX bike, otherwise he was going to tell Donna. He's going to make an excellent politician. Be prepared to fork out for a new car for his eighteenth.

'You have to do whatever it takes to keep this from Mum, okay? It will kill her, and then Donna will kill you, and then my family will either be dead or in prison. Great. I only recently heard from an old school friend that Donna got some gangsters to give Frankie a good seeing-to soon after he beat her up.'

I wonder whether I should tell her the drama not over yet – it just begun.

I goin' leave her mother, I goin' divorce her. Yes, I go do it. *I go do it.* No more toing and froing in my mind, no more cowardice, no more *im*-balancing the cons over the pros. After what happened with Daniel's hoodlums, I can't turn back. It was an accidental catharsis that has led to mental clarity and a deliberate plan.

But how I go tell Carmel, especially without Morris to support me?

'As for Uncle Morris,' she adds slyly, 'I think you need to pay him a visit and apologize.'

'What I have to apologize for?'

'For whatever you did to upset him.'

'How you know I did anything?'

'Because I *know* you. Run along now, put on a pretty dress and take Uncle Morris a bunch of flowers while you're at it.'

She's not wasting no time taking a new kind of liberty.

Maxine stands up and uncoils all snake-like, stretching up and knocking the chandelier with her hands.

She looks ridiculous in those heels as she resumes clearing up.

'Maxine, why don't you slip out of those shoes while you doing the domestics?'

She hops from one foot to the other. 'You're right: my feet are dying a slow death, but if I take them off I'll never get them on again and I've got two meetings this afternoon and the opening of a five-star boutique hotel in Chelsea tonight, owned by *Russians*.'

She rubs finger and thumb together.

'And on that note,' she says, pretending it's an afterthought, 'I've almost finished my business plan for the

House of Walker for my Fashion Angel. I'll bring it round soon.'

By the time Donna has returned with the shopping and some Chinese takeaway, Maxine has done what she can with the front room and made her excuses after telling us off about trans-saturated fats, monosodium glutamate, blocked arteries and heart attacks.

I see her to the front door. 'Promise you'll go and see Morris later, all right?'

'Scout's honour.' I raise a hand, oath-style.

She pecks both my cheeks, the way everyone does these days, as if we're all suddenly French and Italian. No wonder disease spreads so quickly.

She has to walk sideways down the steep, stone steps, with her arms spread out for balance. The fashionable bag over her shoulder is so large she could put herself in it and get someone to carry her.

'Maxine, that camp thing,' I whisper, following her outside, closing the door behind me. 'You saying I'm effeminate?'

She laughs me off. 'You're an old Caribbean queen, but don't worry, most people won't notice. You're a dying breed, Daddy.'

Thanks.

She's talking nonsense of course. Being fanciful again. I goin' ask Morris.

'Just wait until you meet my gay boys. They will absolutely *love* you.'

When I return to the kitchen, Donna is humming as she puts away the shopping. She lays out a feast that practically covers the whole table: prawn crackers, spring rolls, chicken-and-sweet-corn soup, sweet-and-sour pork, prawn and beansprouts, beef with black-bean sauce, spare ribs, chicken satay, lemon chicken, crispy duck, mixed vegetables, noodles, special fried rice, egg-fried rice, boiled rice.

'The leftovers will last you a few days,' she says, clocking my astonishment. 'Mum asked me to make sure you were eating. See, we do care really.'

We sit down, just the two of us, which, as with her son, never happens neither.

Seeing as Maxine has accused me of not understanding people, I study Donna while she piles so much grub on her plate I'm not sure there'll be any leftovers.

I come to the conclusion that even though she don't look her age, she acts older, moving her body like she needs to spray WD40 on to her joints.

How come one of my daughters is prematurely ageing while the other one is preternaturally youthful?

Donna's still got good skin, but her face getting harder, and her eyes are dark fortresses that defy you to enter them. Any potential suitor would have to slay some dragons to get past those ramparts. My daughter been alone too long.

I pile on the rice and beef, pork and chicken, noodles and spring rolls.

'I'm sorry,' she says out of the blue, somewhat defensively.

'For what?'

'For being a bit over the top earlier about Daniel.'

Today *is* the day of shocks.

'What I mean is, I went overboard and was a bit . . .'

'Rude?'

'I was panicking about Daniel and lost it. I shouldn't have spoken to you like that.'

224

Some beef catches in my throat. I prefer it when my girls is disrespectful: at least then I know where I stand with them.

'I'm well aware that Daniel can be a little prick when he feels like it, but he's all I've got.' She keeps stabbing at a pork ball but not eating it. 'He's the only thing that's mine.'

The only person that boy belongs to is himself. You should-a started saying the long goodbye soon as he hit thirteen. I wanted to tell you then.

'When he leaves home for university, that's it. He's said as much. I know he won't be coming back except to bring his dirty washing . . . the way *men* do.'

Stab, stab.

'Donna, at least it frees you up to find the kind of nice fella you deserve, someone to treat you good.'

The way she glows makes me wonder when I last spoke nicely to her or showed any real interest in her.

'Don't think I haven't tried, but I'm not like Maxine, with her anorexic BMI that even black men go for these days – betraying the race. Anyway, there are simply no good, available men out there. The eligible forty-year-olds go for 25-year-olds; the fifty-year-olds are with thirty-year-olds, which leaves the geriatrics for sad sacks like me.'

'That is rather hyperbolic, my dear.' I keep my voice and face compassionate, friendly, unhostile. 'I'm sure there are still some good men out there within your . . . *appropriate* . . . age bracket.'

'I'm the expert here, Dad. And trust me, there aren't. The good guys are all taken and the rest are either commitment-phobic dogs like Frankie; or too ugly, too old, too poor, too badly dressed, too unfit, too uneducated, too boring, too low class, too gay or too into white or nearly white women, which is a whole other issue you wouldn't understand.'

I don't know what to say.

Me and Morris often chinwag about how many of our men can't settle with one woman at a time and how many of our men sow seed, then don't hang around to watch it flower, like Frankie. It is embedded in our psyche from centuries of slavery, when we wasn't allowed to be husbands or fathers. We was breeders for the stud farm, and our pickneys' *totemic* (and morally criminal) father figure was the owner of the plantation, who held the power of life and death over us.

We living with it today, because it's corrupted our psychological DNA and disrupted our ability to have committed relationships with each other.

Our men don't know how to stay with our women.

Our women don't know how to raise men who do.

Not me, though. I was a good father to my girls. I stayed married beyond the call of duty. And I been good role model for Daniel. I followed in my father's footsteps, and no one can call me on that. At least not until now.

As for Donna, there must still be plenty good men out there; she just ain't seeing them.

Par exemple, about fifteen years ago Carmel told me some very nice St Lucian fella (a social worker with an unfortunately large nose, apparently) was chasing Donna and asked her out for a drink. At the time she wanted another child but wanted a partner first.

She told her mother she turned him down because she didn't want ugly babies.

'Donna, dear,' I ask, finally, 'what kind of man you looking for?'

'Do you really want to know?'

'I do, my dear.'

'Really?'

'Yes, really.'

Donna puts down her knife and fork, picks up her knapsack, which is on an adjacent chair, opens a purple leather purse and takes out a well-thumbed piece of paper.

'I wrote this four years ago as a way to clarify my aims and objectives. If you write your goals down, it helps you to achieve them. I read this when I need to feel hopeful and inspired. This is the very least I'm looking for in a man.'

This goin' better than expected.

She proceeds to read from it, quite solemnly, like it's a mantra.

~ My husband will be Caribbean or of Caribbean descent.

~ My husband will be a very successful and *solvent* professional.

~ My husband will be aged between thirty-five and forty-nine.

~ My husband will have no children from previous relationships.

~ My husband will be very intelligent and educated to at least degree level.

~ My husband will be taller than me, ideally six-foot plus, of muscular build and *without* a pot belly.

~ My husband will be handsome but not so handsome other women chase him.

~ My husband will not have a hairy chest, back, hands, nose, ears or ingrowing hairs that he expects me to pick out with tweezers.

~ My husband will be . . . (Dad, this is the bit you *don't* need to hear.)

~ My husband will love cooking for me, unlike Frankie, who never so much as boiled an egg.
~ My husband will never lie, cheat or ogle other women.
~ My husband will be a sweet and kind but still *very masculine*.
~ My husband will be a great listener.
~ My husband will accept me completely for who I am with no criticisms.
~ My husband will not snore.
~ My husband will want to hold my hand in public.
~ My husband will adore me even when I am old and wrinkled.
~ My husband will love Daniel.
~ And Daniel will adore him too.

'That's it,' she says, gloomily laying down her precious document on the table.

'Donna,' I venture softly, trying not to insert no judgemental inflection into my voice. 'Have you thought you might be being a bit too fussy?'

Wrong move, Barrington.

'*Too fussy?*' she roars. 'I wasn't fussy enough with Frankie, was I? I was taken for a right mug, because I had low self-esteem. I've done enough self-empowerment courses since to know that I'm worth more. Now look what you've gone and done, put me right off my food.'

She takes up her plate, slouches over to the bin and shovels in the remains.

'I can't believe that I confided in you for the first time *ever* and you ruined it. You just don't get it, do you?'

'Get what, dear?' I reply, trying on Morris's tone when faced with prickly contenders.

She's looming over me again.

'That *you're* to blame for my man problems. I don't trust men, because you caused Mum pain all her married life. I've done enough therapy to know that subconsciously I don't expect to end up in a happy partnership because of you.'

Lordy, lordy, if my middle-aged daughter wants to blame me for her inability to catch man, nothing I can do about it. I ain't had no power of attorney over her reasoning since she became a pig-headed teenager.

'I couldn't say anything before because . . . well . . . you've paid for Daniel's education and . . . my house and everything, and, while I appreciate it, of course I really appreciate it, it's also made me . . . well, I might as well say it, *beholden* to you.'

At this point in the proceedings our relationship looks like it's toppling over the precipice into the Valley of Death. 'Anything else you want to get off your chest,' I ask, just to help it along on its way.

'You terrified me when I was little, when you came home drunk and started picking fights with Mum. I'd be wetting myself in bed, *literally*. Home is supposed to be a sanctuary for children. In any case, I rarely saw you, because you were out all the time. Then Princess Maxine came along and you spoilt her rotten, and it's been that way ever since. She got the father I never had.'

I stand up, and she'd better move out of my way or I will have to shove past her and then she will add GBH to my list of war crimes.

She steps backwards, arms bolted straight at the elbows, like she's struggling not to deck me.

I start packing away the Chinese. Yes, it will suffice for the next few days.

I take my time, stack the boxes neatly in the fridge.

I start to walk down the hallway in slippers made of lead.

Except Donna ain't done yet.

I sense she has moved to the doorway, watching me.

'I saw you,' she says in a tone that makes me feel an axe is about to be lodged in my back.

She leaning against the doorframe, arms folded.

'April 1977. I was on my way to a party, and Mum said you'd just popped out to the offie to get a bottle of whisky, but you'd been a while and to look out for you. I reached the bottom of the road and there you were, sneaking out of that outdoor brothel known as a cemetery, looking so shifty . . . with a woman dressed like a prossie *right behind you*.'

Nothing to salvage.

Nothing to deny.

Nothing to declare.

'A few nights later we were all watching the telly, and as soon as it got dark you said you were off to have a drink at the pub. I tailed you and you went straight into the cemetery again, like the rest of the dirty old men. About twenty minutes later you came out and headed off to the pub. The whole of that summer you were at it. Then you got beaten up by some pimp or whoever, and I just thought, serves the bastard right.'

Where is Morris? I want my Morris.

'I could never tell Mum because it would have devastated her. She was, and still is, too innocent and fragile. And I couldn't destroy Max's fantasy about what a great father you are, in spite of how you treat Mum. I've kept it in for thirty-three years. Protecting you. Protecting Mum. Protecting Maxine.'

She waiting for me to say something.

I mount the stairs, one foot at a time.

When I reach my bedroom, I heave up the window and put my head out of it for some air. As much as Donna might like me to, I do not throw myself out of it.

I undress and climb into my nice clean bed, made up with the fresh sheets Maxine must have found in their secret hiding place.

A few minutes later I hear the front door slam.

13.

Song of Power

2000

Hackney Council should train their housing teams in detective skills, what with all of the nonsense you have to put up with from existing and prospective tenants

which is what you tell the new housing assistants when you're inducting them, the fresh-faced know-it-alls straight out-a university with no experience of life but a whole lot of attitude

that you knock out of them, because, after over twenty years in the job, and as a *Senior* Housing Manager, you is now a *boss lady* with power, responsibility and experience

Look here, you tell them, *you've got to have your wits about you in this line of work, because it's tough out there on the mean streets of Hackney. Just imagine you're in the LAPD working South Central LA . . . but worse*

which always raises a nervous laugh

you warn them about the lengths people will go to jump the queue on the coveted Housing Waiting List, which might otherwise take twenty-five slow years to climb, if at all

how to detect the shit in the bullshit, although you don't use those words exactly, such as

teenage girls with cushions stuffed beneath jumpers, like you an idiot born yesterday chancers claiming to be sleeping on park benches for months, but they can't explain how come their shoes is so polished, their clothes so clean and smart

the forged documents and false Hackney addresses

the tenants who sublet their homes, who terrorize estates, build extensions and knock through walls like they own the joint, thereby contravening the tenancy agreement they signed on the dotted line, which you've been known to thrust into a face or two as proof (you even got a black eye for your efforts once)

tenants who keep donkeys, goats, pigs, chicken, sheep, raccoons and monkeys in their back gardens, even a fully grown bull that was brought in as a calf for a child's birthday, which you had to arrange to be craned out over the roof

the rehousing and maintenance you got to authorize, especially after gas leaks and explosions, arson attacks, negligence, front doors battered down by raging beasts or police raids

families who outgrow their allocation of bedrooms

families on the Social Services register who are usually a multigenerational headache

the crazies, overcrowders, jailbirds, probationers, noise polluters, rat infesters, domestic-violence perpetrators, non-payers, whore houses, squatters and crack-house proprietors up for eviction and the heavies you got to send in when they don't go quietly

you and Reuben used to engage in friendly banter about these issues, but he always sided with the dregs of society, blaming capitalism and the Milk Snatcher for everything (privatization, monetarism, the miners' strike, poll tax, right-to-buy, police brutality, rich people, poor people, racism, colonialism, famine, natural disasters) while you always sided with the philosophy of hard work and self-betterment

ten years later you still miss hearing his entertaining politico rants

while you was both cuddled up on his lumpy bed under the patchwork quilt made by his great-grandmother back in Hungary (which you made him take to the dry cleaner's for the first wash of its life, *probably*)

you still miss making love on the *nice clean-smelling* floral linen you bought and ordered him to put on fresh any time you was goin' visit, otherwise you wasn't returning again to his *archetypal bachelor pad* to sleep on grey sheets that was once white

you still miss your games too, especially after you eventually allowed him to buy you sexy lingerie from a shop in Wardour Street, which gradually opened up a whole new vista neither of you could get enough of

silk scarves, cuffs, candle wax, latex, a paddle

boy, you was one *sizzling hot mama*, up for things you'd never even imagined

after a lifetime of restraint, you was up for *everything* . . .

boss lady at work *and* in the bed, which was how he liked it

Carmel, you was shocking . . .

. . . really

slipping down the steps to his side-entrance flat Friday nights and staying late under the pretext of goin' out with the girls, which they was all in cahoots about

not that Barry ever doubted your lies; in fact he encouraged you to enjoy yourself, to go to the pub or see some blockbuster movie

you still miss being cocooned in Reuben's *functional* one-bedroomed basement flat on Rushmore Road that you'd made as homely as you could, in spite of the rough planks of wood piled on to bricks that served as bookshelves, the crude political posters instead of framed, pretty pictures on the walls, a kitchen without a toaster or an electric kettle, and a garden with a wooden table with two bench seats attached that he'd stolen from a pub and wouldn't return, no matter how many times you told him it was criminal

so you made the flat less functional with dried flowers in vases, potpourri in bowls, purple floral throws and cushion covers, a swirly pink-and-purple shag-pile rug, floral towels, flannels, soaps, scented candles, room deodorizers, a whole new set of cutlery, floral crockery, glassware, tea towels, toaster, microwave, electric kettle to replace his antiquated gas whistler

he let you do your thing, bemused, saying he didn't notice décor

that the most important thing in his life was you

and with him you became a bigger, nicer version of yourself, one who didn't snarl and squabble, who didn't feel hard done by

he even loved the things you hated about yourself, like the mampie rolls on your stomach you couldn't shift and your ugly feet with childhood scars and bunions that he massaged and even *kissed*

to think a fella would love you so much he'd want to kiss your *trotters*?

and even though you knew God was watching, you couldn't help yourself

even though you still went church (on an increasingly irregular basis) you reasoned you was no more a hypocrite than everyone else, like that bastard Pastor George, who was a secret homosicksical

and, as much as you sweated over committing the sin of adultery, you couldn't give Reuben up, and even ten years after the last time you saw him, you still miss being wrapped up inside him and rummaging through his thick curly hair, which had gone from *Cairo to Barcelona to Budapest to Barnet to Hackney to you, Carmie*

he was your Sephardic Shepherd – come and gone

O, how you bathed in his warmth, lady

so that when you left his flat you was glowing all the way home and had to tone it down when you walked in the door and Barry was around

and you never once talked to Reuben about your marriage, so you wasn't disloyal in that way

never told him you'd leave Barry, because, for all the hell he put you through, no way was you goin' back on your marriage vows, because marriage is a gift from God, Jesus sacrificed himself for humankind, same way you got to sacrifice yourself for your marriage

no two ways about it

even though by now Maxine had left home and was at art school, wearing noses rings and playing around with papier mâché, milk cartons and bricks like she was on *Blue Peter*

bragging how she was goin' be the most famous artist the world has ever known (even more full of herself than ever)

which changed once she'd left college and become a fashion stylist *whatever that is* and finally realized she was no more special than anybody else

(at least she took your advice to get a proper job rather

than live on the dole, hoping that someday somebody would discover her)

then, in 1993, Donna had Daniel, and you was glad your family hadn't broken up but expanded

as it should – you and your Antiguan husband, your children, your first grandchild

as God ordained it

it was meant to be

unlike you and Reuben, who was a perfect match in the bedroom, but a perfect mismatch outside it

you would never have fitted into his culture of socialist rallies and people with no dress sense, *futons,* films with subtitles, riding bicycles and reading boring books that wasn't page-turners like the Jackie Collins novels that was now your favourites

nor would you want to

and he certainly wouldn't fit into your world

except he started saying how lonely he was without you

how lonely he was without a partner and the children he desired

how he'd got a job in Town Planning at Lambeth Council

bought a flat in Stockwell and said he had to break off all contact

and you had to let him go, because you had no right to try to keep him

you had him for five years and for that you give thanks

even though you stood outside his flat a few times in the dark of night

looking through his curtainless window at white walls, Che Guevara poster, bookshelves

thinking if you was there you'd have put up proper nets, *at least*

     not daring to ring the bell
     catching the last tube home

and then
     coincidentally
     a few months later Barry asked for a divorce
     and you made sure he knew better than to ever ask again

after that, you spent the 1990s goin' church more than ever
before
     Mrs Walker, Miss Merty and Miss Asseleitha became the
stalwarts of the Church of the Living Saints
     Wednesday evenings, Friday nights, Saturday afternoons,
Sunday all day
     you been begging the Good Lord for forgiveness ever
since
     but the problem is – those five years was the best of your
life
     truth is, you begging without regretting
     so you damned, girl, you damned

14

The Art of Being So-called

Saturday, 22 May 2010

I standing outside Morris's block of flats, prepared to beg forgiveness.

His hump has lasted longer than I can endure.

In a minute I go ring the bell and be buzzed up to his bolt-hole.

If I ring the bell and he don't answer, I know he really is planning on winning the Hump Olympics. I know this, because the intercom system comes with a camera. I also know this, because it is 7 a.m. and unless he changed a habit of a lifetime, that man will have roused himself an hour ago.

And I feeling nervous, is true.

C'mon, you got to let me in, Morris. But what if he don't?

En route to here, I marvelled at the World Outside, the spring blossoms, the clattering milk carts, even the rush-hour traffic, as if I'd been incarcerated more than just the past few days of my life. I felt like a veritable Persephone, skipping through the meadows after a terrible winter spent in the underworld with that filthy dog Hades.

Even though, *even though*, I still feeling the weight of Donna's revelations offloaded on to me. It's one thing sensing your child loathes you, but it is quite another hearing it straight out of her mouth.

Was I a terrible father, an evil ogre? And, if I was, what can I do about it now?

It seems to me that Donna would've preferred it if I'd gone for good. I can't believe that for over thirty years Donna's been going around with the secret knowledge, in her mind, that her daddy visits prostitutes. No wonder she been so vexed with me. What if she knew the truth?

Maxine phoned last night, asking how I was feeling, to which I replied 'Cool', saying what she wanted to hear. I don't blame her. She don't need to carry my heavy load.

'Maxine,' I told her, 'I'm going to see Morris first thing on the morrow, and should he be agreeable, I want us to meet these bezzies of yours. So, my dear, how about you take me and Morris to a bar in Soho tomorrow night?'

Maxine's intake of breath was audible.

'You're right, and you need cheering up in a *safe environment* to take your mind off things. I'll make sure you're home by half eleven – *sober*. Lovely. I can't wait to haul you two out of the 1950s and into the twenty-first century.'

As Mr William Butler Yeats wrote all of those years ago, *Things fall apart; the centre cannot hold* and seeing as *mere anarchy* is loosed upon my world (and a domestic revolution is imminent), I might as well explore this *gay* life that's on offer.

Maxine also said she'd spoken to Carmel on the phone, which came as a shock, because I really didn't think those two was close enough to be chatting to each other long distance. Turned out Carmel had bumped into Odette in St John's, whom she'd not seen since Odette left London in 1989. Apparently Carmel's staying at Odette's spa hotel for a while and has postponed her return.

More bad news.

It goin' be revelation with breakfast, defamation with lunch, revenge with dinner.

'When she coming back?' I asked Maxine.

'She won't say, Dad. I get the feeling she doesn't want to come back.'

I might not even have anything to tell Carmel when she gets back, because when her and Odette start catching up, it will all come-a tumbling out. But when *will* she reappear? This has gone on too long a-ready.

Morris's voice cackles down the intercom: 'A-who dah?'

'You know full well *a-who dah*.'

Him and his blasted foolishness.

'Is that you, Mr Walker? Is that really you? Come to apologize? Come to kiss my arse?'

'I'll do more than kiss your fine little arse, you ole fool. Now beam me up. You know you want to.'

By the time I reach the door to his flat, it is open and he is moving back down the hallway, the red dragon kimono I bought him from Selfridges billowing behind.

At the square junction of kitchen, living room, bathroom and bedroom, he turns to face me, his kimono hanging open – saluting me with his fifth limb.

'Yes, Private de la Roux. Is just this kind of respect I deserve. I is *de* general, *de* potentate of our micro-universe, and you will do my bidding or your punishment will be severe, yuh hear?'

I run him up and down with my eyes, so that he is in no doubt I goin' devour him alive. I can't believe he can still charge up my electrodes so bad. Who'd-a thought it? How can one person get you goin' from childhood right through to (youthful) ole age?

I shed mi jacket, mi shirt, mi braces, mi string vest, mi trousers, mi boxers and mi hat. I kick off mi shoes and pull off mi garters and socks.

Now there's nothing standing between him and my Conquering Lion of Hackney.

I roll forwards, making sure I hold in my stomach, and when I reach my destination my heat-seeking tongue makes contact with his and engages in some muscular, energetic gymnastics. This is always the best way for us to clear the air, avoiding a round of incriminations and recriminations.

I feel him up and slip his silky robe off of his shoulders and slide my hands over the supple contours of his moisturized epidermis.

I bite into his neck and suck out the marrow of his goodness.

He smells shower-fresh, minty-toothpaste clean, smoothly shaved and cologned. Smashing.

I drop to my knees (well, more like lower myself carefully, in stages), while he cradles my head, closes his eyes and purrs.

He lucky. How many fogies get such indescribable pleasure from such a willing and proficient lover?

Is my way of telling him I sorry for being such an arse. Don't need to spell it out.

I lead him towards our Chamber of Love and the black satin sheets with red stitching I bought for him in multiples when he moved in.

Come hither, sirrah. Come here, my spar. *Come hay, nuh man. Abee a guh cook.*

I push him lightly on to the bed, so that he flops face down on the pillow without damaging any joints.

I go do you the way I always done you, the way you

always like me doing you, and when I finished doing you, you go be spinning towards the stars, my friend.

While he lies in a state of deliciously explicit and excited expectation of the delights I got in store, I close the curtains and put Shabba Ranks's 'Mr Loverman' into the tape-player on the bedside cabinet. Oh, yes, Ranks might spout homophobic doggerel along with that batty-baiter Banton, but this one song is our perfect *wine an grine* theme tune.

I climb (also in gentle stages) on to his back and start rubbing his shoulders. Morris a-love that.

We can take our time, because we got all the time in the world; and after we taken all the time in the world, with Shabba growling in the background, we stare up at his magnolia ceiling, catching our breaths.

Little shivers of pleasure shoot up and down my legs.

'Morris, you can pass for one of those buff middle-aged fellas who still pump iron in the gym, *easy*. Why don't you put an ad in one of those periodicals I keep in the garage: "Mature gent: 8 inches, uncut, muscular, horny, ass-play, versatile".'

(He's not 'versatile', but I like to humour him. Not eight inches neither.)

'Very funny, Barry, but I'd have to pay *them*. And I'm sure there isn't a single twenty-year-old in the world who would think I look buff. More like "Extra-mature gent: wrinkly, dinkly and shrinkly".'

'Morris, you must be suffering from that body dysmorphia condition people in rich countries have just invented because they got time to waste creating psycho-illogical problems for themselves. It's all about perspective, and from mine you *are* buff.'

'Maybe I've got a bit more buffed since I last saw you,

then, seeing as I already been to four Pilates for Pensioners classes. Yuh think a six pack is showing already?'

'Sure thang. You getting results a-ready.'

I turn towards him and drape him with myself.

'Don't care how buff you is, I still want you. Love still goin' strong, Morris. Love still goin' strong.'

Did I just say that? What *is* the matter with me? I feeling so happy just being with him.

'I grateful to you, Morris. Yes, I grateful. In this my hour of need you taking my mind off my troubles and woes.'

'Yuh goin' all soft on me, Barry? Yuh getting in touch with your feminine self, ehn? Tell me, what-a go-wan? Something's gone down this past fortnight, because you different.'

And I do tell him, breaking it down into chronological scenes: Daniel, Meltdown, Maxine, Donna, and finally, the possibility, or rather the inevitability, of his ex-wife and my soon-to-be ex-wife plotting to destroy our reputations while having their feet massaged by Antiguan gigolos looking for sugar mammies.

By the time I've recounted the whole kit and caboodle, omitting Donna's 'graveyard snooping', Morris is looking at me like he can't decide whether I'm mad or he should be proud for me being so *offended* by the posh thug.

'Barry,' he says, calling my name unnecessarily, the way we both do, like it's not just the two of us so close our breaths are vaporizing into each other's mouths, 'take my advice: next time you feel like losing it, ask yourself what the Dalai Lama would do and follow suit, all right, Boss?'

'All right, Boss.'

'Because coming out to Daniel and his friends in the dead of night was scaling the heights of stupidity, even for you. At least you had seventeen years of knowing him. You think

I ever goin' be babysitting my latest grandson Jordan again if Clarence finds out what I am? My boys are always complaining about racial discrimination, but they so full of discrimination themselves. You know what? As a father, I fucked up in that respect.'

'Don't talk to me about fucking up fatherhood, Morris.'

I might as well join Morris in his glass half-emptiness world-view, because I ain't feeling so Pollyanna right now.

'Barry, you are still leaving Carmel?' he says, sounding a little worried.

'Yep.' If only Morris really knew the internal trials I been enduring to get to this stage.

'Good – so you must tell her as soon as she walks back in through the front door and then we take it from there. Okay? Whatever happens, we go deal with it together. All righty?'

'All righty.'

'So . . . just to be clear, you goin' leave Carmel and move in with me, right?'

'Yes,' I say emphatically this time. It feels good to say it – real, purposeful, a decision wrought by recent dramatic events, doubts and extreme personal anguish.

I feel say I could flex myself again. I *could* – with the assistance of my kindly, reliable but rather expensive friend, Dr Viagra.

Ten hours later we are in Madame Maxine's Gay-ho, the narrow thoroughfares around Old Compton Street riddled with motor vehicles trying to run you down, bar crowds overspilling on to the pavement like they own it, and those irritating rickshaws that appeared in the West End about ten years ago, I ask you. Is this Shanghai? Is this Bombay? Is this Ho Chi Minh City?

Hordes of fellas on the cruise too, not in parks or cemeteries at night, where location alone is proof of intention, but out here in blatant, flirtational, public view.

It's not as Village People as I expected. Fellas are dressed quite normal and not all *Gay-Pride-Parade-Wearing-Only-a-Sequinned-Thong-and-Peacock-Feather-Headdress*. Actually, me and Morris is the ones getting *anthropological* looks, with our smart fifties suits, spats, fedoras and, in my case, a chunky gold chain around my neck. I give them anthropological looks right back. Don't they understand that we the *visitors* here, not the natives?

Halfway down Old Compton Street we walk past the Admiral Duncan pub that got nail-bombed by that Nazi nutter in '99 – the quarter-brain who couldn't get a woman, blamed gays, blacks and Bengalis and decided to blow us all up as revenge. The pub's got flamboyant pink lettering and purple walls, with that Freedom Flag flying at full mast. When I heard the news of the bombing back then, it became one more reason why I shouldn't go anywhere near these bars. Stick to the parks, Barry. They might beat you up, but at least you won't end up with your legs down one end of the street and your head down the other.

This is when it hits me. For the first time in my life I got no doubt that *everybody* in the vicinity knows that me and Morris are 'gentlemen of doubtful virtue'. Ain't no fakery here. Lord, they *know* us. Oh my, I don't even know where to put myself because some of these fellas make such *prolonged* eye contact with me they should apply for a resident's parking permit. Not for a minute are they thinking we are two spruced-up husbands, fathers, grandfathers, cutting through the West End on the way home from a wedding reception, funeral or Pentecostal church service. No, sah, *dis*-a not

Hackney, *dis-a* not Brixton, *dis-a* not Leyton. This go be *Gay-ho*, and they thinking, 'Look at those two ole Caribbean queens.'

If I had more courage, I *would* hold Morris's hand for, say, *one second*, though. All of my life I've watched couples holding hands, kissing in the street, on the bus, in pubs. I've watched couples walking arm in arm, ruffling each other's hair, sitting on each other's laps, dancing closely, romantically, jazzily, funkily, badly, bawdily.

And never, not once, have I felt able even to link arms with the man I love.

Me and Morris exchange sidelong glances, and flicker.

He grabs my hand and squeezes it for a few seconds.

It is our first public display of physical affection in sixty years.

The first bar Maxine lures us into is called the Yard. She's dressed relatively sensibly today in not-so-sprayed-on jeans and so-called 'ballet pumps', having '*totally* wrecked' her feet in the clodhoppers from a few days ago. I say relatively normal, because she's wrapped her head up again to resemble one of those bulldozing Nigerian matriarchs who roll down Ridley Market three abreast and will mow down anyone who don't step aside.

The bar is so densely packed with young beefsteak, fag hags and, as Maxine pre-warned us, 'voyeuristic hen parties', and thumping with such ear-splitting so-called 'music', that Maxine has to screech operatically, hitting a high C, just to ask us what we want to drink. I screech operatically back that me and Morris need to sit down to avoid having heart attacks, but there are no empty seats. We hightail it out-a there, try a couple of other bars similarly afflicted, before

Maxine suggests we 'jump into a taxi', as she knows 'just the place'. On the way she phones her bezzies to tell them we relocating to the Quebec, just around the corner from Marble Arch. I tell her I ready to call it quits, because I ain't bar-hopping like a student. She reassures me it's aimed at the older gay clientele and also known as the Elephants' Graveyard.

'Charming. Why don't you just take us to the undertaker's and be done with it?'

'Daddy,' she retorts, 'you're not planning on being a grumpy old man *all* night, are you?'

I didn't expect to be and I don't want to be, but I can't shake off the fact that the wife is at this minute sticking pins in a voodoo doll of me; that my elder daughter been carrying around a lifetime's resentment; and my only grandson has been *shamed* by me and will never talk to me again.

The doorman asks us if we know what kind of bar it is inside, and Maxine retorts that we are regulars, brushing haughtily past him. Soon as we enter fellas take a sneaky butchers at the newcomers. Most of them look like retired bank managers and schoolteachers, your run-of-the-mill demographic of middle-class gents from the suburbs.

I realize that as a newcomer to these gay habitats I really did expect to find *habitués* who are attention-seekers, but not a bit of it. They're just regular guys, older versions of the ones I used to *al fresco* with back in the day. Just goes to show how even my assumptions might, upon occasion, be misconceptions.

The long, narrow pub's got a wooden bar the length of a medium-sized yacht, faux-Victorian carpet, wallpaper, chandeliers and, ruining any nostalgic inclinations, ugly air-conditioning pipes hanging from the ceiling that are more suited to a dank hospital basement than a pub. A flat-screen TV suspended on the wall also pursues a theme of the contemporary *commingled* with the antique, along with a pinball machine that's being worked furiously by some sweaty Oriental fella with Mah Jong in his veins.

'It's the oldest gay pub in London, *darlings*,' Maxine announces as she beelines over to an empty table.

Since when does my daughter get to call us darlings?

'It opened in 1936, although I don't think gay pubs existed then.'

She settles us down in our seats like a fusspot (whispering in my ear to check that I'm okay), all but pulling the chairs out for us and helping us take off our jackets. Why doesn't she just measure us up for our coffins at the same time?

'Oh, I don't know,' Morris says, his eyes roaming the room like it's the Sistine Chapel. 'I wonder if Quentin Crisp used to come here? Gay fellas had their meeting places too back then.'

'And what an adorable little muppet *he* was.' Maxine rubs her hands together. 'A lovely bundle of pink bouffant. *If at first you don't succeed, then failure may be your style.*' She laughs. '*Tell* me about it.'

'Indeed, Maxie,' Morris *co-enthuses*. 'What about this one: *Life was a funny thing that happened to me on the way to the grave.* Now tell *me* about *that.*'

'Daddy, if you and Uncle Morris had come out in the sixties, you might have known him.'

'If we'd so-called come out then,' I tell her, smiling indulgently, 'you wouldn't-a been born. Besides, neither of us has actually so-called come out, not properly.'

'No, not *yet*,' Morris agrees, resting his hand briefly on mine on the table, so that his lighter fingers fall into the cracks between my longer ones.

My instinct is to dash my hand away, but it really is okay for him to do that here.

Nonetheless, I *should* have withdrawn my hand, because he suddenly goes and plants a kiss on my cheek. Maxine's eyes nearly pop out of her head in be-*thrillment*.

Step by step, Morris. Don't expect me to be another Quentin Crisp in five minutes.

Her mobile rings. 'They're here!' Maxine jumps up as her three bezzies pile in through the double wooden doors with a blast of youthful exuberance.

Why did they call her when they was right outside the door?

'Look!' Maxine squeals as they approach, making a show of herself and pointing at us like we're a pair of monkeys tap dancing on the table. 'Aren't they *wonderful*, ladies?'

The bezzies gather round, while Maxine coos and quivers. They shake our hands and slap our backs, stopping just short of pinching and prodding us.

'*I* discovered them,' she declares, hugging both of us in turn, cheek to cheek, like a proud parent. 'So hands off and *be-have*, especially *you*.' She wags her finger at the blond one. 'This is Dad, *Uncle* Barry to you, and this is *Uncle* Morris.'

You wouldn't think none of them was gay fellas, except maybe Blondie. They just look like arty-types. To be honest, Maxine is clearly the campest person in the room.

She takes the order for drinks, which rather surprises me, seeing as I ain't never seen her actually offer to pay for anything in the history of our relationship. True to form, she not goin' let me down now. 'I'll start a tab,' she says point-edly. 'Dad, it'll be a Coke for you.'

Will it?

'I'll have a Coke too,' Morris chips in. 'But put a double shot of rum in it.'

The others place their orders, Maxine goes off to the bar, and me and Morris are left with three pairs of expectant eyes waiting for us to whistle through our backsides.

'Chaps,' I say, clearing my throat, 'you seem to know who *we* are. What about you?'

The first one to introduce himself is Blondie, who can't keep his eyes off Morris.

'Pierre Duchamp, cosmetics entrepreneur,' he says, holding on to Morris's hand way too malingeringly. Indeed, such is the current of desire flowing towards my man I could go skinny-dipping in it.

What is he, a gerontophile?

I sneak a glimpse at Morris, who looks flattered. Getting big-headed a-ready.

Blondie has green eyes that almost glow in the dark. Around his neck is a thin black collar with silver studs, a theme that extends all the way up his earlobes and all the way down the sides of his black leather trousers.

'He might be Pierre Duchamp to you,' another one jumps in with a rather highbrow voice. This one's a tall fella with a long face and dreadlocks piled high into a spaghetti twist on his head. 'But he's Benjamin Brigstock to his parents. I've seen his passport.'

They all fall apart at that.

'For Crissakes,' Blondie retaliates, 'Benny Brigstock is never going to sell the metrosexual make-up range I'm developing.'

'I can't see there's much potential in make-up, myself. Not for *real men* anyway,' I say while putting my arm, yes, my *arm*, around Morris, who stiffens.

Blondie looks offended. The others chuckle, unsure.

He skulks off, muttering something about helping Maxine with the drinks.

'What about you? What is *your* name, young man?' Morris asks, doing what he does best, alleviating tense situations with friendly social discourse.

This is one helluva handsome fella, a latter-day Eros with curly *Italianate* hair, dramatic features, seductive sloe-eyes and juicy blow-job lips. I bet he's a *dutty* bastard. I can always tell.

'I'm Marcus,' he says, blatantly aware of his beauty.

I can't take my eyes off his mouth. Lord, it's so big the *Titanic* could have sailed in it . . . and me, back in the day.

'And what do *you* do, Marcus?' I ask his mouth.

'I'm Head of Visual-Merchandise Design at Miss Selfridge,' his mouth replies. 'I was at Saint Martins with Max.'

'What is this visual-merchandise business when it's at home?'

'Pretty much anything to do with the display of merchandise in stores,' he says, like his job is as vital to human survival as agriculture or medicine. 'Anything from window displays, creating props and accents, organizing clothing placements, marketing campaigns. I'm the in-store *aesthete*, if you like. Their greatest asset, or so my manager keeps telling me.' He snorts.

'Don't be deceived,' Spaghetti Head butts in. 'What he means is that he puts wigs on mannequins during the day, and in the evenings he puts condoms on anyone who'll take him, like his manager.'

'You weren't complaining when you were the one rolling *my* condoms up your dick,' he snaps back.

'Now, now, chaps.' Morris intervenes a little too prematurely for my liking. 'Let's keep this occasion nice and convivial.'

Why?

I examine Blow-Job Lips. Apart from his mouth, his nostrils are a bit too wide and his skin a bit too tawny for him to be entirely of the Anglo-Saxon persuasion.

'Where yuh people from?' I demand. He looks taken aback but answers his elder obediently.

'Jamaica.'

'They black?' I ask.

'Um, yes, no, red-skinned, as they say over there.'

He's flushing.

'Thought so,' I reply. 'Just like people back home who wanted to pass.'

I see Morris squinting at me through my excellent peripheral, as if to say, 'Don't start on this one too. Chill out, nah man.'

'I'm not passing, because I'm hardly properly black, am I?'

'Not if you can pass.'

Whoah! Barry, yuh starting to sound like one of those radicals. What's got into you? You not a race man. What do you care? Leave the boy alone.

I just killed the conversation stone dead. In which case, I'd better give it mouth-to-mouth resuscitation before Maxine gets back. I turn to Spaghetti Head. 'What about you?'

He throws up his hands and blurts out, 'Guilty! Guilty! Arrest me, lock me up, behead me, put me before the firing squad.'

That relaxes the atmosphere just in time for Maxine's

return with the drinks, Blondie in tow, clearly reassured that Maxine will protect him from the Evil Ogre.

'Good to see you're all enjoying yourselves *at last*,' she says, handing out drinks. 'And no one's being a trouble-maker, *as usual*.' She slams down my glass of Coke in front of me with such force a chunk of ice leapfrogs out of it.

Except my princess can't stay angry with me for long because who am I but her privy purse?

'Dad,' she says in my ear, 'they don't keep tabs at the bar. Er . . . can you help out at all, pretty please?'

I slip her a fifty-pound note. 'Get a double shot of rum for me too or I want the change.'

She frowns. but she's been bought. I watch her all but skip off, happy as when I used to give her twenty pence for a lolly from the ice-cream van.

Me and Morris are seated side by side. Blondie has parked his arse on the other side of Morris, strategically just out of my immediate eyeline. Maxine is at the end of the table, Blow-Job Lips is next to her and opposite Morris, and Spa-ghetti Head is facing me.

Maxine proposes a toast. 'Here's to Daddy and Uncle Morris. The elders who blazed a trail. Respect!'

Blazed a trail. How, exactly? In the wardrobe?

'Respect!' they toast, and we all down our alcohol-infused drinks that will charge us up nicely for an evening's carousing.

'Young man,' I say to Spaghetti Head, while the others start fawning over Morris. 'Tell me about yourself. You a Rasta?'

'Christ, no, never in a million years. It's just a style thing.'

Is *that* what he calls it?

He flashes me a crisp white smile that goes with his crisp

white shirt, open at the neck to reveal a dark, *chocolatesque* chest. He sits back and spreads his crisply clean, *be-jeaned* legs wide, showing off long, lean thighs and a decent enough package.

This one's not a young Adonis like Blow-Job, too intelligent-looking, although his body makes up for it. His face is too long to be handsome, and his nose too short relative to it; he's got a chunk missing from his forehead, and he talks lopsided.

He catches me observing him and gives a sly smile. Nonetheless, I do believe I could take a trip to the toilets with this one.

Lord, an ole man can have his harmless fantasies.

'Before you ask, my name is Lola,' he says.

'*Lola?*' I splutter, nearly choking on my drink.

'Short for Damilola,' he says, grinning, unfazed by my reaction. 'Which I only use in the Big Bad Homophobic World Outside. To my friends, I'm Lola.'

Right . . .

'Nigerian,' he further explains, picking up a stray strand of spaghetti that's fallen over his face and tucking it back into the meal on his head. 'Born there, raised here. I'm twenty-nine, so a lot younger than this bunch, but, I'm afraid to say, so much the wiser.' He nods over at his cohorts before backtracking. 'Not Maxine, of course. I *worship* her. She's not immature at all.'

Oh, yes, she is.

'As for Marcus and Pierre, they're only good for a night out on the tiles, which is great when I need to blow off steam.' He leans forward in a posture of confidential disclosure. 'I call them my Friday Night Hedonistic Friends, as distinct, you understand, from my Saturday Evening Dinner

Party Friends, my Art House Movie Pals, African Academics Debating Society and Gay Support Group (London Chapter for the Under-Thirties).'

I try to suppress the ripples of laughter bubbling up deep within my wicked soul.

'Those two usually end up completely trashed and giving complete strangers lap dances. Don't expect them to have heard of James Baldwin or Bayard Rustin. RuPaul and Danny La Rue? Yes. Langston Hughes? No.'

I wonder if Blow-Job will include me in the 'complete stranger' category? And, if so, would Morris mind?

Spaghetti Head ploughs on. 'It's impossible to engage them in a weighty conversation, as I think you've just discovered. I know from Maxine that you're a bit of a thinker. A kind of *autodidact*, in fact?'

Alarum! Alarum! Is this *rass* snob suggesting I'm some kind of sad sack who wasn't clever enough to go to university? Oh, shut up, Barry.

Breathe deeply and repeat ten times: *I am the Dalai Lama, I am the Dalai Lama.*

I assume a friendly, non-confrontational countenance. 'So you and Marcus was lovers, then?'

'For seven months,' he replies, looking a bit miffed that I've detoured the conversation. 'Until I discovered I was just one of many fuck-buddies – nocturnal visits on my moped *et-cet-er-a* . . .'

He takes a sip of his white wine, a drink I wouldn't touch with a barge pole. It's a woman's drink, and, Lola or no Lola, he's a man.

'I take it you're not one of the so-called fashionista crowd, then, *Lola*?' I inquire, sounding all upbeat, because one of my *better* interpersonal skills is to stop folk sinking into the sludge of self-pity.

'Christ, no! "Love art, hate fashion" is my mantra.'

Suddenly revitalized, he rolls up his shirtsleeves to reveal sculpted, gleaming, forearms. Our people usually moisturize good. Englishmen don't, which is why they end up crusty.

'You know how people in fashion are always proclaiming passionately "I *love* fashion!", like they're saying something meaningful instead of spouting the most annoying platitude *ever*?'

I nod my head. Yes, dearie, I notice it all the time.

'You see, Uncle, what I myself *personally* find great is how artists like Rotimi Fani-Kayode, Isaac Julien and Yinka Shonibare subvert the kinds of hackneyed cultural and historical iconographies that usually go unchallenged.'

This one's a speechifyer for sure. Only problem is that he takes the motorway to go to the shop round the corner. He's still not told me what he does.

'What is your profession? You an artist?'

That would excuse the hairstyle, *at least*.

'Unfortunately not. No talent in that department, sadly. I've two degrees under my belt, and I'm in my third year of a Ph.D. at Brunel University, where I'm president of the LBGT Society. I'm interrogating the history of homosexuality in Africa, focusing on the privileging of heteronormativity in Nigeria and the constitutionally enshrined persecution of homosexuals there as elsewhere on the continent, except South Africa, where it's at least legally legal, so to speak. I could talk about it all night. In fact . . . I often do.'

No wonder Blow-Job Lips dumped him.

Just then the lower end of the table erupts with mirth.

This might be the high-brow end of the table, but some low-brow nonsense is preferable on my historic first night out of the wardrobe.

'Lola,' I say at last. 'To be quite frank with you, I am not fully cognizant of Africa's pan-continental yet heterogeneous homosexual history, nor do I know anything about institutional and attitudinal prejudices thereof. It is not an issue that ever enters my sphere of interrogative probity, in truth.'

Oh, yes, I can speaky-spokey too.

'Let me tell you, then,' Lola replies. 'These *myth-makers* are actually arguing that, unlike the rest of the human race, Africans were quite incapable of having same-sex relations without being shown how to do it by the Europeans. What's more insulting? To say that Africans were sexually infantilized until the Europeans arrived? Or to admit that they were evolved enough to get their groove on through same-sex attraction?'

Of course men have been at it with each other since time began. Sticking it in any ole bodily orifice they can.

'Let us not forget,' he continues, 'that prior to Christianity sub-Saharan Africa had indigenous religions with their own moral beliefs. The Zande Warriors of Zaire, the Berbers of Siwa in Egypt, transvestism in Madagascar, a boy's rite of passage in Benin. This is what's so twisted about it all. It's *homophobia*, not homosexuality, that was imported to Africa, because European missionaries regarded it as a sin. Take Angola, prior to colonial intervention, homosexuals were accepted, not persecuted. It was the Portuguese who criminalized it.'

He leans back in his chair, closes his eyes and seems to be recovering from his verbalization, extemporization and philosophization.

Maxine right. I really do feel like a grumpy ole man today. This is too much for me. Maxine's bezzies are too self-confident, too in-yer-face. It makes me want to puncture their egos.

I like the pub, though. The regulars are quiet, discreet, none of the braying braggadocio of your usual male bar crowd. Our table is actually the rowdiest. I might even come back here with Morris and meet some fellow *elders*, although if any one of them shows any signs of dementia I'll be out the door in a flash.

By the time I finish drifting, Spaghetti Lolanaise is taking a rather graceful sip of wine. Oh, yes, radical today, banker tomorrow. A real radical would be drinking cheap beer or cider.

He drains the last of his wine and waves it in Maxine's direction like a hypnotist. She rises to the bait. 'Same again, everyone?' And she's off to the bar. Silly girl should know better than to be played. Let him get his own bloody drink.

'Uncle Barry, I want to know *all* about you,' he says, finally noticing my mood shift. I'm never sure whether I'm immune to what I observe in others – the attempt to camouflage negative thoughts and emotions.

'Sod African history for the moment, you're *living* history.'

Thanks . . .

'Max tells me you –'

'I'd rather talk about you. When did you first realize you was a pooftah?'

He deflates into his seat. 'Poof . . . tah?'

Morris turns around sharply. 'Barry, you behaving yourself?'

'Yes, *Cherub*, I only joking.'

'Good.'

'Lola,' I say, all nicety-nicety with Morris listening in at my side, 'I take it you've come out to your family?'

'And how. My dad's response was to declare that *adodi*, which in Yoruba means "one who fucks in the arse", should be necklaced. My Nation of Islam brother Bolade said I was mentally ill. I told him that his hero, Malcom X, was *adodi* too, and that his childhood friends had testified to his homosexual activities from a young age. Bad move. He attacked me with a solid glass ashtray and I ended up in A & E. You see this?' He points to the crater in his forehead. 'Christmas 2004 – present from my brother.'

I think I might almost start liking this lad. I pat him on his hand, and he sinks into his seat.

'You braver than me, Lola,' I say. (See, I got a heart.) 'I did something even crazier the other night, this so-called coming out thing to a group of drunken teenage boys including my grandson. I didn't mean to do it, I just vomited the words up.'

I can't believe I'm discussing this openly, being so influenced by these gay fellas so quickly.

'Whereas you did it knowing what you was up against. Me, I was drunk and out of control. I ain't no hero.'

'Me neither,' says Morris, listening in and shaking his head somewhat tipsily. 'And Barry, did I tell you that was an idiotic thing to do?'

'Oh, but you *are* heroes. Both of you. I certainly don't see any other black men your age here, do you?'

He right, but it don't bother me, not no more. So long as folk treat me decently, equally, I fine with them. I never came to this country expecting to be in the majority. Look at Peaceman. I'd rather sit down and chinwag with him more than anyone else other than Morris. Don't matter what colour a person is; some folk just get a connection. Next time I see him I go tell him about me and Morris. Yes, I go do it.

Peaceman will probably say, 'Barry, I have been waiting for you to take me into your confidence on this matter since we first met in 1965.'

'You be a hero for all-a-we,' I tell Spaggy.

'Yesh, you be a hero for boshofus,' Morris concurs.

Spaggy smiles appreciatively. 'I'll try. I've been interviewing gay men at private parties in Nigeria. "Kings and queens" is their equivalent of "butch and femme".

'You'll never believe this . . .' His eyes glitter. 'But I'm actually seeing a brigadier in the Nigerian Armed Forces. Mean, keen and *utterly* devastating in his army uniform. Also Muslim, married with two wives and the father of seven kids. Hello? Welcome to the Nigerian down-low.'

He waves his glass at my daughter again. I quickly thrust a fifty-pound note at him so I don't have to see her act like a puppet.

'Are you sure?' he asks while grabbing it.

'Get another round, Lola.'

The rest of the table suddenly look up, all attentive. Funny how the mention of free drinks can do that.

'Dad,' Maxine says across the table, 'it'll be a Coke for you, with no pollutants.'

'Yes, Barry,' Morris butts in. 'Go easy now.'

'Since when has four shots of rum been anything other than an *aperitif*?'

The bezzies laugh, but Maxine and Morris stare me down. They goin' whup my ass if I step out of line. They right, though: I shan't let my alky-holiday turn into another alky-hell.

I goin' stay sober until my showdown with Carmel – and this waiting is increasingly killing me – and then I goin' stay sober until the divorce done.

I look around at Maxine's bezzies, all lively and, if I'm honest, they are being nice to me, even though I was a bit harsh on them earlier.

Morris right: I shouldn't be so judgemental, so down on people, especially my *own*.

Suddenly it's like divorcing Carmel is not enough, I feel the need to so-called 'come out' to her too. What is the matter with you, Barry? That is the barmiest thing you can do.

'Lola, get me a *pure*, *healthy*, *sugar-free*, *chemical-free* Coca-Cola and . . . before I forget, what is this LBGT thing?'

'It's an abbreviation for Lesbian, Gay, Bi-Sexual and Transgender, standing for a diversity of sexuality and gender-identity-based cultures.'

'Whava very good idea.' Morris nods his head vigorously. 'We gender-benders have got to shtick up for sholidarity.'

The way he's carrying on, I wouldn't put it past him to get his nipples pierced tomorrow.

'Are you saying that I am now lumped together with those "born-a-boy-die-a-girl" sex-changers? I'll have you know I am quite happy with my fully functioning cock.'

'Hear-hear,' says Blow-Job, joining my fray. 'Me too. Lola hasn't been boring you, has he? Droning on about how Jesus was really an African lesbian?'

Everybody cracks up, even Lola, who whisks himself off to the now-crowded bar.

Maxine comes over to me and gives me a hug.

'I'm so proud of you. You've been so well behaved, even though you've got so much on your mind. Lola's a bit intense for most people. We'll be debating who's going to win *X Factor*, and he'll start lecturing us about tribal warriors buggering each other in Africa hundreds of years ago.'

'Tell me about it,' agrees Blowy. 'And he can be very condescending for someone who's always going on about equal rights.'

'Ignore him,' Maxine says. 'We need brainiacs like Lola.'

'What about me? I'm a great believer in equal rights,' Blondie butts in. 'I *love* black men. Their booties are *unrivalled*.'

'Ignore him too. He loves winding people up.

She thrusts a scruffy piece of folded paper into my hand and whispers, 'Here's my business plan. Don't read it now but do get back to me pronto, *Papa*.'

Blondie calls over, 'I'm trying to persuade Uncle Morris to come to Madame Jojo's with us afterwards. What about you, Barry?'

'Not for me. Is no fun if a man can't drink.'

'Then me neither,' Morris says, putting a hand on my shoulder.

Lola arrives back with the drinks, and I take a sip of my Coca-Cola but push it aside.

'Maxine, gentlemen,' I announce, 'I ready to retire from your delightful company. Forgive me for being a kill-joy.'

'Me too,' says Morris, joining me. 'Make that two kill-joys.'

Lolanaise looks upset. I think he might have Donna's so-called 'abandonment issues'.

Maxine sighs. 'Not that I'm going to meet the man of my dreams at Madame Jojo's.'

She raises her shoulders and drops them in mime-like

exaggeration. 'I should become a lesbian, really. I think I'd be in demand.'

I see the drink is starting to take effect.

'I'm all alone in the world and no one cares!' she all but shouts.

'Poor dear,' Blowy says with deeply felt insincerity, because he's probably heard it all a thousand times before. 'You're far too good for those useless straight men out there. Look at you, in your forties and still such a head-turner.'

'*Turning* forty,' she replies snippily.

'Turning forty, looking twenty, *what-evs*.'

They've dimmed the lights, the music just got louder, the place busier.

I rise to leave, and Morris rises with me, dutifully, loyally.

I turn to the assembled group of bezzies, because I feeling the urge to make another declaration.

'Children, when my wife returns from abroad, I will tell her that our fifty-year marriage is null and void, and she will have to face the prospect of spending the rest of her life alone. Likely she'll come at me with a carving knife. If I tell her I have always loved Morris and never loved her, she might go at herself with a carving knife. Good night.'

For the second time this evening, I just murdered the conversation.

Maxine looks aghast.

What did she expect after the drama of Daniel?

That I could just lock myself up again?

It seems to be dawning on Lola that he don't know a thing about me.

Marcus and Pierre are sitting across the table like they're

watching a weepy at the movies and are desperate for a happy ending.

'Maxine, you coming? I think we need to talk about this, yes?'

And we three musketeers leave and hail a black cab back to my yard.

15

The Art of Taking Care of Business

Thursday, 27 May 2010

My bonkers-mad daughter provided some light relief while I spent my days waiting for Carmel's Return.

Take Maxine's so-called business plan, which, when I got round to reading it, was so ridiculous it made me briefly forget the imminent confrontation.

When I showed it to Morris, he did the bellyache laugh he's been doing a lot lately, a laugh that sped down the hallway and gusted merrily up Cazenove Road and out into the ether beyond.

BUSINESS PLAN: PHASE ONE

HOUSE OF (Maxine?) **WALKER**
By Maxine Walker, OBE ☺

Outgoings
(Annual/spasmodic (casual) per contract/or salaried &/ London Weighting inc.)

Stamps – £150
Stationery – £250
Marketing – £10,000
Photocopying – £300.50

Domestic travel/expenses – £13,999 (= taxis = time management = cost-effective)

International travel/expenses – £25,000 (source fabrics: Bali, Zanzibar, Marrakech, Tokyo)

Fabric & materials – £80,000, give or take

Bose Wave Music System – £778.99 (= staff morale)

Phone & internet – £1,500

Seamstresses – £20,000 at £10 p.h.

De'Longhi Espresso Machine – £849.95 (money saving = lifelong guarantee)

Credit card interest – TBC ☹

Studio – £30,000

Drugs = (Jokes!) ☺

Models × 15 – £150,000 (*supers* = Lon Fash Wk = Mwah! Mwah!)

Bang & Olufsen Flat-Screen TV (to view Fashion TV, etc.) – price TBC

Minions (Oops – Support Team!!) – £30,000 (stylists!!! etc.)

Misc./petty cash/money for sweets (Lol) – TBC

Hunky male escorts for stressed and lonely designer = 52 × 500 = £26,000 = ☺ (Jokes!)

Photography – £100,000 (Testino/Meisel/Rankin or other)

Interns: Poppy, Daisy, India, Jemima, Amber!!!!! = mass savings! (spoilt rich bitches ☹)

Hospitality – £12,999

Assistant –£18,000 p.a. plus NI =?

Head Designer salary – £100,999 p.a.

New car as befits a top designer (doh!) – price TBC

Total Outgoings: TBC

Incomings

Sales to the rich, famous (probably Russian & Chinese!!!)

At our first business meeting together in my kitchen (where else?), Maxine argues with po-faced defensiveness that her 'business plan' has merits that can be built upon, and that it's *supposed* to be 'fun and creative', because 'Do I look like a boring administrator?'

I'm sitting on my medieval throne. She's sitting to my left, wearing cut-off denims that are on the wrong side of decency, especially for a woman her age.

Morris is in attendance to my right, enjoying the performance.

'Maxine,' I tell her up front, 'listen to me good: your so-called business plan is the most ridiculous thing I have ever set eyes upon. In any case, it is not a plan; it's a joke pretending to be a budget.'

'Dad,' she bats back, 'I can't *believe* you're being so heartless. I expected more from you. I'm your *daughter*.'

'Yes, you are my daughter, but this is business and you acting the fool. I still want to support your creative endeavours but on my terms. I will be the sole investor in the House of *Walker* (no *Maxine* about it), which makes me the sole Proprietor. Your role will be that of (mad genius) Creative Director. Take it or leave it.'

Storm clouds are gathering on her face.

'I will appoint a business manager specializing in fashion retail who'll oversee the business. He or she will report to me, and *you* will report to both of us.'

'That's just plain wrong, insulting and offensive,' she says, ready to burst – her emotional impulse to throw a strop engaged in mortal combat with the mental awareness she got to behave herself.

'Dad, you and I have got to be *equal* partners, because I really don't need to have anybody bossing me around at this stage in my life? The whole point of having my own company is that *I'm* in charge.'

'Look at my big h-ugly face, dearest. Tell me, what dost thou seest? A hard-headed businessman with a wealthy property empire or a damned jackass who ain't got two pennies to rub together?'

She starts snivelling into a tissue, although, strangely, I don't notice no actual water spurting out of her Cleopatra eye sockets.

'And you can stop the crocodile tears, dear. You sure you ready to have your own label, Maxine? You sure you're grown up enough? You sure you can handle working for a father who's goin' treat you equally by not making any allowances because you're his daughter? And yuh think Daddy can't be a bad-ass? How many wutliss tenants you think I evicted since I started renting out in the sixties? I'll show you the list: it runs to over three pages. Maxine, I serious about helping you, but I equally serious about pulling out if you mess me about.'

At this stage in the proceedings Morris intervenes.

'You should hire me as Arbitration Counsellor between Proprietor and Creative Director. Although' – he coughs – '*although* such a person would normally be called in *after* folk been working together for some time.' Cough, cough. 'And relationships have reached crisis point.' Cough, cough.

'Fear thee not, Morris. I'd hire you as my Adviser any day, because that is what, *de facto*, you already are, *mio caro consigliere*. I go pay you a fat salary every month too.'

It feels good to talk openly, freely, lovingly to Morris in front of Maxine. I realize how much I starting to feel freed up a-ready.

Maxine's crossed-over legs start spasming so much any-one getting in their way would receive a meaty kick from a pair of glittery hobnail boots.

'No, thank you, Mr Walker.' Morris arranges his face sanctimoniously. 'I don't believe in nepotism.'

'Yes, that's nepotistic!' Maxine agrees before catching herself.

What Morris don't know is that I secretly set up a trust fund in his name a long time ago, seeing as he still won't let me support him. Should I depart this earth before him (which I hope happens, because I'd rather die than live without my beloved spar), he's goin' be looked after good for the rest of his life.

Needless to say, Maxine conceded to my Terms and Conditions, because, quite frankly, she ain't got no choice. We agreed I'd set everything in motion once the divorce done and dusted.

I also told her that, although I expected teething problems, I wasn't goin' put up with no histrionics and infantilized behaviour. I told her I'd give her eighteen months' probation to show me she ready to rise above the crowd and become a success, not just a pie-in-the-sky dreamer.

She told me she'd show me she's got what it takes, then gushed about a future project called City Couture, with outfits inspired by black cabs, traffic lights, skyscrapers; cigarette-butt earrings and even shoes with dog-turd heels, as well as a casual 'mugger range'. 'Daddy, the city dweller *becomes* the city in clothes that encapsulate attitude and architecture, street style and street furniture – thereby closing the divide between the human race and the urban space. How ironic and post-modern is that?' she declared rhetorically, proudly.

I told her that today's innovation is tomorrow's installation, and that she'll be due a retrospective at Tate Modern or MoMA twenty years from now.

She thought I was taking the Michael.

But I wasn't. Do I believe in my daughter? I do believe I do.

The weeks continue to pass without a word from Carmel or her elder daughter, who has sent me to Coventry for crimes committed against humanity, a war tribunal at The Hague.

Every time I asked Maxine what was up, she reported Carmel was still sorting stuff out and would be back soon, but soon never came soon enough.

Maxine kept popping round offering advice. 'We'll take your coming out one step at a time. Today the Quebec, next year Civil Partnership. I'll be your Maid of Honour, and just make sure I catch the wedding posy *or else*. Pierre can be the over-emotional mother of the bride, Marcus can be the little pageboy, and Lola can deliver a sermon about the pleasures of black-on-black buggery.

Thank God for Maxine.

But the suspense got so bad I even contemplated flying to Antigua myself to utter the dreaded declaration: I divorce thee, I divorce thee, I divorce thee.

Except I ain't never flown in my life and I not about to start now. As I confessed to Morris, 'Why the hell would I risk getting blown out of the sky in revenge for two wars I am not responsible for and end up clasping an airplane wing in the middle of the Atlantic?'

As we waited, we discovered that Morris's first night in his lover's marital bed was to be his last.

'It don't feel right,' he said, sitting up the morning after some frolicking-befuckery, his back up against a herd of grazing elephants. 'What if Carmel comes home unexpected in the early hours and barges in on us?'

'It don't feel right to me either.'

My king-sized bed had always been a desolate no-man's-land, the site of a couple who'd trained their bodies to not so much as brush up against each other in sleep.

I gave up telling Carmel I was moving into another room decades ago. Like a divorce, she wasn't having it.

When I think about it now, I really can't believe that I didn't relocate to another bedroom. Why did I intensify the dysfunction of our marriage by sharing the same bed? Guilt? Fear? Cover-up? *Weakness?* What was the matter with me?

Anyways, it's too late now to turn it into a peccadillo pleasure zone.

Nor could I stay over at Morris's, because if Carmel *did* return unannounced at night, my absence would fan the wrath of her flames.

We decided to spend our days together and our nights apart.

I went to sleep alone and woke up wondering if Carmel had turned up and was sitting in the kitchen to surprise me. I could-a bolted the front door, but I knew this would equally vex her real bad.

Morris turned up for breakfast every morning with his red-top and my broadsheet and a pint of milk or a loaf of bread if we was running low. One morning he brought in a mysterious white paper bag that he dangled in front of me before proudly arranging five *croissants* star-style on a white dinner plate.

Oh my days, what is the matter with him?

'Yuh really getting the gay bug, ehn, Morris? First croissants, next it'll be those *earth-moving* cupcakes they keep banging on about in the supplements and, before you know it, flower-arranging classes. Croissants are just the beginning of the slippery slope, my man. Stick to Mother's Pride.'

Morris was humming loudly before I even finished talking (cheeky arse) as he tried to butter and marmalade croissants clearly not designed for that purpose. Anyone can see that croissants are just a conglomeration of pastry flakes that should be rolled into a tight ball and stuffed wholesale into your gob, which is what I did.

Suddenly he dived like a swooping bird on to the floor, because he must-a seen a crumb. He picked it up betwixt forefinger and thumb and crept to the kitchen bin like he was holding the tail of a mouse, whereupon he put his foot on to the black pedal and deposited it.

He and Carmel are similar in that regard: they see dirt where it don't exist. That's where the similarity ends, *for-tu-nate-ly*.

After breakfast we started the habit of reading the books lent to us by Lola, after he insisted on meeting us for coffee at Starbucks over at Angel and thereupon delivering a lecture, out of the blue, about the hip-hop down-lows.

Long, short and tall of it, he won't be happy until 10 per cent of all black fellas come out of the closet.

I quipped, 'You mean some of the hoodrats of hip-hop might be homos on the down-low?'

He didn't find me funny.

Morris started on *Invisible Life* by the African-American novelist Mr E. Lynne Harris, Esq., while I got stuck into *The*

Gay Divorcee by Mr Paul Burston, Esq., which I thoroughly enjoyed, though I couldn't for the life of me work out exactly what a West End Wendy or MDMA was. ('Muscle Mary' was self-explanatory.) Waiting in the wings was a Mr Diriye Osman, Esq., a Mr Philip Hensher, Esq., a Mr Alan Hollinghurst, Esq., and a play called *Bashment* by a Mr Rikki Beadle-Blair, Esq.

All of this gayness is starting to affect me, preparing me for a new life, and, yes, as Lola said, helping me come to terms with what I been fearing and hiding all my life – although I won't admit it to no one. And certainly not the 'gay therapist' Lola recommended I visit. (I ask you.)

One day I might even write an essay about these books for Queer Studies: *The Exemplification, Amplification, Ramification and Occasional Campification in Contemporary Gay Literature*. 2,000 words. *Easy.*

Yuh see? I made a spectacle of myself that fateful night with Daniel's hoodlums, and I got complications ahead, but I can't stop what's happening here.

Yes, sah. Yes, Morris. Yes, Lola and fellow *attention-seekers*, I feel myself coming out, no *so-called* about it.

16

The Art of Speechlessness

14 September 2010

So here we are, late morning, mid week, reading quietly, peaceably, harmoniously at the kitchen table about an hour before our perambulatory expedition down to Dalston for some lunch, when I hear the key turn in the lock and guess who swans in through the front door with Donna in tow, dragging the kind of man-sized suitcase favoured by immigrants?

Lord-a mighty, what happen to wifey? I barely recognize her.

As she moves closer down the infamous hallway that has been witness to many a Walker drama over the decades, I notice she not only walking a bit straighter, but limping a lot less.

What is more someone has taken a hammer and chisel to her former self and starting chipping away, because the woman who must-a been hiding underneath is starting to show.

Her eyes appear bigger, glossier, glowing.

Her face is smoothly tanned, quite radiant. Are those actual *cheekbones* peeping through?

As for her hair. *What-a thing.* When I first met Carmel, her hair was the product of a hot-iron comb; as she got older she dyed it; and when it started to thin prematurely from all she put it through, she bewigged herself.

Now look at her: *au naturel,* and, I have to say, it looks bloody lovely: pretty little grey curls shaping her head.

Yes, it really suits her. Wifey looks classy, makes her look younger too.

I stand up as she enters the kitchen, wearing a floaty white kaftan with blue diamond embroidery and white linen trousers that flap over a pair of canvas sandals with platform heels. *Heels?*

She's wearing a turquoise bangle and raindrop *earrings? Lipstick . . . nail polish?*

What happened to her offensive nylon trousers with tights worn underneath? You could hear her a mile off with all that rub and bristle.

Way she looks now, I could pass her on the street and not recognize her.

And since when does she carry shoulder bags? Carmel's bags have always been modelled on the Queen's.

I don't stop Morris as he takes his leave, silently, diplomatically, scooping up the two novels (wisely) in the process.

Me and her face each other.

Me standing by the window, hearing rain splatter against it, wondering if she goin' send me through it.

She watching me watching her, enjoying my astonishment as I absorb her newly renovated self.

She don't appear angry, don't appear hurt. She appears . . . *confident . . . magnificent.*

I been rehearsing my speech so long but the thought of delivering it . . .

This is not the person I thought I'd be divorcing. Who *is* this person?

Donna, dressed in a smart black work trouser suit, has

taken up position as sentinel and is blocking the kitchen doorway.

She should get lost, because I really need to have an *entre nous* with her mother.

As if Carmel can read my mind, she says, 'Thank you for your help, but you can leave us alone now, Donna. I can handle this one.'

What? I goin' be *handled*?

'Okay,' her guard dog mutters reluctantly, like she don't want to miss the histrionics. 'I'll see you later.' She goes over to her mother, gives her a peck on the cheek.

As she leaves, she flashes me a smirk that insinuates she'll be returning to help her mother pack my body parts into black rubbish bags and bury me in the garden under cover of darkness.

At this point I realize I am trapped, because if Carmel decides to pull a knife on me there's a massive kitchen table blocking my exit.

Except this too is strange. Carmel don't look like she ready to serve up my intestines.

'Sit down, Barry.'

I do as she says, and she takes her position at the opposite end of the table, not slouching.

'Yuh looking good, Carmel.'

'*That's* an understatement, yuh no think?'

'Uh, yes . . . You looking absolutely splen—'

'I *know* what I look like, Barry. I don't need you to tell me anything. Now, *this* is what I goin' tell *you* . . .'

She eyeballs me, but I used to that, except it ain't resentment coming off her but something else. Pity? Is *pity* she feeling?

'Carmel,' I say, realizing I'd better get my speech in before

277

hers, 'I'm aware you not been happy for sometime now. We've both been lonely in this –'

'Barry,' she says, cutting me off, *'shut up.'*

She waits for me to appear suitably chastised.

'Now, contrary to your assumptions, I am quite contented, as per the *unusually.'*

She takes her time, fiddles with the bangles on her wrists. Her *turquoise* nails are long, shapely, manicured.

What *has* she been up to?

The rain is now thrashing against the window, signalling summer's left us and winter ain't far behind.

'After the funeral, I stayed on to sort out Papi's business. He left everything to me, his *only* child. Don't worry, my lawyer is seeing off those scavengers.'

She tchupses and skins up her nose, ruining her new image.

'Talking of lawyers, I've returned to wrap up my life here and start a new one over there. Yes, you wasn't expecting that, was you? First thing I got to do is "lawyer-up", as Donna puts it, because I starting divorce proceedings and you not getting off lightly.'

She takes off her wedding ring, which, seeing as she's thinner, comes off easily. She flicks it so it rolls like a wheel across the table, dying a death right in front of me, where I leave it.

'I caught up with Odette over there and, like you always saying, when women get together they natter.

'She told me I got to forgive, same way she did. *Unforgiveness is the poison you drink every day, hoping the other person will die*, she kept reminding me. Well, I working on it. Yes, I working on it, because you got the sickness in you and therefore can't help yourself. But it hard, Barry. It so hard, because, way I see it, I spent fifty years of my life betrayed by your lie. Missing all of the clues that was staring me in the face. I been through some bad times over there, Barry, realizing my whole adult life been wasted. Odette says you gave me two daughters, so it's not wasted, but she wrong.

'Here's another thing I found out: you was being talked about even from when you was at school. It just as well you married me when you did, but that was the whole point, wasn't it? Fifty years with a man who used me as his cover story to protect his disgusting business, making a mockery of me. How yuh think that make me feel?'

She arises without her customary huffing and puffing, fetches a glass of water to drink. Carmel? Water?

'Yuh see, Barry, I'm not lonely no more. So don't you start telling me I am. Remember Hubert from school? Of course you do, because you *stole* me from him. Well, he back in my life and we getting on just fine. More than fine. You shock again, eh? He got a Ph.D. at Howard University in *Washington*, where he became a maths *professor*. He's not a skinny sixteen-year-old neither. He taller than you, slimmer than you, more hunky and not bald neither.'

She registers everything that flickers over the face that I am now convinced shows everything.

'I goin' back to him. My life here is done. Don't worry, I ain't in the business to dish the dirt. What good that do me, eh? Let everybody know what a fool I been?

'Donna's taking a fortnight off work to help me with everything. I'll be here every day from 10 a.m. to start sorting through stuff, and you better not be here, neither sight nor sound. I sending in the packers next week, and I don't want you here then either. Don't worry, I'm not stripping a house that represents half a century of misery.

'As for that Jim Reeves record you scorn so much? Ditto. I can't wait to take a hammer to it. You lucky I ain't taking a hammer to you, but you're not worth a life sentence. I done my time already.

'I don't want to see or speak to you again, unless you contest the divorce, which you won't.'

'Carmel, Carmel, dear, I –'

'Shut up. You a sick man, Barry, and the only person who can help you now is God.'

17.

Song of Freeness

2010

returning home after thirty years, landing at V. C. Bird International, blasted

by the sticky heat you not used to no more and feeling out of place with all of the English tourists pouring off the plane in their shorts and sunhats, because your little Antigua has become a number one *islan' in de sun* destination since you was last here and when

the ole straw-hatted Calypsonian strumming his guitar on the tarmac nodded at you

like maybe he knew you, like maybe you went to Miss Davis Primary together, or he was a childhood neighbour perhaps, or even a half-brother, because although you'd concede it to nobody, least of all Barry and not even Donna, given Papi's track record with Loreene and all of the other whores Mommy told you about, you wouldn't be surprised if you was related to half of St John's

and you nodded curtly back as you piled into the tiny Arrivals Room and joined the queue for foreigners, rummaging in your bag for the United Kingdom of Great Britain and Northern Ireland passport that you was once so desperate to get hold of

except it felt both right and wrong because

after so long away you don't really belong here no more, do you Carmel?

but how can you not belong where you born, girl?

and Cousin Augusta drove you straight off to Holberton Hospital, where you felt such rage when you saw Papi so comatose and pathetic, unable to register you'd come back

for him

to forgive him but now

seeing him there

tucked up in white sheets in his own private room

dying comfortably in his sleep, all shrivelled and innocent-looking after he'd caused Mommy so much pain her whole married life . . .

last time you saw him was thirty-two years ago, when she was being lowered into the grave and

all of those feelings came rushing back and you had to squash them down, use all of your self-control not to release a torrent of abuse at a man who'd lived longer than he deserved

because Barry was right: you *despised* him, so why was you play-acting the dutiful daughter?

and Cousin Augusta said you must stay at hers until Donna arrived, but you needed to see your childhood home, *his* home, immediately, urgently, otherwise you'd be floundering without an anchor

but you was so *shock* at how everything had remained the same but changed

same grandfather clock in the hallway – one hand missing, no longer ticking

same parade of family photographs – darkened under a patina of dust (the Millers, Gordons) same mahogany tallboy at the end of the corridor – one drawer hanging off

same wicker chairs in the sitting room – unravelling

same round teak dining table – water marks disguising the inlay, and damp corrupting the wood

Papi's prized Viennese armoire – cornice and carvings chipped

Papi's prized French Directoire desk – its rolltop stuck halfway up

Mami's 'Parisian' sofa suite in her bedroom – sunken, stained, dirty stuffing sticking out

your childhood brass bed – without a mattress and its full complement of springs (upon which you *finally* lost your virginity two weeks after your marriage and the day before you travelled to England)

everything stale and silent, mouldy and moulting, smelly and musty, cobwebs and dust, ashes to ashes, just like Papi, barely holding on

Papi, who was still everywhere and nowhere

and before him the long-ago forebear who squatted this uncultivated plot of land that became Tanner Street in the days when your people wasn't allowed to buy a little bit of your own island

and you and Augusta talked on the veranda, you on the rusty Hollywood swing still there (unbelievably), the floor creaking and sagging with age (like you)

the garden overgrown beyond recognition, wild bush and bramble, soggy date-palm leaves heaped on the ground, weeds pushing up through the paved pathway already cracked by tree roots intent on returning the island to forest

like Papi's mind, she said, all gnarled up, all tangled up

283

he wouldn't have nobody helping him, even though his hands shook so much he could barely hold his breakfast mug of rum, and he could hardly walk even with crutches and he could-a got a house boy or a house girl, but no, it was as if he was punishing himself because

your daddy changed, Carmel, ole age softened him like his flesh

Augusta recalled sitting on this very veranda three years earlier – *for seven years* she'd pop by weekly with his shopping – and *he sat there, Carmel,* and wept over his younger self who'd done unspeakable things to his wife because of the uncontrollable monster inside of him, just like his father, and even his grandfather – a long line of angry Miller men goin' back to slavery days – who took it out on their wives

O my offence is rank, he said, *it smells to heaven . . .*

which is why when your mother died, he never remarried

just had a few women comin' and goin', and the last one was some ghetto guttersnipe who let her pickney tear up the place until he kicked them out

then he was alone these past nine years, upset at how he'd been abandoned by his daughter, by the granddaughters who barely knew him, the great-grandson he'd never even met, all of his brothers and sisters long dead – Eudora and Beth, Alvin and Aldwyn

everybody gone, Augusta, everybody gone . . .

and you felt so bad, so guilty, so regretful you hadn't come back earlier and reconciled with him

and when his spirit finally passed it was like Mommy dying all over again but worse

and you was so relieved when Donna arrived to help you manage your feelings and his estate, which wasn't much, because he'd outlived the demise of the Early Bird stores

a mobile-phone shop and cheap clothes shop was where his stores used to be, which made him such a big-big man in this small-small town

that was smaller than both you and Donna remembered

but you marvelled at Redcliffe Quay and Heritage Quay and what a shock – English Harbour redeveloped beyond belief, with expensive properties and gated communities for the ex-pats, returnees and holidaymakers, and the international yachts, the regattas, the cruise ships stopping off on their round-Caribbean trip

which gave you an idea it might be a nice thing to do – a cruise

you, Donna and Maxine seeing the other islands, but Donna said Maxine would be too much of a handful, and you tried to stand up for your younger girl because you know Donna has always been green-eyed about Maxine

who you actually feel sorry for these days because you her mother and she ain't happy

and Donna backed down and said okay, Maxine can come too

and then she had to go back to work in London and you was left alone

sorting through Papi's finances you bumped into Odette in town, just outside the First Caribbean International Bank, looking nothing like the poor, distressed creature who left England twenty-one years earlier

wearing this orange kaftan with big sunflowers all over it and *bald*, yes, she *bald*, just like that Madeline Bell from the sixties, with big white hoop earrings, but not because she got alopecia but because she'd decided to go from high-maintenance to no-maintenance hair *on principle*

liberating herself from the *billion-dollar fortune the hair moguls extract every year out of we coloured ladies*

over lunch at Rum Baba at English Harbour she took hold of your hands across the table

I hope you don't mind my saying this, Carmel, but you look so tired, so down-in-the-dumps, dear, like you not been looking after yourself. I know you must be grieving for your daddy, but, to be blunt, you've really let yourself go. Years of marriage to that man has taken their toll on you, what you need is some TLC

which was such a relief, because you'd been waiting for someone to reach out and pull you up, and who better than Odette, who was always such a great girl, always dancing and making joke, and you hated it when Barry used to slag her off all the time

and felt sorry to see her crushed to pieces over the years of being married to Morris too, not realizing the same thing was happening to you

a destroyed woman who needed rebuilding, you both agreed, after you'd spent hours discussing what your respective husbands been getting up to *with each other* behind your backs

How could I have not noticed, Odette? What's wrong with me, Odette?

you was so devastated at what she told you that she drove you back to Miss Odette's Boutique Hotel and Spa and stayed praying with you all night long and ordered you to stay as long as you wanted, as her guest, until you stopped feeling either suicidal or homicidal

so you stayed there in a bungalow on the hillside along

with all of the rich African-American ladies of a certain age who paid plenty for some TLC yoga retreats at Odette's

and you met Marcus, Odette's retired architect boyfriend of six years, which was the biggest surprise, and he treated her so nicely and

you started using the cross trainer in her gym for ten minutes every morning to get your metabolism goin', as the trainer instructed, even though every muscle in your body hurt, because you'd never done any proper exercise in your life except for housework, walking to the shops or church

started doing some gentle yoga too and water aerobics in Odette's lovely *infinity pool*, started taking Alexander Technique classes to get your posture corrected, and finally you had a massage

which you'd resisted for ages, because you don't trust people who choose a job that involves groping naked people all day and in any case

nobody has seen you undressed since Reuben in 1990 and you wasn't about to strip for a stranger, not even down to your bra and undies

and at first you couldn't relax in case the young woman tried anything funny, but in the end you gave in and was sobbing so much she had to stop and she said

she'd never come across such rock-hard knots in all her years as a masseuse

There's a lot of pain trapped in your body, Mrs Walker, and you've got to let it out as part of your healing process, which you did, three times a week, until the knots started to melt away

like your rheumatoid arthritis, which virtually disappeared in the heat, like you was being reborn again and starting to enjoy yourself, enjoying breakfast one morning, eating a big plate of fresh fruit salad as per Odette's instructions

which you'd never done before, preferring instead your usual home breakfast fry-up of eggs, sausages, ackee, yam and, lately, even when you're stuffed, adding a couple of pancakes with syrup, which Odette said was because you was overeating to avoid dealing with the difficult issues in your life and that *food is for nourishment and not for numbing the emotions, Carmel*

and you was enjoying the clear, sunny morning of your island, as if you was a regular tourist like the ones you'd been watching getting on to a catamaran to spend the day cruising the coast

when, from behind the breakfast deck, by the steps that led to the paths that led to the bungalows spread out on the hillside, you heard

Is that my Carmelita? Carmelita! Carmelita! What a pretty name that is. What a pretty girl she is . . .

and the longer you stared at this somehow familiar stranger, the more you realized it was Hubert, but not the skinny, stuttering Hubert of before, but an older, handsomer, manly version with a gorgeous head of white hair

looking at you adoringly, and you thanked the Lord he hadn't seen the wreck you was when you first arrived, especially

when he told you he was a widower, goes church every day, only listens to Bible radio, reads the scriptures one hour every morning and one hour every evening, and moved back to Antigua permanently after forty-four years in America, where he'd been a professor at Howard University

Always carried a torch for you, Carmel . . .

which he didn't mind anybody knowing about, even on

that first day when you went walking around English Harbour holding hands like you was childhood sweethearts again, like he was *proud* to be seen with you, like you was already his woman

you telling him all about your BA in Business Administration and your *career* in Housing Management, responsible for 2,000 properties.

(not speaking much about your evil *anti-man* husband, except the divorce you planning)

until it got dark, but you didn't want to let go your hands, so you asked God to forgive you for being a bit premature and spent the night at his very nice house overlooking English Harbour (on land his grandfather squatted a hundred years ago, which was now real estate worth millions)

and it felt so natural, so normal – to be with him

as was the way he brought you peppermint tea and toast in the morning without asking, both of you sitting outside his bedroom veranda watching the pelicans glide by like little spaceships

and that evening you danced to Barry Manilow, Harry Belafonte, Michael Bublé, Barry White, on the deck outside his living room, because this is a man who says not a week goes by that he don't dance

your bodies smooth and in sync, the gentle way he led, moving his *very* supple hips, which eventually freed up the fluidity in yours, and you got a little shimmy thing goin' on which you *know* he appreciated

you tried to remember when you last danced and came to the conclusion it was probably in the 1970s

but never mind, because you determined to look to the future now and not waste any more time regretting the Big Bad Decision that changed the course of your life because everything about Hubert feels right

God has brought him to you and you thanks God and God is Love and Love is Healing

and you get to thinking about how you could build a Christian retreat on the island (once you've taken Barry to the cleaners) with its own church, put all of your housing-management experience to good use

Merty as Head Housekeeper, putting the fear of God into the staff, Asseleitha as Head Chef with all of her international cuisine experience from Bush House, seeing as those two been dreaming about coming home for so long

and Odette keeps saying it's better to stay active as you age or else you vegetate

maybe something for Drusilla and Candaisy if they want to come over too, or maybe they just goin' come over anyway, because they all got English pensions that go a long way in Antigua

so you can all be together on home soil after fifty years away

from where you first started out

the Ole Ladies' Society of Antigua, O Lord

to rest our weary souls, O Lord

cleanse our hearts and minds, O Lord

bring us closer to God

to walk in Jesus' name, O Lord

give thanks, O Lord! Give thanks!

18.

The Art of Travel

Sunday, 1 May 2011

Me and Morris are in the drive, circumnavigating my cream-coloured 1970 Buick Coupe Convertible, which is gleaming sleekly and purring gently in the afternoon sun.

'*Dis-a* one helluva sexy beast,' I say, stoking its warm, hard, polished bonnet. 'Man, I could do *indecent* things to this animal.'

'That's known as motorphilia,' Morris says. 'And, if it isn't, I just coined a term. Mind you, I wouldn't put it past some folk, though, Barry. You see these sickos out there who are into necrophilia? Well, I read the other day in my *very informative* red-top about dendrophilia. You know what that means? People turned on by trees.'

'I say we get turned on by taking this baby for a ride, and the only philia I interested in is Morrisphilia. A-wha' d'ya say, pardner?'

The car ain't been for a spin since 1975, when it broke down on Clapton Road and we pushed it back here with the kind of manpower that could substitute for horsepower in those days.

Now it's restored to its former spiffing glory, an idea hatched after what became our First Christmas Together Major Barney.

★

Morris had roasted a turkey courtesy of *Delia's Complete Cookery Course*, which had all of the lashings and trimmings, smashings and swimmings, including some fancy, five-fruit stuffing. Didn't do a bad job either. I told him if he kept it up I really *would* civil partner him. He said I was sexist and hadn't I heard of the Women's Liberation Movement? I replied that unless he'd had a sex change, he was a fella last time I looked.

'Yes, Barry, but your problem is that you got a very *gendered* attitude that's stuck in the dark ages.'

Morris should stick to reading gossipy biographies instead of those PC-socio-illogical-smear campaign books he's been burying his head in since Lola gave him his own *personalized* reading list.

Later that Christmas afternoon I persuaded Morris to come up to Park Lane with me so I could show him a little surprise. We cruised there in my Jag, voyeurizing the Christmas lights and yuletide spirit of late-afternoon celebrators and strollerators. I parked in the underground car park at Marble Arch, and we walked down Park Lane. We was wrapped up good in our new navy Crombies, our new cashmere scarves (his grey, mine red) and a muskrat fur hat (with external ear flaps) for me, and a sheepskin steppe hat (without external ear flaps) for him, all of which I'd bought us for Christmas in Conduit Street.

As we caught sight of ourselves in a passing window, I said, 'Nobody can accuse us of being two ole Caribbean queens in this get-up, ehn? More like two retired ambassadors from the Caribbean, or maybe two retired African dictators. Or, rather, I am the erstwhile dictator, while *you* are my erstwhile Chief-of-Staff.'

He didn't respond, so I teased him, 'Or maybe you look like my well-dressed manservant.'

'Barry,' he said, rising to my bait, 'anyone ever tell you your mouth bigger than your brains?'

'All right, then, we look like two *equally prosperous* Nigerian oil millionaires.'

'You mean those fat cats who get rich on the profits of oil drilling in the Niger Delta while the locals starve?'

Why does Morris always have to get so serious just when we having fun?

'Morris, ole dear, ease up. I merely want to walk into any toity-hoity shop in the land and not be refused entry.'

We arrived at the car showroom that, unfortunately, was closed.

'Anyways, you think these purveyors of exorbitant commodities for the super-rich worry about where Mr Moneybags gets his money from? Corrupt petrodollar or no corrupt petrodollar, the only thing that talks in this world is filthy lucre, and I still got plenty of it, even after Carmel procured half of it. Who da boss?'

'Barry, you an *eedyat*, you know that?'

That didn't stop his jaw hitting the pavement when he saw the streamlined red Lamborghini in the beautifully lit window, veritably palpitating with dewy, succulent gorgeousness.

'Morris,' I said, taking hold of his arm, 'I brought you here for a reason.'

He turned and looked up at me, eyes widening, then narrowing, like he already knew what I goin' say.

'I go purchase one of these ve-hi-cals. Yes, my good fella. A Lambo-mi-getti!'

A late-life crisis couldn't pass by without my getting the kind of car that would make other men so sick with jealousy they'd want to throw themselves under a speeding train.

Morris rotated his head slowly from car to me, from me to car, before uttering his most damning verdict: 'You see that *ve-hi-cal* over there? That Lambo-you-getti? Is a work of art a-true, but how can you even contemplate such a vulgar display of wealth when there's a recession on, and in some parts of this country you could buy several houses for the price of that car? How long you think it goin' last in your piddling garage in Hackney, of all places, before it's a case of Lambo-theft?

'You know what everybody thinks about the Lambo-gits who hare around town in these *ve-hi-cals*, blasting exhaust pipes so loud it's like bombs dropping and giving everybody shell shock? They saying, *There goes a man with a big ego and a small dick*. Yes, boss, everybody laughing at the Lambo-pricks. Yuh sure you want one?'

Needless to say, Christmas Day ended badly and I didn't bother speak to the Great Defender of the Downtrodden until the end of Boxing Day. I ain't normally the kind of person given to childish sulks (I leave that to everybody else around here), but Morris took it too far and had to enact a grovel of a certain nature to win me round.

Whereupon, after my mind had been lightened along with my load, I decided he right, yes, he right, as usual. I goin' Lambo-for-getti.

At which point I got the brainwave to do up my ole Buick instead.

We started stripping it down on the second of January 2011, the day the builders moved in to obliterate all traces of my former life, wife and strife. They knocked through the front room and back room to create one large living room with wooden floors (plantation-style furniture), French windows and a patio out into the garden that Magic Fingers Morris (all of a sudden) was intent on redesigning into a Zen Peace Garden with ponds, mini-waterfalls, gravel, rocks, oriental hedges, a pagoda, bamboo screens and even a little bridge, I ask you.

We had the kitchen gutted, its back wall replaced with a (parlour-palmed) conservatory. Upstairs the marital bedroom joined forces with the marital bathroom to become one massive bathroom with a bath, commode and a new power shower with a built-in seat. The two remaining bedrooms became one large *master* bedroom, and the attic became Morris's 'studio flat', but only for the purposes of his sons, whom Odette still hadn't told, and other nosy-parker bigots should they inquire or visit.

At the same time, we dismantled and remantled the Buick, chased all over London getting parts; ordered from the States whatever we couldn't find.

We rebuilt the engine, put in a new body, installed a new ignition box and had a spare distributor built, replaced the radiator, installed a complete set of 15" × 7" Buick factory chrome wheels, refitted the inside with a Tilt steering column with Sport steering wheel, had a new Sony AM/FM/CD receiver mounted out of sight under the driver's seat, and rear speakers, tinted glass, new carpet and reconditioned second-hand bucket seats to boot.

We finished it off by sandblasting and spray painting it from rusty beige to metallic blue and then finally . . . May Day . . . and our baby was a-ready-a-go vroom . . . vroom . . . *vroom*.

*

So there we was, prowling around our handiwork, about to spend a charming spring afternoon hitting the high road, when a one of those shabby rattle-trucks favoured by rag-and-bone men pulls up right outside the drive and toots the horn. I don't recognize the driver – some scruffy middle-aged fella with a grey beard who waves and nods at me like I should know him – or the light-skinned lad in the seat in the middle.

But I do recognize Daniel when he jumps out and stands on the kerb like he don't know what to do. Neither do I, because I ain't seen the boy in practically a year.

I stand there while he stands there all shamefaced and embarrassed. Thankfully Morris beckons the boy forward, and he walks hesitantly up the drive, shoulders hunched as if bracing a wind, dragging his feet, trainers scraping the gravel, hands in his pockets, looking very sheepish.

What happened to the aspiring Master of the Universe, ehn?

He grown an inch, at least, and he's got the beginnings of a moustache. It don't suit him, but teenage boys don't care, soon as they start to sprout fluff they want to show it off.

Daniel stands there fixated by the ground. I am fixated by him. Morris, typically, is fixated on breaking the ice.

'Right, I'll just pop in and put the kettle on,' he says chirpily, clapping his hands and rubbing them together like he's Hilda Ogden in *Coronation Street* circa 1964.

'Morris, stay, you don't have to go nowhere.'

'Yes, don't go,' Daniel says with a tentative, hopeful grin. Everybody knows Morris is a soft touch. 'Granddad, I just wanted to –'

Apologize?

'Apologize about what happened.' I notice his voice ain't so high and mighty. He can't style it out when he's on the backfoot, ehn?

'Oh.'

'I don't have anything to do with those boys any more. They're history: *ancient*. All they care about is drink, drugs, sex and screwing their parents for money to pay for at least two of those categories. Benedict is the one who wanted to take you on. How *egregious* was that? Disrespecting my elderly grandfather? I barely knew him before that night and . . . you see . . . I was out of it . . . asleep.'

He studies me to assess whether he's said enough to be forgiven, his eyes goin' all slippery-slidery.

'I take it you're absolving yourself of all responsibility, then?'

'I was drunk.'

'You chose to get drunk, not so?'

'That's debatable. On the one hand, yes, I was paralytic, completely waved, but on the other I didn't actually know my limit, which is why I exceeded it? Therefore we can say that my drunkenness was accidental rather than intentional.'

He goin' make a good politician.

'I see, so it wasn't your fault, is that what you saying? You are in no way to blame?'

He starts to squirm. 'I was younger back then, Granddad, just a child, really, and easily led and you know what it's like, you get into a mess sometimes and mix with the wrong crowd, but I'm a man now, and I don't even drink any more. Getting drunk is for losers. Winners stay sober and rule the world, hey.'

Another revisionist in the family.

I stand my ground, hard-faced but aware, for the first time, that it must-a been tough for the lad to deal with his grandfather coming out to his friends like that.

'Look, these things happen, Granddad.'

'Not to me they don't.'

'Put it this way,' he says, his upper-crust swagger returning relative to the realization Grandy ain't goin' back down so easily. 'If drunkenness is taken into consideration as a mitigating factor in a court of law, as I do believe it is, then why can't you accept it?'

He raises a grandstanding eyebrow.

I wanna give him a grandstanding slap.

This boy's humble-pie act lasted less than two minutes. Either this will end in a verbal head-butting, or we have to make up. Problem is, just as I was getting to know him, I thought I'd lost him. I liked being involved in my grandson's life. I liked being around a member of the so-called 'younger generation', full of plans and dreams, instead of looking at plans for funeral plots, metaphorically speaking.

Truth is, I missed the cocky little sod.

I was a journeyman to grief . . .

O ye.

'How yuh mother?' I ask, detouring from this stand-off.

His eyes lose their defensive battlements position and become animated.

'Mad as hell, as to be expected. But happier too. She's found herself a (hush hush) "special male friend" that she met at a conference, which keeps her out of my hair, at least. He's fifty-seven, white and a high-court judge, which, as she explained to me, more than makes up for his first two failings. (Like, if that's not racist and ageist, then what is?) I have my suspicions he could be a secret "feeder". Cooks her these three-course meals most nights, and it's *showing*. I've got my eye on him because I've got to watch out for Mum. I mean, someone has to, given her mental state.'

'Maxine never mentioned him to me.'

'Auntie Maxine doesn't know. Mum's keeping him hidden away for now. Guess what, though? She told me everything about . . . you two.' He gestures at us, awkwardly. 'But swore me to secrecy, because she'd promised Gran not to tell anyone.

'Then, and this is what she's like, she spent the whole weekend going through her phone book and telling *all* her thousands of female friends that her father's a closet gay with his best friend. I heard her walking around the house dishing the ins and outs. She dined out on you, Grandy, for *months* . . .'

'And what do *you* think of your granddad?'

'I think Mum's conservative with a small *c* when it comes to certain issues.' He shakes his head. 'Whereas I'm actually an all-round Progressive with a capital *P*. You've always been good to me. I won't ever forget that, and I *am* sorry. About what went down. *Believe*.'

'Here,' I say, extending my arms to give him a man-hug.

He reciprocates, which suggests he really might be okay with having a Barrysexual, correction, *homosexual* (la-di-dah) grandfather.

'I can't stay, Grandy,' he says as we part. I grip him firmly by the shoulders before letting him go. 'I dropped by because I wanted you to hear something really important. Listen to this: I applied to Harvard and I've not only been accepted – I knew that back in March and forced Mum to keep her big mouth shut upon pain of death – but I've just heard this morning that I've been awarded a full scholarship.'

Harvard? My grandson? Oh my days. Pass the smelling salts!

'Guess who's going to Harvard!' he shouts at full pelt while doing one of those hip-hop-style dances that look like he's got both hands wrapped around a giant wooden spoon and he's stirring a glutinous stew clockwise in a giant cauldron.

Me and Morris start slapping his back and each other's backs and doing a fancy jig-a we own.

'I couldn't wait to tell you,' he says, relishing the moment. 'When I graduate, I'll apply to Harvard Law School, of course.'

We all gone soppy.

'Don't forget us when you're a hot-shot lawyer charging us £500 per hour for saying Hello or Happy Christmas on the telephone,' Morris says. 'Don't forget the little-little people.'

'Speak for yourself, Morris. I ain't no little-little person.'

Daniel laughs. 'Good Lord, I'm not *actually* going into *law*, Uncle Morris. A law degree is my route into politics, and where better than Obama's alma mater? I'll probably do a D.Phil. in Politics at Oxford afterwards, as I'll need access to this country's elite networks in order to start ascending the slippery slope of a political career. I'm going to form my own party: UK Progressives.'

Just then the truck behind hoots its horn. Daniel turns around, gesticulates he's coming.

'I've got to go now. I'm on my way to my friend's dad's farm in Epping, and we're already late. He's one of my new mates, Nelson, after Nelson Mandela? We met on a Leaders of the Future weekend. As soon as we stopped here, his dad said he used to go out with a girl who lived on this road, then he recognized the house *and you*. I assumed it was Maxine, but he said no, Donna. Can you believe it? My friend's dad used to go out with my mum? That's *crazy*. He said it didn't work out with her, which is probably a polite way of saying she was showing early signs of insanity even then.'

I feel myself reeling.

'Shumba? You saying that fella there is Shumba.'

'His name's Hugo.'

'Yes . . . Hugo used to call himself Shumba. What happened to his rat's tails?'

'What? He had rats?'

'Dreadlocks, Sonny Jim.'

'You mean Hugo was a dread? Wow, that's so cool. I'm not surprised, because he's so alternative. He relinquished a title and sold off a huge estate that he'd inherited to set up a charity that provides water pumps to African villages. How cool is that? Now he lives in an eco-house he built himself on a small organic farm and sells his produce at farmers' markets.'

The horn hoots again.

'I gotta go. See you!'

Daniel bounds away, his long legs flying uncoordinatedly, still gangly.

'Daniel,' I call after him, 'stop by again soon, nah?'

He spins round. 'Of course.'

'We got a studio flat up top. Any time you want to stay. It's your *pied à terre*.'

'Wow, well cool.'

'Will we lose you to America, Daniel?'

'No way, I'm *definitely* coming back. My roots are here,

Grandy. Anyway, I've got to come back for Sharmilla. She's going to wait for me.'

What, four years or more? Yuh think she go wait for you?

Shut up, Barry, let him enjoy his youthful certainties.

'You two have *got* to get on the internet,' he calls back. 'So that we can keep in touch when I'm in the United States of America! Whooo-ooo. *Don't* worry, I'll set it up for you pair of dinosaurs before I leave. Whoooo-ooo, I'm going to Harvard!' He punches the air and does some more hip-hop shoulder dancing. 'Hey, does this mean I've now got two granddads? How progressive is that?'

And then he gone. My grandson gone.

The truck moves off, with Hugo smiling and giving me the thumbs-up through the window.

He seems like a nice fella, still a bit mucky but a philanthropist no less. I was wrong about him, as I am quite sure Morris will remind me from now until we really are changing each other's bedpans.

We stand there a while after the truck has revved off.

Daniel-a part of me. He my future. I will live on through him.

But whereas he's just starting out, his granddaddy's on the home run.

I practically got a sixty-year head start on the boy.

He might be able to spell the word *vicissitude*, but his experience of it will grow as he does.

He might know what hubris means, because he's a clever boy at the age of seventeen, or is it eighteen now? But he will experience it fully if he don't watch out. I should get him to read *Coriolanus*. All aspiring politicians should.

He'll be moulded by America, that's for sure, just by being there. He won't even be aware it's happening. He'll be filled with the American sense of self-belief, and the sense of can-do, and the Harvard sense of entitlement.

I couldn't wish for more for my grandson. Donna's done a good job with that boy. I want to tell her so, because I don't think I ever have. I don't think I've ever congratulated her on anything. Lord, really? Yes, really. Maybe I should try to make up with her even if she slams the phone down or the door in my face. I've been thinking too, maybe her craziness as a teenager was a cry for attention from me, or anger at my favouritism towards Maxine. I been trying to see things from her perspective. I been trying.

As for Maxine, I feel now that I spoilt her so much she never toughened up, but I don't regret it. Loving her more than was good for her. Anyways, my new, hard-line business approach been working. She's growing up. Jesper, our business manager, tells me the patient is showing steady signs of improvement. She's been meeting the deadlines for her collection, which is due to show in October, it goin' come in under budget, she's now producing receipts for *everything* and not spending what can't be accounted for, like her hairdressing bills (which is a miracle), her weekly strops have all but been eradicated, and no interns have left the building crying in the past seven weeks.

'About that cup of tea . . .' I say to Hilda 'Morris' Ogden, steering him towards the house.

Three hours later we are on the M1 heading north, doing a tame 70 mph, rather than an exhilarating 90, seeing as the state-controlled MI5 operatives have placed snoop cameras all along the motorway.

We got the roof down, we wearing sunglasses even though it's overcast, and we playing Shirley's 'The Girl from

Tiger Bay' from her new album at full blast. At seventy-four she's still got a voice to send shudders down mi spine and put any pretenders to the throne to shame.

We're drawing interested glances from fellow motorists, as to be expected. They probably think we are two famous American jazz musicians: Little Morris and Big Daddy B of the Louisiana Jazz Ensemble, and so forthly.

If we feel like it we can drive all the way to Manchester, York or even Glasgow. Why not? Nothing stopping us now. Don't need to report back to nobody. Only person I got to answer to is Morris, and I happy to do that. If it's late we can get a nice room for the night, order room service, watch *Pay TV* . . .

It's only when you drive out of London that you get the sense that most of this country is made up of countryside: wide-open fields and a sky uninterrupted by buildings. I been a citizen of the concrete jungle too long. I never leave London these days and, to be honest, when did I ever? A trip or two to Leeds to visit relatives, taking Maxine to the seaside.

Years ago we was even less welcome in the countryside than in the towns. It was safer to stay within the walls of the citadel. We wouldn't get lynched exactly in the bush, but we'd certainly get frozen out, at best.

All of this space and sky and greenery is like being in another country altogether. As we driving deeper and deeper into it, I starting to feel like a tourist, like we somewhere foreign, somewhere abroad.

I been thinking how maybe it's time to go home too, just for a visit, test the water.

Antigua *mon amour*, we been away too long, my darlin'.

We should go back before we . . . well, we not dying any

day soon but we must-a lost parts of ourselves being in England so long. Yes, a pilgrimage is in order and, seeing as Odette is now some kind of spiritual guru to Carmel (according to Maxine), she might be okay with me and Morris.

Not so sure about Carmel.

I'll never forget her standing there, delivering that sucker punch.

'I spent fifty years of my life betrayed by your lie. My whole adult life been wasted.'

Wifey got to me. I felt the consequences of my actions.

I still feeling it. And I sorry. Carmel, I sorry.

I even wrote her a letter of apology, but what good a letter do when someone's been cheated out of happiness so long, ehn?

I got to carry that with me for the rest of my life, because, no matter what excuses I made, leaving her would-a been the honest thing to do, at least once Maxine turned eighteen. Duty done. In the words of Mr James Baldwin, Esq., 'The way to be really despicable is to be contemptuous of other people's pain.'

In any case, if Carmel's still not okay, and me and him do go Antigua, I'll hide around corners if I see her walking around St John's hand in hand with Hubert, that *lickspittle*. Yes, yes, I'm sure he's changed, as Carmel told me . . . but really? Hubert? She couldn't do better?

Yes, maybe it's time to go back to where it all began. A flying visit, but not flying, of course. We can go by sea, same way we came, leisurely.

But, first things first.

'How yuh doing, Boss?' I ask Morris, who is at the wheel humming along to Shirley.

'I good, man. I good. You?'

305

'Me too, but you know something? I have some *stuff* to get off of mi chest.'

Stuff that's been on my mind ever since I decided to leave Carmel. She's not the only one I did wrong to. It's been keeping me awake most nights, so I go downstairs to read. Morris is so fast asleep he don't even notice.

It's about time Morris knows that I ain't just been living two lives, but three . . .

'Seeing as we starting a new beginning and all of that, I want to come clean, Morris.'

'Eh?'

He shoots a glance over at me like he's trying to get the measure of what I've just said. He can tell I nervous.

I have a faint cold fear thrills through my veins, / That almost freezes up the heat of life.

Even though I know I'm about to lob a hand grenade, I have *fe* do it.

'Stuff, Morris . . . stuff you need to hear . . .'

Let me start with the German construction worker from Munich who was working on the NatWest Tower in the City and rented out one of my early bedsits in Dalston Lane in 1975 – Jürgen. Then there was Demetrius, Kamau, Wendell, Stephen, Garfield, Roddy, Tremaine and all of the faceless dalliances and encounters.

There's a slip road ahead leading to services, and before I can say anything more Morris is signalling left and we pulling into Toddington.

We in the car park.

He's killed the engine.

He turns to me, serious, grabs my wrist tight.

'What am I now? A Catholic priest you got to confess all of your sins to? If you start down that road, I got to recipro-

306

cate, and I ain't so sure you can handle that. You want to know where this conversation will lead, my friend? A dead end, that's where.

'Listen to me good, Barry. I have known you since 1947 when we was nippers. That's sixty-four years, yuh hear? You and me has finally got a future to look forward to together, so let we not go digging up our past misdemeanours, right? Just sit back comfy and easy and listen to the one and only Miss Shirley Bassey and let we just enjoy the vibes, man, enjoy the vibes.'

Acknowledgements

My deeply felt gratitude, as always, to my brilliant editors, readers and the team at Hamish Hamilton-Penguin: Simon Prosser, Anna Kelly, Lesley Bryce, Donna Poppy, Caroline Craig, Anna Ridley, Ellie Smith and Marissa Chen, and everyone else who makes things happen behind the scenes. A big thanks, as ever, to my agent Karolina Sutton at Curtis Brown. Thanks also to the generous and critical readers of this novel at various stages of its incarnation: Denis Bond, Roger Robinson, Blake Morrison, Mel Larsen, Oscar Lumley-Watson; and to the people who helped with research: Brenda Lee Browne, Sharon Knight and Ajamu X. Thanks most of all to my husband, David, my primary reader, rock-solid supporter and fellow banterer.

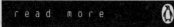
BERNARDINE EVARISTO

THE EMPEROR'S BABE

Londinium, AD 211

Meet Zuleika: sassy girl-about-town, hellraiser, the feisty and precocious daughter of Sudanese immigrants, now married off to a rich, fat, absent Roman and stranded in luxurious neglect. Until one day, that is, when the Emperor himself comes to town bringing with him not just love, but danger, too . . .

Dazzling, brilliant, streetwise and audacious, *The Emperor's Babe* has been hailed as one of the most original novels of recent years.

'Readable, sexy, delicious . . . I loved this book!'
Helen Dunmore

'A glittering fiction whose words leap off the page into life. Brilliant'
The Times

'Youthful and daring, with hidden depths of wisdom and hilarity'
Independent

'Manages to move the reader from laughter towards tears. Unforgettable'
Daily Telegraph